PRO

A RYKER RETURNS THRILLER

ROB SINCLAIR

BLOODHOUND
— BOOKS —

Print ISBN 978-1-5040-7783-5

ALSO BY ROB SINCLAIR

1

Orange rays from the low autumn sun streamed in through her bedroom window. She brought her hand up to her face to shield from the glare as she stared outside, looking across the rolling landscape – green fields, pine forests, all interspersed with grey, craggy rocks rising up to the mountainous summits.

Before long snow would arrive once again. By the end of the year she'd see nothing but white out of this window, and the area would be flooded with people who'd descend to take advantage of the many ski slopes. She hated the winter. Hated the crowds. The spring and summer were quieter, but still not quiet enough for Sophie, when various adventurers and outdoorsy types – walkers, runners, cyclists, mountaineers – arrived to exhaust themselves on the myriad peaks. At least with them came some good weather.

As for autumn? Probably her favourite time of the year. The quietest time, even if it was the wettest and the gloomiest.

Not gloomy today though, even if her mood was.

She sighed and moved away from the window and sat down on her king-sized bed as she stared at the screen of her phone.

No message. She hadn't received anything from him for more than four hours. Why was he ignoring her?

She typed out another message, her long nails on the glass screen sounding like a dog scuttling on a tiled floor. Her finger hovered over the send button...

She pushed her finger onto the 'x', held it down until all text had disappeared, then stood up from the bed. Sound outside. A deep rumble. Car engine. Unusual to have a visitor, at this time of day. Her gaze switched from the closed bedroom door to the world outside as she put the phone in her pocket and moved to the window. She didn't get there before she heard the vehicle crunch to a stop on the gravel. She stopped a couple of steps from the glass. Close enough to peer down if she craned her neck. A van?

The doors opened. Two dark-clothed figures stepped out as her mum's voice drifted up the stairs.

'Sophie, your dinner is ready.'

'Mum?' Sophie said in response, her voice raised, the first signs of distress already evident.

She turned and rushed for the door. Pulled it open. Dashed across to the landing to look down to the grand entrance hall below, at the bottom of the swirling staircase.

'Mum!'

Movement ahead of her. The door to her parents' bedroom swung open and...

'Dad,' was all Sophie could muster as she stared at her father. He'd thrown on a pair of joggers and hoody after his shower, his hair was still wet.

His eyes narrowed as he moved toward his daughter, a silent question. *What's the matter?*

Sophie looked over the banister, drawing her dad's attention that way. The next beat, Sophie ducked and cowered as an explosion sent the sturdy oak front door banging inward. A scream from somewhere beyond downstairs. Not Mum. Clara. The housekeeper.

A rush of footsteps and angry shouting followed as the two black-clad figures barrelled into the house.

'No!' Sophie's dad said before setting his wide eyes on her. 'In here,' he said, indicating behind him, to his bedroom.

The panic room.

Then he spun, as if to rush back there, but Sophie reached out and grabbed his hand.

'Don't leave them. Mum. Pierre.'

A gunshot downstairs – her dad flinched, Sophie froze. A scream followed the shot. Clara. Another gunshot. She stopped screaming, but next came the petrified cries for help from Sophie's mum and brother.

'What's happening?' Sophie said, her voice choked.

'Get yourself safe. Don't open the door except for the police.'

Sophie didn't respond.

'Sophie, please?'

She nodded and they both rushed off. She carried on straight ahead, to the bedroom. Her dad veered right, to the stairs. She heard him padding down quickly, then more slowly as he neared the bottom.

'I'm here!' he shouted out. 'I'm here. Please.'

Sophie raced through into the bedroom, heaved the chest of drawers aside. Slammed the button on the wall and a three-foot square section of the wall clanked from its position, revealing the hidden space beyond. Sophie pulled the door further open. A dim light came on as she ducked and moved into the cramped space. She spun and grabbed the door handle. Pulled it toward her. Paused. Another bang and crash downstairs. Angry voices. Pleading too.

If she closed the door... she'd be safe... but her family...

Her dad's words echoed in her mind.

She yanked the handle and the door closed with a *woomph*. Locks engaged. The lights in the room amplified. Sophie's eyes flitted across the space. The room was all of six feet square. Not much more than six feet high. Nothing but a few bottles of water inside. Plus the screens on the wall. Mostly CCTV coverage of the house, but also a smart-screen controller for the house's security system. Internet and phone access too.

She jabbed the smart-screen with a finger to bring it to life. Looked at the status bar at the top. No internet. Phone? She had to call for help.

But now her gaze was drawn left, to the two screens for the kitchen. In one of the screens, the bloodied body of Clara lay unmoving. Her parents were both on their knees, hands clasped – cuffed? – behind their backs.

Pierre?

She looked to the other screen. There he was. One of the masked intruders held him by the back of his jacket, hauling him up like a mother dog would her pup. In the man's other hand... a gun. The tip of the barrel rested on her younger brother's head.

Sophie gasped in shock.

Both of them looked toward the camera. The other masked man came into the view. Lifted a finger to tap his ear. Sophie knew what he meant. She reached forward and turned up the volume.

'My friend is coming up the stairs now,' shouted the man holding Pierre. 'You have one minute to come out. If you don't, I'll shoot your brother in the head, right here.'

The second man moved out of view, toward the exit for the hall. Sophie whipped her eyes back to her parents. To her dad. Expected him to say something. To beg the man, or to remind her of what he'd already said about not opening the door. But he didn't say a word.

4

Moments later a light tap came from the other side of the panic-room door. A muffled voice too, the thick metal drowning out the clarity of the words.

Back on the screen, the man renewed his grip on Pierre, causing Sophie's brother to squirm and whimper. Her mum cried, pleaded with the man, sounded so hopeless and helpless.

'Twenty seconds,' the man shouted to the camera.

What other choice did she have?

Sophie reached forward, toward the lock release button. Her hand paused there, hovering.

'Ten, nine, eight–'

She slammed the button and hung her head. As the door opened she held both her hands out, palms up, showing she wouldn't fight.

Strong hands grasped her, dragged her out through the low door and to her feet. A gun barrel pressed into the small of her back.

'Walk.'

A prod with the barrel got Sophie moving. Tears streamed down her face and her legs were heavy and wobbling. They reached the stairs.

'Keep going.'

They went down. To the kitchen. As Sophie stepped in her eyes rested on her parents, Pierre now on his knees next to them.

The look her dad gave her... disappointment?

'Get her in the van.'

'No, please!' her mum shouted out.

The next moment Sophie's hands were cuffed behind her and she was rough-handled out of there as her mum begged and pleaded. Her dad? Still nothing. What was he thinking? Planning?

Did he know what was happening?

Sophie shivered as she stepped out into the early evening air.

Her brain rumbled with thoughts about what she should do... comply, was the only solution she kept coming back to.

The masked figure opened the van doors and shoved her in and without her hands to protect her she landed on the cold metal floor of the van with a thud, her shoulder and temple taking the brunt of the fall. She groaned in pain, writhed, as the van doors slammed shut.

She pulled herself into a sitting position, up against the van wall. Tried to calm her breathing so she could listen to the world outside her confines. She heard nothing. Until footsteps pierced the silence. The doors opened. Pierre. The man tossed him inside, and he landed as awkwardly as Sophie had. The masked man cackled before closing the doors and retreating once more.

Pierre propped himself up, a similar position to Sophie, on the opposite side. She stared toward him, but with the last of the evening light as their only illumination, seeping in through the grimy, partially covered back window, she could barely make out his features.

'You're okay?' she asked him, trying to sound calm. She didn't.

'I'm scared,' he said, his voice breaking.

'Me too. If we do what they tell us, we'll be okay.'

'Why are we in here?'

Sophie didn't answer straight away as ominous thoughts whirred. 'I don't know.'

Footsteps once more. Their parents. Both of them were hauled in. One of the intruders climbed in the back too. The doors closed once more. The engine started. A jolt as the van moved off.

'Stay still, all of you,' the man said, taking a seat on the bench by the metal divider that separated the back from the driver. The man's gun lay on his lap.

Silence after that. The van banged and clanked on rickety

suspension. Each jolt sent a painful judder through Sophie's body. She looked over her family members. Tried to gauge their moods in the dim light. Her eyes rested on her dad, sitting closest to the armed man.

'Where are you taking us?' her dad asked, his voice stern.

'Be quiet,' the armed man said.

'You have everything you asked us for. Let my family go.'

What did that mean?

'I said be quiet!' The armed man reached out with the gun and swiped it across her dad's face. With his hands behind his back the only defence he could manage was to turn away from the blow. Sophie flinched at the crack. Her mum cried, as if feeling her husband's pain. Pierre whimpered.

Her dad... he reeled away but then sprung up and launched himself forward, knocking into the man. They both fell sideways. The gun clattered free.

Sophie glanced to her mum next to her. She squirmed, as though about ready to drop to the floor to try to pick the gun up. But then a scream put paid to her movement. Sophie froze too as her brain processed the sound. Not her dad screaming, but the man. Her dad had sank his teeth into the man's neck. The man desperately tried to free himself, smacking his fists down onto her dad's back, over and over.

The van went over a bump in the road. Then veered right. The momentum was enough to cause her dad to release his grip. The man shoved him off, dove for the gun. Lifted it up.

BOOM.

Sophie squeezed her eyes shut, a piercing, disorientating ringing in her ears consuming her thoughts. The ringing subsided and was replaced by an even worse sound. The screaming of her family members. All three. Her dad's the worst as he writhed on the floor, holding his leg to his chest.

'I should put a bullet in your head right now,' the masked man said, as he propped himself back on the bench.

'No, you won't,' came the shout from the unseen driver.

The man huffed but said nothing more. Sophie's dad continued to moan with pain, her mum and brother continued to sob. She continued to... do nothing really.

The journey lasted only a few minutes more before the van came to a rocking halt. The back doors opened and with two guns trained on them the family of four were ushered out, Sophie's dad doing his best to move with the bullet in his thigh.

'Where are we?' her mum said, terrified.

Sophie looked around the dark. The van's headlights lit up the pine trees ahead of them.

'This way,' one of the men said, shoving Sophie's dad in the back and causing him to stumble to the ground.

One of the attackers dragged him back to his feet, then the two armed men led Sophie and her family forward, moving in line with the van's headlights, into the trees.

'They're going to kill us,' Sophie's mum whispered to her. 'We have to try something.'

Try something? Like her dad had? Look how that had worked out.

They didn't move for long before they received the command to stop. The gunmen lined Sophie and her family up on the soggy, needle-covered ground, the last of the illumination from the van's headlights reaching only a few feet in front of them.

'On your knees,' came the barked instruction.

Sophie complied first. Pierre next. Sophie looked up to her mum, gave her a pleading look.

'You got what you wanted,' Sophie's dad said. 'Why don't you–'

BOOM.

Sophie screamed in shock as her dad's body dropped to the ground in slow motion, the back of his head a mess of blood and hair and skull.

'Run!' Sophie's mum shouted out.

She went to turn around. Another gunshot. She cried out and fell to the ground.

Pierre jumped up and darted left. Sophie bounced to her feet too, looked this way and that. She flinched at another gunshot. Not aimed at her. No scream either. Her mum again?

She ran forward.

'Hey!'

She raced as quickly as she could. Jumped over a fallen tree trunk. Without her hands to help balance she nearly lost her footing...

Another gunshot. Then another. Aimed at her? She couldn't tell anymore, but she hadn't been hit.

She kept going forward. In the darkness she didn't see the exposed root. Her foot caught underneath it. She lost her balance and fell forward, face first. She just about managed to roll into the fall, her shoulder again taking the brunt of the impact, but at least saving her face.

But she couldn't stop her momentum. She tumbled, then...

Free-fall.

An unseen edge. She imagined her body plummeting hundreds of feet to a sorry end.

Wind rushed against her face. She braced for impact. But only a few panicked heartbeats passed before she hit the treeline below. Thick, furry pines scratched and scraped her. Her forehead smashed off a thicker branch. Then her back cracked off another, sending her into a helpless spin before she landed on the forest floor with a painful thud.

Alive, at least, but even in darkness she felt the world around her spinning.

She strained, trying to focus on her senses. No more gunshots from above. No sounds of anyone up there at all.

She knew what that meant. Her family were all dead.

Despite her attempts to stay awake, her eyes slowly slid closed.

2

_____

THREE MONTHS LATER

Perhaps his decision was counterintuitive. Given the chance to live a nomadic life, many Europeans would sooner travel south, toward warmer climes, as the winter approached, but instead, James Ryker headed north. Honestly? He'd had enough warm sunshine and glistening ocean over the last few months and wanted a change. His recent companion, fifteen-year-old Henrik, seemed happy with the perhaps more familiar territory, given he'd grown up in northern Norway where harsh winters were a way of life.

Ryker sighed and shuffled in his seat. His back ached from the constant vibration and jolts of the rickety train. Something of a relic, the carriage reminded him of those he'd seen from old movies from decades ago, with individual wood-panelled cabins, a frosted glass door separating the cabin from a corridor that ran down one edge of the carriage. Were trains like this used to give the tourists who came to the region a sense of nostalgia? Or was this simply a replacement service of sorts. Certainly the previous trains they'd taken, from the Med, all the way up to Milan, were sleek and modern in comparison. Some of them superfast too.

This one... at least it gave plenty of time to take in the glorious mountainous scenery and snowy peaks.

A tap on the door snapped Ryker from his thoughts and he looked across at Henrik who slowly opened his eyes as he woke up. The door opened and a smartly dressed ticket inspector – cap and all – stepped inside.

'*Buongiorno.*'

Ryker and Henrik took out their tickets and showed them to the man. He eyed the pieces of paper a little suspiciously – at least in Ryker's mind – before handing them back.

'It's the next stop,' he said to them in English. 'Less than an hour.'

'*Grazie,*' Henrik said.

The inspector gave him a curious look before moving on out. Ryker's focus returned to the window and the wintry scene outside.

'You're missing her already?' Henrik asked.

Actually that – *she* – hadn't been on Ryker's mind at all. Not the whole time anyway.

'No,' Ryker said.

Henrik smirked. 'Liar. I can understand it. She was very beautiful.'

She being Eleni. A spy, of sorts, with ties to both the American and Greek governments, but an unbreakable loyalty to neither.

'She was.'

'Dangerous too. I think that attracts you more, or am I wrong?'

Ryker didn't answer. He didn't really want to have this conversation with a fifteen-year-old boy. With anyone actually. He liked Eleni, even if he'd never fully understood her. He'd enjoyed spending time with her, but both of them knew it was never intended to be permanent.

'You could always go back. To Greece. To Athens.'

'Maybe one day.'

Henrik laughed. 'I can understand why you were attracted to her, but the other way around? You're...'

'What?'

'I don't even know how to explain it. But you'll have to teach me your tricks.'

'Tricks?'

'How you get beautiful women like that, to like *you*.'

Ryker smiled. 'Perhaps when you're older.'

'So you're saying we'll still be travelling together then?'

'*I'll* still be travelling,' Ryker said. He couldn't bear the thought of staying in one place too long anymore. 'Who I'll be with is a different question.'

He noticed a flicker of hurt on Henrik's face, though he'd only spoken the truth. He'd never intended to spend so long with this young man by his side after their disparate lives had clashed together in a mess of secrets, lies and violence months before. Yet the two of them – two lost souls, in many ways – had certainly bonded, more so than Ryker had ever expected. He'd never seen himself as a father figure, not with his dark past, and his ever uncertain future, but he noticed the way Henrik looked up to him, looked to him for answers and advice, even if he remained unreasonably headstrong at times.

'So you know this place?' Ryker asked.

Henrik had chosen their next stop-off location – St Ricard – a small town near the French-Italian border, within the Alps.

'I've never been,' Henrik said. 'But I know of it.'

He didn't add anything more. Ryker continued to stare until Henrik looked over at him.

'And you know what about it?' Ryker asked.

Henrik shrugged, trying to be nonchalant, Ryker thought. 'That it has four hotels, three ski lifts, about fifty different routes down. Six bars at the bottom, not including the ones in the hotels. It'll be busy this time of year.'

Ryker wasn't sure he wanted busy. But he'd looked online on the journey here and the town, out of season, had less than three thousand residents. How much bigger could it be during ski season? Perhaps double, triple its out of season population, perhaps, but that still only made it a small town in his mind.

'So you want us to go skiing?' Ryker asked.

Henrik shrugged. 'Let's see,' he said with a strangely knowing smile.

An hour later, they stepped from the taxi in the centre of St Ricard. The town's wooden cabins rose above them to the north, the white of the mountain rising several times higher still, its peak out of sight. To the south, rolling white hills stretched into the distance. To the east and west further peaks lay visible on the horizon. Definitely not a big place, but people walked the slushy, gritty streets here, there and everywhere.

'You can see Mont Blanc to the north-west,' Henrik said, sounding enthused as he tossed his backpack over his shoulder. 'We could climb it before we leave.'

He said that so calmly and confidently. As though it was perfectly feasible for the two of them to simply roll up one morning and scale Western Europe's highest peak in the middle of winter. Perhaps he was right. Ryker had never climbed Mont Blanc and had no clue how accessible it was.

'First things first,' Ryker said, adjusting his own, larger and more heavy backpack. 'Let's find somewhere to stay. Then let's eat.'

Henrik laughed, Ryker wasn't sure why. They looked over all of the town's four hotel options. The first two were full. The next was too expensive-looking so they didn't even bother to go inside. They had more luck at L'Hotel Alpine, which was as lacklustre as its name, from the dreary reception staff to the tired exterior and interior, but it had vacancies at least. Ryker paid cash for two single rooms. After a shower and some downtime, he and Henrik met outside the hotel restaurant on the ground floor.

'I'm not eating in there,' Henrik said, staring into the grotty-looking interior where a large, brightly lit buffet bar took up one side of the space. There were no diners inside. A smell of grease and boiled vegetables and fried something or other wafted over.

'Agreed.'

They traipsed through the streets, still busy now that darkness had descended – which happened pretty early in deep winter. Ryker shivered in his coat. A decent coat, for most occasions, but the temperature on the clocktower in the main square of the town read minus eight Celsius. Quite a difference to Athens where they'd started their journey not long ago. If they were staying here long, they'd need to stock up on appropriate gear.

They found a bar, proudly displaying large neon signage at the front that advertised some of the offerings inside – beer, wine, cocktails, burgers, pizza. Nothing particularly local-sounding, though as they stepped into the bustling interior, it didn't seem as though people minded much.

They sat in a booth and Ryker watched the punters as Henrik scanned a menu. The clientele included quite a mixture of people, ranging from families with kids, to groups of twenty- and thirty-somethings, to couples of all ages. A few groups of teenagers too. Locals mostly, Ryker thought, the largest group of which were clustered at the far corner of the bar, taking up the space which contained two pool tables and a variety of arcade machines.

He looked back to Henrik and saw he was staring over in that direction. When Henrik turned and caught Ryker's gaze he gave a slightly sheepish look. As though he'd been caught out.

Had someone caught his eye? Or perhaps he was only looking at the teenagers because they were so... normal. Henrik was anything but a normal teenager.

Did he envy them or pity them?

'What do you want?' Ryker asked.

'Chicken burger and a large beer,' Henrik said.

'Chicken burger and Diet Coke it is.'

Ryker headed to the bar. Squeezed into a space between a couple in their thirties and a group of three women drinking brightly coloured cocktails. He caught the attention of one of the bar staff and ordered the food and drinks, choosing to speak in French rather than English, which resulted in a confused look from the barman, even though Ryker knew his words were spot on.

As he stood and waited for his drinks, he realised one of the women to his right was staring.

'I saw you and your son arriving earlier,' she said to him in English, though her accent was European. Obviously his French had given away where he was from. 'You don't look much like skiers.'

'What do skiers look like?'

She squinted, as though unsure whether Ryker's question was serious or not.

'So, are you?'

'A skier? Not really.'

'Thought so. Shame though. I could have showed you the runs.'

'I'm a quick learner.'

She smiled. Ryker looked over to Henrik who stared at him.

'Just you two here?' the woman asked.

'Yeah.'

'His mum–'

'She's not here.'

A slight flicker in her eyes as though she wasn't sure whether she'd made a mistake in asking. The truth was, Henrik's mum was alive and well. She just couldn't have cared less about her son's whereabouts, and hadn't done so since he was taken away from her as a toddler. His life since then... complicated.

Henrik's stare turned to a frown.

'He doesn't like his dad flirting?' the woman asked.

'We're flirting?' Ryker said, eyebrow raised.

She looked away playfully and Ryker was about to say something else but the woman's words played on his mind. Twice she'd indicated that she thought Henrik was Ryker's son. Twice he hadn't corrected her, though in previous situations he always had. Why the change now?

'What's your name?' Ryker asked the woman as the barman pushed his drinks across the scratched top toward him.

'Amelie.'

'I'm James.'

He picked up his drinks.

'Maybe see you around?' she said hopefully as Ryker went to move away.

'Maybe.'

He took the drinks back to Henrik whose eyes didn't leave Ryker the whole way.

'All thoughts of Eleni gone now then,' Henrik said, a little aggravated, which surprised Ryker, given their earlier conversation on the train.

'Not at all,' Ryker said.

'You like her?' Henrik said, indicating back to the bar.

'I don't know her.'

'But you like how she looks.'

'I don't *not* like how she looks. Does that bother you?'

'I'm not bothered, just... curious really. Trying to figure out what type of man you are. And wondering whether I want to be like that too.'

Ryker thought about that for a few moments, but the answer to Henrik's thoughts were too complex to delve into fully, he decided.

What type of man *was* Ryker anyway?

'She thinks you're my son,' he said instead.

'And what did you tell her?'

'I didn't tell her otherwise.'

'So I'm your son while we're here? Is that what we tell people?'

What did Henrik want the answer to be?

'Yeah, why not,' Ryker said. 'To avoid any confusion. Or unwanted questions.'

Henrik's face screwed in suspicion. 'Yeah, sure. To avoid confusion. Like when you're talking to pretty ladies who like the idea of a single dad, perhaps? Will you say your wife died unexpectedly, or that she ran off with your best friend? Which gets the most sympathy do you think?'

Ryker laughed and shook his head.

'Actually that's not what I meant at all.'

'Yeah, *Dad*, of course, I believe you,' Henrik said with a cheeky wink.

Ryker said nothing as he glanced back over to the bar.

———

A chicken burger and two drinks each later, Ryker came back from the toilet to an empty booth. He looked across to the games area and spotted Henrik hovering by one of the pool tables. Not the one with five teens sitting on the table, but the one where two boys played an actual game, with others looking on. Ryker watched for a few moments, analysing the situation. No one spoke a word to Henrik though he received plenty of dubious glances from the others. Not outright hostility, but not far from it. Henrik was far from a shy teen, but he also wasn't the most sociable and Ryker thought it would have been an effort for Henrik just to approach the alien group. Was his silence a sign he now regretted that decision?

Ryker's thoughts tipped toward feeling sorry for his friend, but then Henrik stepped forward confidently and placed some money on the table – Ryker couldn't tell the denomination of the note – and started talking to the two playing. Both glared at him but then Henrik laughed and so, too, did a few of the onlookers. The two players didn't.

Okay, so no need to feel sorry for Henrik after all. He'd handled all manner of horrible, sometimes evil adults. He could handle a few kids.

A strange stand-off ensued until Henrik reached forward to offer a handshake. The two guys hesitated but then took Henrik's hand in turn. Then Henrik turned and indicated to one of the onlookers. A young woman, a little older than Henrik, Ryker thought. Tall, slender, blonde hair. She gave Henrik a pout and then Henrik re-racked the balls and the game began. Henrik and the girl versus the two boys.

'You want some company?'

Ryker looked over to Amelie, hovering at the end of the booth. He'd sensed her approaching and had willed her to carry on to the toilet or the exit. As pretty as she was, his first responsibility right now was Henrik.

Amelie glanced over to the pool game. 'He's not shy,' she said.

'Apparently not.'

She sat down without further invitation. She held a fancy cocktail in her hand, barely anything left of the electric-blue drink – just the sight of it made Ryker's insides curdle.

He downed the remaining half of his beer.

'You want another?' he asked.

She looked at him curiously.

'Sure.' She laughed. 'But perhaps not another of these though. A gin martini please. With a twist.'

Ryker headed to the bar, one eye on the pool game as he went. Judging by the looks on the faces of the two guys, the game was not going in their favour. Henrik's partner potted a shot and she jumped up in the air and Henrik – face beaming – high-fived her. Ryker smiled and ordered the drinks. Amelie's friends remained at the bar but they paid Ryker no attention before he walked back off with the drinks.

'How long are you staying in St Ricard?' Amelie asked when Ryker had settled back into his seat.

'Not sure yet.'

Ryker took a large swig of his beer. One of the two lads potted what must have been a decent shot because he balled his fist and cheered and his teammate gave him a manly slap on the back, their bravado increasing in line with Henrik's and his partner's exuberance. What was Henrik's game here? Woo the girl? Pick a fight? Either way, Ryker didn't feel particularly comfortable looking on. But perhaps that's exactly why he'd never make a good dad in real life. He'd never be able to let go and let his kids go off and live their own lives, make their own mistakes.

'Not much of a talker, are you?' Amelie said, grabbing Ryker's attention.

He looked back to her and noted the disappointment in her eyes.

'Sorry, just distracted.'

'It's nice, that you're so protective of him.'

Ryker didn't say anything.

'How old is he?'

'Fifteen.'

'He seems older.'

'He does. Sometimes.'

'Where's his mum? Sorry, that was–'

'In Norway. That's where he's from. But she... he hasn't known her for a long time.'

'So it's just the two of you?'

'It is now.'

He took another gulp of beer. For some reason, as those last words passed his lips, he had a thought of Eleni. Of the time he'd spent with her in Athens, Henrik there too. Nothing like a 'normal' family of three, but together they'd been content.

'What about you?' Ryker asked. 'Are you here long?'

'Only three more nights,' she said. 'But I come here a lot with my friends.'

He looked to her hands, on the table. No ring.

'Those friends?' he said, indicating the two at the bar.

She nodded. 'We travelled here together from Lyon. We've known each other for years. My friends are both married now, but I'm... I'm not.'

She fixed a sultry look on Ryker. He smiled and she carried on talking about her friends, but Ryker was distracted again. He'd sensed the mood worsening over by the pool table, as Henrik and his partner congratulated each other more and more, and the two boys sulked and glared daggers more and more. Most of the crowd seemed to be with Henrik – likely because he'd been the underdog – but not all of them. A group of three lads stood sullen-faced by the two players. If it all kicked off...

A cheer went up as the girl potted a ball – the black? She looked up to Henrik, beaming, and he wrapped his arms around her and lifted her up in the air like she was a trophy. Others closed in and ruffled their hair and patted their backs.

The five glum-looking boys stood watching. Henrik released the girl and shook the hands of his opponents but moments later was back in among the crowd of supporters.

'He's made quite an impression,' Amelie said, craning her neck.

Did she mean good or bad?

Ryker tried to take his focus from Henrik and onto Amelie, but he struggled. To keep the conversation flowing, Ryker asked wide questions to get her talking so he could keep an eye on Henrik. He certainly didn't want to be rude, and he'd be lying if he said he wasn't attracted to her, and she was obviously interested in him... Without Henrik there, Ryker had no doubt he'd have been as keen as Amelie, but Henrik *was* there and... he couldn't even explain it in his head, never mind out loud.

'What about you?' Amelie asked.

'Sorry?'

He looked back at her. Just the slightest annoyance in her features.

'What do you do?'

She'd just been talking about her job in advertising. He'd expected the reciprocal question sooner or later. He looked into her eyes a moment. He'd wondered more than once since she came over what she'd want the answer to this question to be. He could tell her the truth. That as an unruly teenager he'd been recruited to the UK's intelligence services. Groomed, effectively, and turned into a clandestine, deadly agent sent around the world to carry out the government's dirty work under the radar. That he'd carried out that role for nearly two decades, killed scores of people. But had also seen so many people killed because of him. Including the people he'd cared about most in the world. That their deaths weighed heavily on him every day. That he'd left that life behind several years ago in part because of the guilt. That during those years his past had caught up with him time after time, no matter where he went or why. That because of all that he tried as far as he could to stay on the move and to not get too close to others for fear of them getting hurt, because of him, and his past.

He glanced over to Henrik as those thoughts rumbled.

'James?'

'I'm taking a career break,' he said. 'But I used to teach martial arts. Self-defence.'

'Oh yeah?' she said, a little more animated. 'I know some Krav Maga. I mean, probably not as much as you.'

'You'll have to show me what you know.'

Ryker smiled then took a swig from his drink. He started a spiel about the various fighting techniques he'd been schooled in, many years ago, and their pros and cons in real life. And she seemed interested enough. Clearly this choice of lie as to his career was better suited to Amelie than his more usual practice of saying he was a consultant. As he talked he switched his focus back and forth to Henrik. With the conclusion of the game, Henrik seemed to be the toast of the town with the girl and her friends, with plenty of smiles all around, but the five boys remained sulking, a few glares here and there. No more pool on either table.

Soon the initial jubilation died down and Henrik and the others settled. He remained close by his playing partner, the two of them glancing at each other longingly every so often. But then the girl's face turned more neutral, as though Henrik had said something he shouldn't have. She gave him a couple of forced smiles but the mood between the two had changed. And others had taken notice. A boy peeled away from the group and went over to the fivesome by the pool table. Whispered into one of their ears. That was followed by a hushed, heads-together conversation by the five. Then one of those five – the tallest and bulkiest of them – moved off and over to the far side of the bar where two men were propped on stools drinking beer. The men looked about the same age as Ryker, possibly older. As the boy relayed whatever the problem was, both men glared from Henrik to Ryker and back again. Then one of the men stood from his stool – a big guy – and even if Ryker had no idea what Henrik had said to take the night in this direction, he knew exactly where the situation was headed.

Ryker sighed.

'Are you okay?' Amelie asked him, a look of concern on her face.

'Me? I'm sure *I'll* be okay,' Ryker said. 'Unfortunately I can't say the same for others.'

He sat back in his booth and waited for the inevitable.

3

The man walked purposefully toward Ryker as the youngster scuttled back to his crew. Amelie looked up at the guy as he approached.

'Hugo?'

'You need to get your boy and leave,' the man said, in heavily accented English, as he glared down to Ryker.

Ryker brought both hands onto the table, got himself ready to spring to action, just in case.

'Because?'

'Just leave. I'm giving you a chance. Take it.'

Ryker glanced to Amelie. Wariness had taken over. But wariness of Hugo or Ryker?

'Your boys are that bothered about losing a pool game?' Ryker said then paused. No answer. 'I can get Henrik to come back over here if it's really necessary.'

'No. You're going to get up from that seat, and both of you will leave this bar.'

Ryker's attention diverted to the kids. Two of the lads had broken away from the five and strode up to Henrik. One tapped him on the shoulder. Henrik spun. The lad shouted in his face, gesticulating. Then poked his finger into Henrik's chest, causing Henrik to back-step.

Enough.

Ryker went to get up. The speed with which he moved caused Hugo to flinch.

Then Henrik threw a punch...

Ryker groaned inwardly. The boy's friends descended on Henrik en masse. Ryker went to shove Hugo away but, sensing the threat, the guy cracked his beer bottle against the wooden back of the booth and the glass shattered into pieces leaving the jagged neck in his hand.

'Too late,' Hugo said, teeth bared. 'You don't move until it's over.'

Ryker decided not to point out the inconsistency in the man's mixed instructions. Instead, he reached out and grabbed Hugo's wrist. Stamped down onto the side of his knee to cause his leg to buckle. Twisted his arm and brought him to the floor, his hand holding the glass propped in the air on the edge of the table. One push was all it would take for Ryker to pop the elbow joint, or with a bit more effort snap the forearm if he really wanted to...

Amelie scuttled back in her seat, apparently terrified of Ryker all of a sudden.

'Drop the glass,' he said to Hugo.

Squirming in pain, Hugo did so.

'Leave him!' Ryker shouted over, with enough force to get the attention of everyone in the bar.

The skirmish between the teens faded to a stand-off. Henrik, clothes and hair skewed, brushed himself down. Most of his supporters had deserted him, keeping their distance from the fight. His playing partner looked on, seeming as shocked as she was disappointed, and she didn't attempt to give Henrik either aid or comfort.

Ryker let go of Hugo and shoved the guy away before storming toward Henrik.

'Come on.'

Henrik seemed reluctant at first, as though he'd wanted the fight and was angry with the interruption. But they both made their way to the exit as Hugo, and one of the teens, hurled abuse in their native French. Ryker understood most of the insults, which largely centred around their mothers and sexual acts. Not the most hurtful of taunts for two people who'd barely ever known their mothers.

They carried on out, Ryker intent on marching straight to the hotel before having it out with Henrik as to what the hell had just happened. But they made it all of five yards from the bar before the call came from behind them.

'Hey!'

Henrik stopped and turned. Ryker groaned and did so too.

Men and boys and a few women piled out. Hugo, his friend, the five from the pool table, others too.

'You told us to leave,' Ryker shouted. 'We left.'

'Have you any idea who you're talking to?' Henrik shouted in turn, much to Ryker's annoyance.

Naturally, the testosterone-charged group didn't take kindly to that.

'Why don't you come and show us.'

Stepping forward were two men. Well, one was nearly a man – the burly teen – plus Hugo's companion from the bar. A bigger, bulkier, meaner-looking man than Hugo in fact. Which made Ryker curious as to why it was Hugo who had arrived at Ryker's table to do the dirty work initially. But he was even more curious why these people felt so riled by his and Henrik's presence.

'Come on,' Ryker said, pulling on Henrik's coat. 'We don't need this.'

Henrik shoved him off. 'Don't we? They were six on one against me. And what? You're going to walk away from that?'

'The odds are even worse now. So yeah, I'm walking away.'

'So much for protecting me. Some father you'd make.'

'This is protecting you. Now let's go.'

Ryker went to grab Henrik again but the boy wrestled free once more, then patted down his jacket and his jeans.

'You looking for this?' said one of the pool players, stepping forward with a phone held aloft.

Henrik stormed forward. Ryker rolled his eyes and set off after him.

'Give it,' Henrik shouted.

'Henrik!' Ryker said. 'Leave it.'

He went to grab Henrik but then the agitator tossed the phone to the ground and lifted his heel and stomped his foot down onto the device.

Henrik growled and raced toward him. Ryker raced too. He reached out to try and grab Henrik yet again but the two youngsters barged into each other, fists flying, grappling. Ryker got a hold of Henrik's coat, around the neck, but no sooner had he grasped the fabric than a big meaty hand took hold of him in the same position and pulled him free.

He spotted the arcing fist. Ducked out of the way and sent his own balled fist into the man's stomach. A hard shot. An equally hard target, nothing but muscle. Ryker sent another to the kidney which caused a groan of pain from the man who responded with an uppercut. He was big, and strong, but not too fast.

Ryker saw the next shot coming and darted to the side then hammered his elbow down on the man's back before using the heel of his shoe to push him forward, sending him scuttling and sliding to the soggy ground.

Ryker moved for Henrik again. Three on one for him now.

Ryker grabbed the arm of a youngster and yanked hard to toss him away. Then he seized Henrik's arm as he tried to send a fist to someone's face. Ryker took a blow to the back. Another to the side of his head. He ducked and used his elbow to fend the attackers off and wrestle Henrik free. He swung Henrik around so the boy was behind him – relative safety.

Men and teens circled in front of Ryker. One of the young men Henrik had tussled with jerked, as though to race forward, to get around Ryker and to Henrik, but Ryker sidestepped and lifted his fists, rocking on his toes like a boxer, and the boy backed down.

Hugo didn't. He darted forward. Ryker ducked. Grabbed the guy around the thighs like a rugby player, lifted him off his feet and tossed him onto his back with a painful-sounding thud.

Ryker remained crouched, swung left and right on the spot, ready for any further attack.

None came this time. In fact, the previously boisterous crowd looked a lot less confident all of a sudden. Hugo and his burly friend stood side by side, nursing themselves. The bigger man glared over.

'If we see you here again…'

He never finished the threat. Instead his eyes rested on a spot behind Ryker.

Ryker glanced that way, but only to check there was no ambush coming. He didn't spot anyone, but stayed poised, ready for another attack.

None came as the group skulked back into the bar, one after the other. When he was sure no threat remained, Ryker put his arm around Henrik and turned around. Looked to the spot where Hugo's friend's gaze had settled. Two bright headlights shone back at Ryker from across the street. He lifted his arm to shield from the glare. Moments later the engine rumbled and the car sped up and disappeared in a flurry of slushy spray.

Other than the car was big and dark, Ryker couldn't be sure what vehicle it was, and had no clue who was inside.

But Hugo and his chums obviously knew.

'Not quite how I expected tonight to go,' Ryker said as he and Henrik set off for the hotel.

'No. But I bet you're interested to find out more now, right?'

Ryker didn't respond and they walked in silence for a few moments, Ryker waiting for an explanation.

'So?' he prompted as they neared the hotel.

'What?'

'What the hell where you doing back there?'

'Self-defence.'

'No. Before that.'

Henrik tutted, as though offended by Ryker's question, or perhaps his apparent lack of trust.

'I only wanted to play pool.'

Ryker laughed sarcastically. 'Yeah. Try harder.'

'And I liked the girl. Ella.'

'You made quite the team.'

'She was decent. But I'm better. I only had to watch for a couple of minutes to know I could have picked any partner and beaten those two.'

He spoke with such natural confidence. Ryker didn't know whether to be impressed or not. He'd never realised Henrik was a pool shark. The young man continued to surprise Ryker. Not always in a good way.

'How much did you bet them?'

'Fifty euro,' Henrik said with a wide grin that, caught under the twinkling lights of a bar they passed, looked more than a little sinister.

'You can pay for our next meal then,' Ryker said.

Henrik rolled his eyes.

'And what happened after the game?'

'You saw. They started a fight with me. They weren't happy that they lost, and they weren't happy that Ella was giving me attention.'

Ryker chewed on that for a few moments. He fully believed that a group of teens – even a group of adults, in a bar, all filled with alcohol – would start a brawl over something so simple, but Ryker didn't buy it. Henrik wasn't like that. He wasn't that... one-dimensional. He'd gone over there to the teens with an ulterior motive. A motive that he was reluctant to share with Ryker.

'I don't believe you,' Ryker said.

Henrik tutted again. 'You never do.'

Except the story didn't add up. Particularly when put together with the reaction of the adults. A reaction which had actually pre-empted the teen fight. Hugo had come to Ryker's table, up for battle, even before Henrik threw the first punch. Why was he so intent on warding off Ryker and Henrik?

'I don't believe you,' Ryker said again as they reached the doors to their hotel. 'So this is what we'll do. We're going to our rooms. We'll sleep on it. In the morning, you'll tell me the truth.'

Henrik stayed silent.

'You want to know what I think?' Ryker said.

Henrik sighed. 'I think you'll tell me whether I want you to or not.'

'Cute. But I'm thinking you chose for us to come to this town for a reason. A reason you haven't told me about yet. So, in the morning, you *will* tell me. Otherwise we're done here, and I'm leaving, with or without you. Understood?'

Henrik glared at Ryker, looking riled by the order, or perhaps just by Ryker's calmness as he delivered it, as though what he'd really wanted was another confrontation.

'Goodnight, Henrik,' Ryker said before walking off to his room

4

Henrik lay on his bed, still fully dressed. Angry. At those boys from the bar. The men too. Ella, a little bit. Ryker? Perhaps Ryker more than the others, actually. Yes, Ryker had backed Henrik up – physically at least – exactly as he expected Ryker would. But... Henrik couldn't even explain it. Simply that he was angry at Ryker because clearly he didn't fully trust Henrik. Didn't fully trust anyone, Henrik knew, but that was exactly why Henrik couldn't tell him *everything*. Not yet. Because he knew Ryker would simply shoot him down. He had to find out more first, on his own. Make his case more persuasive.

He stood up from the bed and listened. Nothing. Ryker's room was three doors down, on the floor below – the hotel didn't have two available rooms any closer – but Henrik wouldn't have put it past Ryker to be standing outside the door, lurking, just in case Henrik decided not to stay put.

The guy really had trust issues.

Had he even placed a camera or some other bug in Henrik's room?

No. Henrik pushed that thought away. Ryker was *capable* of that, but Henrik was sure he hadn't.

He picked up his coat and moved for the door. Opened it. Peeked into the corridor. No sign of Ryker or anyone else. He moved on out. Came out of the lift on the ground floor even more tense than before.

Would he find Ryker sitting in the reception area?

No. No one there at all.

Feeling more than a little surprised – and also just a hint of guilt – Henrik made his way out into the cold night. He hesitated a moment outside. Plenty of options as to where to go from here. Back to the bar was one option he seriously considered. Either straight inside to finish the fight, or even to lurk outside, somewhere dark, until those lads left. He'd pick them off. Make them pay. But doing so would achieve little really. He also thought about Ella. He hadn't expected to find someone like her in that bar but... No, not tonight. He'd see her again soon enough though. He wanted to.

The fact was, the reaction to him in that bar had been strong, and he knew why. Well, not a reaction to him as such, but to what he'd said. What he'd asked about. Who he'd asked about. He'd had no reply to those questions, but the fight, in a way, was answer enough.

Okay, he knew exactly where he needed to go tonight after all.

With a quick look around him to make sure he was alone, Henrik set off through the darkness.

5

Did he trust Henrik? Ryker thought as he lay in his bed. Not really. Henrik was fifteen years old and impulsive. Ryker had had doubts before about whether he needed to watch the boy more closely, but to what end? He really wasn't the kid's guardian. More than once on their travels together they'd shared a room, meaning Ryker was able to keep a close eye on, and control the boy's movements, but Ryker didn't believe either of them really wanted that in the long term. The way Ryker saw it, if Henrik wanted to keep Ryker by his side, he'd have to learn to be open and honest. Simple as that. Trust was built by being trustworthy.

That thought didn't make Ryker feel any more comfortable as he tried to sleep. But what was the alternative? Other than going and spying on Henrik's room through the night to make sure he was there, and stayed there. Ryker wouldn't do that. In many ways, he had to leave it up to Henrik to make his own mistakes. As long as Henrik realised that Ryker wouldn't always be there to bail him out.

Content with his decision, Ryker slept relatively well. He woke just after 8am and showered and dressed before heading to Henrik's room. He knocked and waited. And waited. Knocked again. His brain spun with thoughts when he finally heard soft footsteps on the other side.

Henrik opened the door, hair mussy, eyes bleary.

'Breakfast?' Ryker said, sounding a lot brighter than Henrik looked.

'Give me ten.'

———

Fifteen minutes later they walked the slushy streets in search of a café.

'Anything else you want to tell me?' Ryker said.

'About what?'

'You know.'

Silence, before, 'No.'

'Okay, so this is the plan. We're checking out of that hotel this morning. We'll go and find an outdoor clothing store. We'll buy a tent and all the gear we need and we'll head into the mountains for a few days.'

Ryker looked to Henrik. He didn't seem too impressed by the proposition.

'It was you who wanted to do some climbing I thought,' Ryker said.

Henrik didn't say anything to that.

'And while we're up there, away from civilisation, away from the people here who already hate us, it'll give us plenty of time to talk. Plenty of time for you to tell me exactly why we've come to this town. Because I'm pretty sure it wasn't just to play pool and flirt with young women.'

'Actually playing pool and flirting sounds pretty good to me,' Henrik said with a smile, and Ryker couldn't help but reciprocate.

'The problem is, Henrik, I know you too well.'

He winked. Henrik looked away as though he'd been found out.

They enjoyed a decent breakfast of omelette and orange juice and coffee before arriving at the store just as it was opening for the day. They didn't take long to choose the appropriate gear and a simple pop-up tent. Ryker had enough cash for the purchases, and they had enough left for a few days of food, but they wouldn't be able to afford another night in a hotel without getting more cash from Ryker's reserves, for which they'd need to move to a bigger town to find a money transfer shop.

Henrik's cheap burner phone was also broken beyond repair so Ryker bought him a new one from a convenience store. The cheapest they had. It wasn't as though Henrik really needed anything extravagant. Other than Ryker, he had no one to communicate with.

Having chatted little neither over breakfast, nor in the shops or subsequently on the way back to the hotel, Ryker nonetheless mentally prepared a list of questions for Henrik once they got moving away from St Ricard. Hopefully in the intervening time, Henrik had been given chance enough to realise he needed to spill the beans. Ryker didn't want to have to force the truth out of him. He'd leave it down to the youngster to make the call.

Ryker kept his eyes working as they walked. The streets were already busy with people in their puffy waterproof ski gear, heading for breakfast, or keen to be the first to the slopes. Ryker remained on the lookout for any of the people from the bar, not just from a defensive perspective but because he'd had more than a passing thought about Amelie and how he'd react if he saw her again. He wondered, too, whether Henrik would welcome bumping into Ella.

Perhaps both of them had burned their bridges there already.

They turned the corner toward the hotel. Ryker's eyes rested on the blue-and-white car parked outside, belonging to the gendarmerie – France's rural police, effectively part of the military.

Ryker glanced to Henrik who looked unsure of himself.

'You don't think...'

Henrik didn't finish the thought. He didn't really need to. Ryker did think the police's presence was anything but a coincidence.

As they approached, a gendarme stepped out through the doors of the hotel and moved toward his car, but a couple of beats later he looked over and clocked Ryker and Henrik. A second gendarme stepped from the car and rose to his feet. Ryker looked up. He had to, because the guy was six-six, possible six-seven, and heavyset. His average-sized colleague looked diminutive in comparison.

'You two,' the smaller, older of the two said in French. 'Come here.'

Ryker sensed Henrik staring at him, and he knew why. Henrik was asking him whether they should comply or run. Or even fight. But Ryker had no inclination to cause a scene. Not another one. This was about a simple bar fight. A bar fight he felt perfectly comfortable explaining, even if he did wonder both who'd called the police, and why it had taken them so long to come after them.

'Gentlemen,' Ryker said as they reached the gendarmes, deciding on English.

The two policemen glanced at one another before the smaller one spoke again.

'You need to come with us,' he said to Henrik, switching to English now too.

He made a move toward Henrik but Ryker put his arm out across Henrik's chest.

'I don't think he does.'

Both officers stepped back and placed a hand to their holstered weapons and Ryker raised his hands in defence.

'He's fifteen years old,' Ryker said.

'So?' the bigger gendarme said. 'He still needs to come with us.'

'You're his father?' the smaller asked.

Ryker hesitated, but only for a moment. 'Yes.'

'Then you can come too.'

'What about the others from the bar?' Ryker said. 'The ones who punched and kicked my son. The one who threatened me with a broken glass bottle. Are you arresting them too?'

Both of the gendarmes frowned.

'What bar?' the big man said.

Ryker glanced to Henrik who squirmed away.

The big man leaned down and whispered into his boss's ear, and the look on the smaller guy's face turned from confusion to some sort of amusement.

'Ah. Okay. So *that* was you two as well.'

Ryker and Henrik said nothing. The big man took his hand from the grip of his gun and took a pair of handcuffs from his belt.

'Turn around,' he said to Henrik.

'He's under arrest,' the boss said.

'Arrest?' Ryker said. 'For what?'

'For trespassing. For breaking and entering. And we can talk about the fight too, perhaps.'

'This is rid–'

Ryker went to move to the side to protect Henrik but the big man caught him off guard, grabbed his arm, swung him around and slapped the cuffs over his wrists.

'For your own safety,' he said, before Henrik's hands were cuffed too.

'Now, *gentlemen*, please, this way.'

The gendarmes escorted Ryker and Henrik to the back seats of their car then got into the front. As the car peeled away from the hotel, Ryker found himself looking to a spot on the pavement across the street. A spot where three women in ski gear looked on with interest. His eyes found Amelie's for just a second before she shook her head and looked away, disgusted.

Yes, bridge definitely burned there, Ryker realised, even if he had no clue yet why.

6

The two lieutenants sat across the basic wooden table from Ryker. The big man was Coupet, and the other was Renaud. Ryker was a little surprised to realise both were technically the same rank, though Renaud was clearly the eldest and most experienced and held sway over his younger colleague.

'Where's Henrik?' Ryker asked.

'He's in another interview room,' Renaud said.

'He's fifteen years old. You can't speak to him without me present.'

'Thank you for attempting to explain my job to me.'

'So?'

'First I want to understand something.'

'Which is?'

'You claim this boy is your son.'

'He is.'

'Henrik Iversen.'

'Yes.'

Not Henrik's real surname. If the gendarmerie were to look into Henrik's real identity – Henrik Svenson – they'd find a missing person profile of a fifteen-year-old boy whose previous foster parents were murdered several months ago in Norway. Ryker had pulled a few favours with old associates to get Henrik his alternative identity. The passport was sufficient to allow him to travel freely, but the identity wouldn't hold up to much scrutiny if anyone searched too hard.

Although, really, what was the worst that could happen if they did find that he was Henrik Svenson? Henrik would be sent back to Norway and put back into the care system there. Not what he, or Ryker, would want: an informal arrangement existed between the two of them that Ryker would stay with Henrik now until he was sixteen, when he was at least old enough to find some work, to pay his own way. But if he was taken away, back to Norway, at least he'd be safe and have a roof over his head...

'You have different surnames,' Renaud said.

'Well done.'

'And different nationalities.'

'Welcome to the twenty-first century.'

Renaud's eyes pinched. Coupet squeezed his fist on the table. Both were clearly a little irked by Ryker's nonchalance.

'Do you have any evidence he is your son?'

'I told you he is. And you can ask him. What else do you expect? For me to bring DNA test results with me on holiday?'

'Where do you both live?'

'England.'

James Ryker, semi-officially, at least, did still have a registered address there.

'Where's his mother?' Coupet asked.

'In Norway. But he hasn't seen her since he was two. She's an unemployed drug addict. I think he's better off with me, but if you really think–'

'And you...' Then Renaud paused to thumb the passport in his hand. 'James Ryker?'

'Again. Well done. You want to know about my parents too? Unfortunately I never knew either of them.'

'What are you both doing in St Ricard?'

'Not a lot so far.'

'Apart from fighting in bars, and breaking into people's houses.'

'Self-defence for the first. The second? I have no idea what you're talking about.'

Though Ryker was concerned. Had Henrik really done that, last night, even after the fiasco at the bar? What was the kid playing at?

If it was true, and not a stitch-up, Ryker wondered whose property Henrik had broken into. Someone from the bar, as punishment? He wanted to know. But he wouldn't ask these two.

Renaud sighed, as though not satisfied, but not sure what else to do without creating more work for himself.

'Okay. Let's go and speak with your son.'

―――――――

The room they ended up in was a carbon copy of the one Ryker and the gendarmes had come from. Henrik sat sullen-faced. No hint of fear. Anger, if anything. Ryker wasn't given a chance to speak to him one on one before Renaud opened proceedings with the reasons for Henrik's arrest, and a reminder of his rights.

'Do you understand?' Renaud asked.

'Yes,' Henrik said.

'This man is your father?' Renaud asked, looking to Ryker who sighed, a little bored of that line of questioning now.

'Yes,' Henrik said, barely without thought.

'And you're happy for him to be your... person with responsibility here.'

Perhaps not the technical phrase he was searching for, but

they were conducting the interview in English, and Ryker at least appreciated that.

'Yes,' Henrik said again.

'Then perhaps we can begin with your explanation for where you were last night, at approximately 12.30am.'

Henrik shrugged.

'You need to give me an actual answer.'

'I don't remember,' Henrik said.

Renaud sighed. 'You don't remember? Were you in your hotel room?'

'Probably.'

Couldn't he at least have said *yes*, Ryker thought.

'I may be able to help here,' Coupet said, before turning over the papers under his fist. CCTV images. One from the hotel lobby showing a figure stepping out into the night, timestamped 11.48. Then another three from a property Ryker didn't recognise. One from a perimeter wall, perhaps, one from the building itself, looking to an entrance, and one from an internal hallway. In all four shots, the figure wore the same clothing, appeared the same height and build. But in all four the figure also wore a hood over a cap, covering much of their face.

Still, Ryker knew he was looking at Henrik. The big question was, how did the police know? Even if Henrik had left fingerprints, the police wouldn't have had Henrik's on record, and wouldn't have known to go to L'Hotel Alpine to find him.

What was Ryker missing?

And all of that disregarded the biggest question of all. Why had Henrik gone to that house?

'Is this you?' Renaud asked.

'No,' Henrik said.

Ryker looked down at him. The boy's face remained passive, in control.

'Why do you think these pictures are of my son?' Ryker asked. 'You can't even see a face on these shots.'

'Are you saying you think it's someone else?'

'He just told you it's not him.'

'His clothing is similar–'

'Dark trousers and a hooded jacket?'

'The description matches to statements we have from two witnesses,' Coupet said. 'Both claim to have seen a teenager. Slim build. Long hair.'

'This figure is wearing a cap and a hood. How can you see long hair?' Ryker asked. 'And are you saying you don't have any other slim teenagers in St Ricard?'

'We probably do,' Renaud said. 'But not one that one of the witnesses saw walk back to L'Hotel Alpine, shortly after 1am this morning.'

Ryker chewed on that for a few moments. Had someone followed Henrik all the way from the property? If so, why? Why hadn't the police simply been called there and then, and Henrik picked up in the night?

The story, the police's actions, didn't add up.

'What do you know of Monique Thibaud?' Renaud asked Henrik.

'Never heard of her,' Henrik said, and the statement sounded strong enough, even if Ryker didn't believe it.

'No? You've been in this town for less than twenty-four hours. You start a fight in a bar here, asking questions about Madame Thibaud's family, then later in the night you break into her house–'

'Hang on,' Ryker said, holding his hand up, the sudden move causing Coupet to flinch as though he was about ready to fly across the table to tackle Ryker if he did anything stupid. 'The fight in the bar–'

'We know about it,' Renaud said.

'My brother works there,' Coupet said, as though the explanation was both needed and sufficient.

'So you do know what happened?' Ryker asked.

'I just said so,' Coupet responded.

'But before you didn't seem to.'

'And now we do.'

What were these two playing at?

'Have you arrested anyone yet for attacking us?' Ryker said. No answer.

'I'm sure if you watched the CCTV from the bar you'd find out exactly what happened. Have you done that yet?' No answer. 'Clearly you've had plenty of time to speak to witnesses and do whatever else related to this apparent break-in, yet the bar fight happened hours before that even.'

Renaud and Coupet both said nothing still, yet Ryker could tell Renaud was clenching his jaw shut.

'Why did you come to St Ricard?' Coupet asked, looking from Ryker to Henrik.

'Haven't you asked that already?' Ryker said.

'Hiking,' Henrik answered. 'You saw the things we bought this morning.'

'You often break into people's houses while hiking?' Coupet asked.

'Was anything stolen?' Ryker asked. 'From Monique Thibaud's home?'

'We don't think so,' Coupet said, and Renaud shot him a look as if angered by the answer.

'And no one was threatened or hurt?'

No answer this time, which was enough of an answer really.

'So whoever did this... it's a very simple misdemeanour.'

'Monsieur Ryker, you're not–'

'So what's the worst you could do here, if the break-in even was Henrik, a boy? A fine? Deport him back home?'

'This is more serious than you–'

'No, it's not,' Ryker said. 'I think we're done here.' He sat back in his chair, arms folded.

'Excuse me?' Renaud said, eyebrow raised.

'You can let us go now. We're done here. And we're done in St Ricard. We'll leave today.'

'That's not how–'

'It is how it works. I've already explained the situation. Even if this was Henrik...' Ryker pointed to the pictures, '... I'm more than a little suspicious as to your steps in getting these images, and coming to us this morning. Who are these two witnesses you claim to have? Where, exactly, did they see this alleged perpetrator? Did they both see him at the property or away from it? If the latter, how do you know it's the same person that both witnesses saw? How did they know it's the person from the break-in? And don't get me started on the bar incident, and that fact you *knew* about that but have clearly done nothing about it, and have also showed no signs that you're intending to do anything about it, even though I explained that we were attacked there. And then we have the fact that Lieutenant Coupet's family member works there too? I'd say you've got quite a mess to wade through here. A mess that might not go where you want it to go if you keep pursuing it.'

The room fell silent. Ryker wondered for a moment whether his monologue had been too much – had the gendarmes understood him? The fact both Renaud and Coupet looked like they were chewing wasps suggested they had – enough of it at least.

'So you can keep my son here, under arrest, and *hope* that you get an outcome that works for you both. Do you get bonuses for fifteen-year-olds paying fines? Or, you can let us go now. As a favour, goodwill gesture or whatever, we'll leave St Ricard today, and we can all move on from whatever it is we think happened last night.'

Neither of the men in front of Ryker said a word. Renaud leaned over and whispered into Coupet's ear. Then Renaud leaned over the other way and stopped the recording of the interview. Then he erased the record.

'You can go,' Renaud said. 'But let me make myself very clear. You *will* leave St Ricard today. And you will leave Madame Thibaud and her family alone. If you don't, next time the response might not be so friendly.'

'I think we can abide by that,' Ryker said. He looked at Henrik.

'Yeah, sounds good to me,' Henrik said, but the look the teen gave was far from convincing.

7

Snow fell from the murky grey sky in big clumps as Ryker and Henrik walked out of L'Hotel Alpine with their things. Ryker half expected to see Renaud and Coupet lurking across the street, intent on seeing the two of them out of town. They weren't there.

As with the night before, when Ryker and Henrik had left the bar following the fight, there was little chat between the two of them as they walked, though plenty that needed to be said. Henrik, in his silence, looked chastised, his head down, as though he sensed what was to come.

'We'll climb up the north side here,' Ryker said, indicating to a brown slushy trail that led from the town and into a pine forest that rose high above them. 'There's a ridge a couple of thousand metres up that we can walk across and if we find somewhere sheltered it should be a good place to camp out, looking out over the Alps.'

Henrik stopped walking and Ryker followed suit and turned to look at him. He seemed... worried.

'I thought... I thought we were leaving.'

'We're leaving St Ricard. We don't have to leave the area.

When we're done perhaps we'll trek back down to another town.'

'But I thought maybe... you'd want to get away from me now. Because I lied about...'

'Lied *again*,' Ryker corrected. Then he sighed. 'Come on, let's get moving. It's a long way up.'

Long, and hard, it turned out. The winter conditions didn't help, with plenty of snow and ice to clamber across on the ascent, but they eventually made it to the ridge which swept around like a giant horseshoe for several miles. The clouds had cleared and the sky above them was azure in colour, though the low sun behind them to the west would disappear behind the peaks soon enough, and then the temperature would drop.

They carried on along the ridge for a couple of miles, the going easier than before, until they found a rocky outcrop that provided decent shelter from the increasingly biting wind. Ryker set up the tent and dug a firepit while Henrik gathered wood. Ryker sat back and let Henrik set the fire – he was a natural at it. Ryker never saw him so happy and relaxed as when he was outdoors, taking care of himself. Skills learned and habits developed living a lonely life in northern Norway.

'Aren't you ever going to ask me?' Henrik said, eyes focused on the fire which he stoked with a thin stick.

'How about you just tell me,' Ryker responded.

Henrik sighed, as though building up to it.

'We didn't come to St Ricard for the hiking or the skiing, did we?' Ryker said, to prompt him.

'Actually I really enjoyed the hike,' Henrik said with a smile, 'though I think I've got a blister from these boots.'

He squirmed and stuck a finger down the back of his left

boot as if to cement his words. Ryker didn't say anything and after a few moments Henrik's face fell again as he realised he still hadn't said what he needed to.

'I read a story online,' he began. 'It happened a few months ago in St Ricard. A triple murder. The victims were all in the Thibaud family. Mother, father, son, who was only twelve years old. Their seventeen-year-old daughter, Sophie, escaped.'

'Thibaud. So the same family as Monique?'

'She's Thierry's sister. He was the father.'

'So what happened? You want to solve a murder now?'

Henrik laughed, a little nervously. 'There's quite a lot more to it than that.'

'Go on.'

'So, one night two armed men turned up at their home, in the hills near St Ricard.'

'Not the same—'

'Not the same home where Monique lives, no. She lives closer to the town.'

Was that why he'd chosen to sneak there, because it was closer? But what did she have to do with the murders?

'The men stole jewellery, cash, and a small amount of gold,' Henrik said, eyes focused on the flames of the fire. 'But... it wasn't a simple robbery. The family were rounded up. The thieves drove them out into the forest in the middle of the night. Then lined them up on the ground. They shot the father in the back of the head. Executed him. They probably intended to do the same to all of the family, except Sophie and her mother and brother tried to run. Only Sophie made it, but only because she fell over a ridge. Some reports said she fell over a hundred feet. The attackers didn't chase after her. She disappeared. The housekeeper was killed in the house, collateral damage most likely. Her husband phoned the police the next day to say she was missing and the police went to check the house and...'

'And Sophie?'

'A huge search was set up to find her, but they didn't succeed. People began to speculate that she'd been kidnapped, or perhaps her body was eaten by animals. Then, a week later, she appeared in the town, malnourished, severe hypothermia. She'd been lost in the mountains, too injured to move more than a couple of miles a day.'

Ryker chewed on the story for a few moments, his brain already theorising what had happened; the motive, what Sophie – the survivor – must have gone through in those seven days. He'd been stranded in a frozen wilderness before. Left for dead with a broken leg, miles away from civilisation. He'd made it back alive, somehow, though the painful memories of that horrific time never eased. He shivered now, as he reminisced. Probably not the best place to be thinking about that time, stuck in the snow two thousand metres up.

'And why are you so interested in this?' Ryker asked.

Though the words *damsel in distress* sprung to mind. No doubt Sophie was an attractive young woman. Was Henrik here to save her? From what?

'Sophie spent a couple of weeks in hospital. Then her aunt – Monique Thibaud – took her in to look after her as she recovered fully, and to help shield her from the press. Her aunt is a rich woman. The whole Thibaud family are rich, actually. Their grandfather started what became one of the largest champagne houses in the country. You must know it.'

Ryker had heard of the champagne. Not the family.

'They're a well-known family, and every paper in France asked questions about this story. Sophie, as the only surviving member of her immediate family, has inherited her father's portion of the wider family's wealth.'

The mention of money certainly changed the landscape.

The amount of death and violence that Ryker had seen boil down to greed and a need to acquire riches...

'So Sophie's recovered and living with her rich aunt,' Ryker said. 'I ask again, why are you so interested?'

'The police put the murders on two men. Didier Lenglet and Ramiz Touba. Lenglet was a known criminal from Lyon. He had a list of offences, but mostly small-time things. Car theft, burglary, assault. There were rumours he worked for a local Algerian gang. Touba was an Algerian national who the police have since publicly claimed to be responsible for three other murders. Gang related.'

'A hitman?'

Henrik shrugged.

'And where are Lenglet and Touba now?'

'Lenglet was shot and killed when the police went to arrest him. Touba was arrested but then attacked in prison before his trial. His throat was slit.'

Ryker winced. Henrik spoke so calmly about all these acts of horrific violence.

'It's obvious, isn't it?' Henrik said.

'What is?'

'They weren't the killers. Or, at least, if they were, then someone put them up to it. And that's why they're both now dead. A cover-up.'

Ryker had to admit, even going only off what Henrik had said, the story didn't add up. That didn't mean the events had anything to do with him and Henrik though.

'What's the theory then?' Ryker asked anyway, unable to stop himself turning the story over in his head now.

Henrik sighed. 'I don't know. The official line is that Thierry Thibaud and his family were targeted because they were rich. They estimate the items stolen had a value of more than two million euros.'

'And the unofficial theory?'

'There's a lot. Some more crazy than others. But Thibaud's wife worked as a lawyer. She was also a big environmentalist. One of her recent, quite public projects, was as the chair of a group who were opposed to the building of a dam in the Fontaine valley, a few miles from St Ricard.'

Ryker raised an eyebrow. Both at the potentially interesting turn in the story, but also the depth of his young companion's knowledge.

'When did you even come across all this?'

Henrik poked the fire again, unable to look Ryker in the eye. 'Weeks ago.'

'And you didn't tell me because?'

'Because I thought you wouldn't let us come here.'

True. He wouldn't have.

'So you think it's a cover-up.'

'It makes some sense, doesn't it?'

Ryker dwelled for a few moments.

'Now explain to me last night,' he said, his tone harder. 'What happened in the bar?'

Henrik shuffled on his perch, as though this was the uncomfortable part he hadn't wanted to get to.

'I thought... if there is a cover-up, then two out-of-towners asking difficult questions would stir things up. St Ricard is tiny. Everyone would know the Thibauds. Most likely, all those teenagers knew Sophie too. I thought if I started probing...'

Inwardly Ryker admonished himself. Most likely Henrik had picked that trick up from him. Asking awkward questions of people with something to hide usually got one reaction only...

'And it did, right?' Henrik said, a little more enthused. 'I knew as soon as I mentioned Sophie's name that the subject was taboo. And so I carried on talking, asking more and more and... look where it ended.'

'The bar fight? Except it didn't end there. Because next you snuck out of the hotel and broke into Monique Thibaud's home.'

'I shook things up a little bit more,' Henrik said, no hint of remorse. 'You know, since she reappeared, no one's seen Sophie for weeks. Why has her aunt locked her away?'

'Because she's been through hell.'

'Yeah,' Henrik said with a petulant sneer. 'Or something else. Like she knows more about what happened. Something she doesn't want others to know.'

'That still doesn't justify you breaking into her home.'

An eye-roll now. Henrik's confidence certainly hadn't been dented by any of this, and now he was getting the story – and his actions – out in the open, he was becoming bolder all the time.

'And what happened next?' Ryker asked.

'Her home is this big old farmhouse, but it's hardly the most secure. She's not like a security conscious kingpin. But she did have these guards. Why? I was chased out of there by two of them. Proper security guards, like you'd expect the Mafia to have or something. But I got away from them easily. There's no way anyone from the house followed me back to the hotel. If the guards had me in their sights... well, they wouldn't have just sneaked around following me to see where I went. Would they?'

'So what are you saying?'

'The gendarmes still found me. Us. Didn't they? Which shows that something bigger is happening in St Ricard. Some of the locals know something about it. Those police probably too.'

Ryker had thought the whole situation with the gendarmerie odd. Was this the explanation?

'And I know that woman, Monique Thibaud, is hiding something too. When I broke in, into the hallway of her home, before the guards came after me, I saw her. I saw the look in her eyes. We need to find and speak to Sophie.'

Ryker sucked in a lungful of cold air through his nostrils to try and clear his thoughts before he spoke.

'It's an interesting story,' he said.

They both went silent. Henrik looked from the fire to Ryker, a frown spreading across his face.

'That's it?'

'What?' Ryker said.

'An interesting story?'

'That's what I said.'

'So we're–'

'Not going to do anything about it.'

'You can't–'

'Can't what? Make decisions for us? That's exactly what I'm here to do. This... whatever happened to Sophie Thibaud and her family has nothing to do with either of us. Only months ago we both very nearly got killed and now–'

'But we didn't get killed, did we? And we only came together in the first place because of a chance encounter like this. You came to Blodstein, a place you'd never been to before, and helped to–'

'This is different. I didn't go to Blodstein knowing I'd get involved in anything. It simply happened that way.'

Henrik scoffed. 'So you can only go to a town and help people if you don't know about their problems before you arrive? That's nonsense. I'm sorry but I really don't see the difference at all. You could have walked away in Blodstein, but you chose to stay and do the right thing. We *could* help here. I know you, Ryker, I know you're a good man, and you *can* help here. And it's not like you have anything better or more important to do, so why *wouldn't* you help?'

Put like that, Ryker could see the point. Yet one of the biggest reasons why he wouldn't help was because of the underhand

tactics Henrik had used. What life lesson would that teach him?
To get what he wanted he only had to lie and trick?

But was it right to punish Henrik, and in the process allow
people – whoever they were – to get away with murder? What
about the victims?

'What do we get out of it?' Ryker asked.

No answer.

'Seriously, Henrik, are you really willing to put your life, or
at least your freedom, on the line, trying to help a young woman
you've never even met before?'

'I don't really have a life. So yes. Why can't *this* be my life?'

'This?'

'Helping people who need it.'

Ryker sighed again. He didn't want to admit it, but he found
Henrik's insistence more convincing than he'd expected.

During the contemplative silence that followed, Henrik
added a couple of logs to the fire. Ryker watched the flames as
the bark on the outside of the new logs fizzed and crackled.

'You know what I think?' Henrik said, looking back up at
Ryker with determination on his face.

'Shhh,' Ryker said, holding a hand up.

Henrik looked confused, but only for a second before his
expression changed to something quite different – fear.

He'd heard it too.

They weren't alone.

8

Ryker turned to the copse of trees leading down into the valley to the west, behind which the sun had disappeared a couple of hours ago. Henrik followed his line of sight.

'What is it?' Henrik asked.

Ryker didn't answer. He kept his eyes on a spot in the trees. Henrik had heard the sound too. He expected a figure to come into view, perhaps more than one, but then he averted his eyes downward to the low moving shape, slinking slowly, prowling.

Not a person. A lone animal. Wolf?

Its bright eyes glinted in the moonlight, its shoulder blades protruding above its dipped head as it sniffed the air and padded toward them, one cautious step at a time.

Ryker rose to his feet.

'Stand up,' he said to Henrik. 'Don't panic. Make yourself tall. Keep eye contact with it. Wolves don't like fire. If we stand our ground here, it'll move on soon enough.'

Henrik noticed Ryker dig his hand into the side pocket of his trousers. For his knife?

Henrik knew Ryker was as tough as any man or woman he'd ever met. But this wasn't his natural habitat.

'A lone wolf is threat enough,' Ryker whispered, 'but it's equally possible this one has simply moved ahead of its friends, and before long we'll have a whole pack circling us.'

'So what?' Henrik said. 'You're going to gut it?'

Ryker shot him an angry glare. For what? Speaking too loudly? Or his choice of words?

The animal kept coming forward, one slow, deliberate step at a time. Henrik shuffled next to Ryker and the wolf raised its head a little, the brown and grey fur on its neck bristling before its gums parted to reveal its sharp teeth. A rumbling growl caused its gums to vibrate.

'Henrik,' Ryker said in warning. 'I said don't move.'

But Henrik stooped down to his rucksack.

'What are you doing?' Ryker said, stern, but clearly trying to sound calm in order to not panic the animal. But Henrik knew Ryker had read this wrong.

Henrik moved slowly but deliberately, opening the rucksack, pulling out a packet of jerky.

'Henrik–'

'It's okay. I know what I'm doing.'

He stood tall again. Took a couple of steps away from the fire, closer to the animal. He sensed Ryker shuffle behind him, as though about to reach forward to grab him and haul him back, then...

'It's not a wolf,' Henrik said, hoping to calm his companion before he did something stupid. 'The colourings are wrong. Its snout isn't long enough. It's too big as well. It's a hybrid. A wolfdog, I think.'

Henrik slowly crouched as the wolfdog renewed its growl. Then Henrik tossed a bit of meat its way. The growling stopped and the animal sniffed, its glistening nose twitching before it took a cautious step to the morsel. It chomped at the snow, taking the meat in its mouth, then looked up at Henrik expectantly, sniffing away.

'This one's got a sled dog of some kind in it, I think.'

Ryker didn't respond as he stared at the animal.

'Most often wolfdogs come about when a stray dog meets a young male wolf. A loner. With a pack, the others would most likely attack and kill the stray. But a lone male? He just wants to mate. And far easier to do that with the stray than to attack an alpha for a female. It's still an unusual situation, but it does happen.'

Henrik glanced over his shoulder to Ryker who still hadn't moved from the spot by the fire. His fingers remained wrapped around the handle of the knife that hung by his side.

'That doesn't mean it isn't a wild animal still,' Ryker said.

'No,' Henrik said, turning back to the animal. 'But it does mean it's not as naturally wary of humans as a pure wolf would be.'

Henrik tossed another bit of meat and the wolfdog once again sniffed the air before moving closer still to pick up the food. Only five yards separated Henrik and the animal, but then Henrik, still crouching, took a step back toward the fire. He didn't want to get too close too soon. Ryker was right. This animal was wild. There was a chance it could be tamed, but it had to be on its terms. Too much too soon would scare it off or cause it to launch an attack, reacting to its own fear.

But Henrik wasn't unused to these situations. He'd met a lone stray at home two years ago. Maverick, he'd called him. An adult dog. At that time Henrik had run away from his foster home and spent several nights at a time in the forests, only going to the town to get – steal – food when he couldn't get enough from foraging or hunting. He and Maverick had made a good team. They'd spent months together. Each time Henrik had left for the town, he left Maverick in the same spot by an old boat shed. The dog was always right there when he returned, even if every time Henrik had a horrible doubt in his belly as he neared. Maverick had never once let him down. They walked, hunted, slept together.

Until one night three wolves appeared. Three very hungry wolves. Perhaps on his own Henrik could have fended them off with fire or noise or whatever, or perhaps that night would have been the end of him. But Maverick... he did what came naturally to him. He tried to protect Henrik, his leader. He did enough. Sacrificed his own life in the process.

Henrik hadn't ever bonded with another being as much as he had with that dog. Well, except perhaps with Ryker...

He'd never told anyone a thing about Maverick. His existence was a secret – a comfort – that belonged solely to Henrik.

This wolfdog in front of him had more than a passing resemblance to his lost friend.

'You know all domestic dogs originated from wolves,' Henrik said.

'I know that,' Ryker responded.

'And how do you think that happened?' Henrik paused. Ryker looked at him as though not sure whether or not he was supposed to answer. 'Thousands of years ago, wolves and humans learned to co-exist. Humans were dangerous to wolves, wolves dangerous to humans, but wolves also learned that humans were a good source of food. Not eating us, I mean we could provide for them. They're basic creatures really. Survival is their number one aim. Humans could provide food, meaning the wolves didn't have to hunt all the time. And wolves provided protection for humans.'

Ryker still said nothing. Henrik dropped another piece of meat right in front of him. The animal set its eyes on the food, unblinking, but didn't make a move for it straight away. It pushed its head forward a couple of times, as though testing how close it could get to the meat without actually moving. Then it made the bold decision, stepping forward and stooping down for the food. Henrik reached out and slid his hand across the dog's neck and back. The dog flinched a little. Ryker did too, Henrik noticed, and he worried that Ryker might leap forward with the knife. He didn't, and the animal simply looked back up, hungrily, as Henrik continued to slowly caress the dense fur.

'And what happens when you run out of jerky?' Ryker said, still sounding wary.

'Either it'll hang around to see what's next, or it'll retreat to the woods and carry on whatever it was doing.'

Henrik looked up at Ryker and smiled as he stroked the fur. Ryker looked... impressed.

'You don't like wolves?' Henrik asked him.

'I don't have any experience with them.'

'Most people don't. You know why?'

'Why?'

'Because it was easier for humans to kill them than to live with them.'

Ryker didn't say anything, but he looked less than convinced.

'Wolves once roamed in every corner of Europe, but humans drove them out,' Henrik continued, two hands on the dog now. 'Not because they were a direct threat to us, but because they were a threat to our new-found farming skills. Easier to just kill them all, rather than to find other ways to protect our livestock.'

Ryker still didn't respond. He crouched back down next to the fire, his eyes fixed on the wolfdog, as if entranced by the growing bond between it and Henrik, who fed the animal another piece of meat from his hand.

'Many countries are now deliberately reintroducing wolves,

to stop them going extinct. Do you know how many we have in Norway?'

Ryker seemed to think about that, as though calculating how many could be spread over the vast, largely forested terrain, where wild animals, particularly those suited to the cold, could thrive.

'How many?' Ryker asked.

'Around a hundred. That's it. And many of those few packs roam between both Norway and Sweden. And you know what?'

'What?'

'Our government removed protections for the wolves not long ago. They actually want to actively reduce the numbers. Can you believe that? We only have a hundred and they want to kill some of those. It's all driven by lazy, but very loud farmers.'

Henrik gave the animal the last bit of jerky and it sniffed around on the floor and in the air and around Henrik's hand as though searching for more.

'Can you imagine the outcry if a country in Africa said they wanted to cull lions to the point of extinction? Or tigers in Asia? Most people love those animals, even though they're just as dangerous, perhaps more dangerous. But most people hate the idea of wolves living near them, even though they've probably never seen one. Like you.'

Ryker raised an eyebrow, as though not sure whether to be offended or not. Then as Henrik scrunched up the jerky wrapper, the dog flinched and pulled from his grip, and stared back to the woods where it'd come from. Henrik tensed, wary of the sudden change in mood. He sensed Ryker renew his grip on the knife as he rose back to his feet. The wolfdog growled. But not at Henrik, or even at Ryker.

At the woods.

Henrik whipped his eyes that way. A crunching sound. He half expected to see another animal appear from the trees – was this dog not a loner after all? But the wolfdog moved into a defensive position, just like when it had first approached them. Two figures emerged from the trees. A man. A woman. The man had a handgun in his grip, pointing toward Henrik's new friend.

'Don't move,' he said, looking at the dog but his instruction clearly meant for Ryker and Henrik.

The dog bared its teeth as its growl intensified. Henrik straightened up.

'I know you,' he said, a deep frown on his face.

Ryker looked from Henrik to the man. The woman, by his side, had her hand resting on her hip. Another gun.

'Yeah, you do,' the man said.

'Well I bloody don't,' Ryker said. 'What the hell is going on?'

His raised tone caught the attention of the wolfdog, who glared at him, its growl dissipating, then...

'Now!' the woman shouted.

The dog bolted. The man opened fire. The dog yelped as it shot off over a rocky edge and out of sight.

'No!' Henrik screamed, racing toward the man, who set off after the dog. The woman was about to move that way too.

Ryker went for her. She pulled out the gun as the man fired another shot, a split second before Henrik barrelled into him. Not enough strength or weight behind the tackle to send the guy flying, but the man did stumble, and his gun hand was pushed away as he pulled on the trigger again.

Ryker slammed into the woman before she could aim at anything. They landed in a heap in the snow, sending fluffy powder up into the air. Her gun came free. Ryker bounced back to his feet as the man grabbed Henrik by the throat and tossed him to the ground. He readjusted his gun, an angry snarl on his face as he swung the weapon toward Henrik's head.

He didn't get a chance to fire before Ryker dove into him,

taking his legs around the knees. An explosion of snow erupted into the air as the two hefty bodies splatted down.

Ryker spun and pushed his weight back to his feet. Henrik writhed on the ground, disorientated. The man growled in anger as he searched in the snow for his weapon. The woman already had hers in her grip once more. Aiming for Ryker's head...

The wolfdog came from nowhere. Launched itself through the air, mouth open. It chomped down on the woman's arm and she let out a blood-curdling scream and dropped her gun once more.

BANG. BANG.

The dog squealed and dropped to the floor. Henrik shouted out in anguish. Ryker raced forward, aiming to pick her gun from the ground. The woman clutched her bleeding arm. The dog... it wasn't finished yet. Survival mode. Pure desperation. It lunged for the woman, grabbed her around the neck. Pinned her.

The man fired again. Headshot. The dog collapsed as the woman, shouting and screaming, pulled herself free, not knowing whether to clutch her arm or the oozing wound on her neck.

'Don't,' the man shouted out. To Ryker. Who was only a step away from the gun.

Beside the man, Henrik remained crouched, his feet planted, ready to pounce. Anger consumed him. Rage.

'*Neither* of you move,' the man added, swinging the gun from Ryker to Henrik as he edged to his friend who scuttled toward him for cover. She was badly injured. Too injured to fight. They were retreating. Would Ryker let them? Henrik certainly didn't want them to get away.

The man and woman back-stepped together, toward the trees. Ryker twitched, as though wanting to go for the gun, but a warning shot, the bullet blasting into the snow a few inches from his foot, made him stay put.

'This isn't over,' Henrik snarled, glaring from the man to the heap of bloody fur.

'Damn right it isn't,' the man said.

They continued to move back to the trees. Then, when they'd passed the first tree, they turned and ran.

Ryker dove for the gun. Lifted it up, pointing it toward the woods. He didn't fire.

Henrik raced over to the dog. Lifted its sorry head. He closed his eyes in despair as he let go and the head slumped into the blood-soaked snow. Images and painful memories of Maverick's end burned in his mind.

'There's a trail,' Ryker said, indicating the blood in the snow. 'We can follow them. We'll find them.'

'No,' Henrik said, grimacing as he clutched his ankle. 'We don't need to. Not yet.'

'Not yet?' Ryker said. 'Henrik, who were they?'

'The woman, I don't know. But I saw that man last night. At Monique Thibaud's home.'

'One of the guards?'

Henrik nodded. 'They followed us here. To kill us.'

'Why would they do that?'

'Exactly.'

Both of them fell silent for a few seconds.

'Still want to walk away from this?' Henrik asked as he tried to keep his anger bottled.

'We don't even know what this is,' Ryker said.

'No. *We* don't,' Henrik said. 'But perhaps they do.'

Ryker kept quiet as he thought.

'So?' Henrik prompted. 'You want us to walk away now?'

Ryker looked from Henrik, down to the dog in the snow.

'Not a chance,' he said.

9

Despite the anger that Ryker knew both of them felt, and that urged them to give immediate chase, he persuaded Henrik that they should stay away from St Ricard, for now. They found a secluded spot in the woods to shelter in for the night. Henrik had twisted his ankle in the fight with the man. Nothing serious, but Ryker hoped the hours of rest would ease the injury sufficiently for the long trek back down to civilisation.

It was possible that the man and woman could head back to St Ricard and gather backup before returning to the mountain for a second try at killing – or was it capturing? – Ryker and Henrik, but Ryker decided the chances of that, given the distance they'd need to cover, and the added difficulties of moving at night, was slim.

Before they retreated to the tent for the evening, Henrik insisted on burying the remains of his new-found friend. Ryker found the tender moment, as they stared silently at the small brown mound surrounded by white snow, both heart-warming and heartbreaking. Henrik had known the animal for all of ten minutes, but the bond was unmistakeable. As was his anger.

Ryker had rarely seen him so emotional. Was there something more to his anguish?

'It was my fault,' Henrik said.

'No it wasn't.'

'If I had just scared him away to start with, he wouldn't have been hurt.'

'You didn't do anything wrong.'

'No. It was my fault. I shouldn't have fed him. I wanted to show you I... I wanted to impress you.'

'You did.'

Henrik huffed.

'He's dead because of me.'

'No. He's dead because of them. And because he tried to protect you.'

Henrik walked away without saying another word.

———

Ryker awoke the next morning to the intense winter sun beating down on the thin fabric of their tent. Not exactly a blissful night, out in the cold, the wind whistling, his brain whirring. But they'd needed the rest. At least the shining sun brought some feeling of positivity.

'How's the ankle?' Ryker said as Henrik emerged from the tent twenty minutes later, by which point Ryker had relit the fire from the night before and had a tin of soup bubbling away in a pan.

'Good enough,' Henrik responded, but he had a noticeable limp, and Ryker could tell he was battling through pain, trying to be brave.

'We can stay here longer,' Ryker said.

'I'm not sitting waiting for them to come back.'

'We could move to a different location–'

'We're going down this morning. I'll be fine when I'm moving.'

Little more was said as they ate and then packed up their site. Ryker kicked heaps of snow over the fire to put it out then tossed his backpack over his shoulders.

'A lot of gear for an assault,' Henrik said.

'We're not going on an assault,' Ryker said.

'Then what are we doing?'

'We're going to find out what's going on.'

Henrik didn't hide his agitation very well, a sneer spreading across his face.

'They tried to kill us,' Henrik said.

'Perhaps they did. Perhaps that wasn't their original intention. Either way, when we get back down to St Ricard, it's not on a revenge mission. I want some answers.'

'And what if they answer your questions by shoving a gun to your forehead?'

'They can try. And then we'll protect ourselves. But this isn't an all-out assault.'

Henrik still didn't look convinced.

'Or we can just forget all about it and go somewhere else. Your choice.'

A silent stand-off. Then, 'Fine. Let's go.'

———

They were tired and hungry as St Ricard came into view below them. Despite the bright start, the sun had disappeared behind thick cloud not long after they started their descent, and given the murkiness, the lights of the town were already on, drawing them in. Ryker was tempted to at least refuel with a proper meal before they headed on to Monique Thibaud's home, but would the gendarmes swoop if they made their presence so obvious in a public space?

Instead, they settled on having some more of the rations from their backpacks while sitting in a small clearing in the woods, the twinkling lights of the town less than a mile below them.

'Should we dump our gear?' Henrik said as they finished off the cold food.

'Probably a good idea,' Ryker said. They needed to be mobile. Just in case. Even if it did potentially mean a waste of good money if they couldn't get back here, or if the items were ruined or stolen.

They hid their backpacks below a mesh of sticks and piney branches, completely covering the coloured fabric from sight, and hopefully providing decent cover from the elements, for a short time at least. They retained their winter clothing, and each of them had a hunting knife, plus Ryker had a pocket utility knife, a compass, and a torch.

In quiet trepidation, they made the final descent, skirting around the outside of the town as much as they could to keep out of sight.

'How far?' Ryker asked Henrik as they crossed over a road which Ryker knew led into the main town square, not far from their previous hotel.

'Less than ten minutes from here,' Henrik said.

They walked past the last of the town's buildings. Ryker glanced behind him at the fading lights as they moved up a steep, twisting road, barely wide enough for a vehicle.

'How did you get in last time?' Ryker asked.

'I went over the wall at the back. There are a couple of spotlights there but I managed to evade them to get to the back of the house.'

Evaded the spotlights, though not the CCTV cameras, it seemed.

'I prised open a window. They're all sashes, pretty old too. It's not a fortress, it's a big old stone house.'

'Security system?'

'There is one. I saw the infrared sensors inside. And a control panel in the kitchen and in the entrance hall. But it wasn't set at all when I was there. I think because she was home, and because she had the security guards patrolling anyway.'

Ryker thought for a moment.

'Is that the plan again?' Henrik said. 'I know we'll get in that way. There's plenty of cover, even in daylight.'

Though there wasn't really much of that anyway.

'But you were caught last time,' Ryker said. 'So your plan wasn't foolproof.'

'I kind of wanted to be caught. I went there to confront Monique. To find Sophie. I wasn't there to steal gems or anything.'

Ryker said nothing to that.

'So?' Henrik prompted.

'So what?'

'Shall we do the same again?'

'No. Like you said, we're not here to steal. We're here to talk.'

'What do we do then?'

'We ask nicely if we can go inside.'

Henrik paused, then, 'Seriously?'

'Seriously,' Ryker said with a smile.

They rounded a bend on the incline and the house came into view in front of them. Perhaps a farmhouse originally, the stone-built building had at some point in its history been transformed into a handsome – and very big – home. The low-rise wall at the front swept up to a pair of wrought-iron gates that were closed, but didn't appear to be locked. No one in sight as Ryker and Henrik approached.

'Like I said, it's hardly Fort Knox, is it?' Henrik said.

Ryker smiled at the colloquial expression. 'Fort Knox isn't that secure either.'

Henrik looked at him, eyebrow raised.

'Fort Knox is just a military base. People confuse the name with the United States Bullion Depository. It's right next door to Fort Knox, but it's not technically part of the military base.'

Henrik stopped walking a couple of yards from the gates. Ryker followed suit.

'Okay. So I should have said, *it's hardly the United States Bullion Depository.*'

'It'd be more accurate. And anyway, even the security at the depository isn't as advanced as it used to be. Nor is the place anywhere near as important, all things considered.'

'There's no gold there?'

'Oh, there's still plenty of gold. A few thousand tons. About half of the reserves of the US. But it's less than half of what they used to store there, and overall gold itself is much less significant these days, when you think about it.'

'Huh,' Henrik said, eyeing Ryker with suspicion now, as though he sensed Ryker knew a lot more about Fort Knox and the US gold reserves right next door to it than most people did.

Which Ryker did, but that was a story for another day. They had company.

'*Bonjour,*' Ryker said, turning to face the man who sauntered toward them from beyond the gates.

'What do you want?' the man asked in French.

Not the same man as had shot the dog up in the mountains, even if he was similarly dressed – waterproof trousers, bulky outdoor coat, black boots, beanie hat. He was short but thickset, mottled skin on his face.

'To speak with Madame Thibaud,' Ryker said as he and Henrik moved slowly toward the gates.

'She's not expecting anyone.'

Ryker looked beyond the man and to the grounds around the home. He couldn't spot anyone else lying in wait. So where were those other two?

He wondered how serious the woman's wounds were.

'I think she'll want to speak to us,' Ryker said. 'My son broke into her home last night.'

Henrik squirmed, as if about to contest that, or perhaps to run, or attack, but Ryker put a firm hand on his shoulder to keep him where he was.

'We're here to apologise.'

The guy stared intently at Ryker for a few moments, as though working over the information, and the proposal.

He reached to his side. Ryker tensed, but only a little. A radio. The guy turned his head, covered the handset to muffle the conversation. Then he pulled the radio back down and glared at Ryker but didn't say anything.

After a few moments of silence, Ryker stepped forward again, right up to the still-closed gates. He put his hands out onto the cold metal.

'Don't,' the man said, holding a palm out to Ryker.

Then the radio crackled and he lifted it back to his ear for the response.

'Madame Thibaud says, if you don't go, she'll call the police.'

Henrik sighed. Ryker held in any reaction to the pretty much expected response.

'Tell her if she doesn't let us in, we'll gladly speak to the police about your colleague trying to shoot me and my son in the mountains. Where is he and his delightful companion anyway?'

The man didn't respond. Just gave Ryker a death glare as he grit his teeth.

'Go on then,' Ryker prompted.

The man lifted the radio. With him distracted, Ryker moved quickly as he slid the bolt across, then grasped the open gate with both hands and swung it forward, using it as a battering ram of sorts. The heavy metal thudded into the guard's shoulder, sending him stumbling. Ryker slunk in through the gap, grabbed the guy's arm, twisted. Swiped his feet away and eased him down to the ground, arm held aloft and pushed to breaking point. The radio dropped from his grasp as he squirmed and winced.

'Sorry,' Ryker said. 'It's quicker this way.'

The man said nothing as Henrik bounded up, then crouched down. Patted the man's side.

'Got it,' he said, lifting the handgun from the under the man's coat.

Henrik stepped back with the gun. Ryker really didn't want the kid to have that. Too risky. He let go of the guard's arm and reached out to Henrik, who reluctantly handed over the weapon. Ryker stuck it in his pocket, then looked down to the man in the snow, whose face was creased with rage as he nursed his arm.

'I'm going to–'

'Save it,' Ryker said, putting an end to whatever threat or ultimatum the guy had his mind set on. 'I've heard it all before. Get up and show us which way to go.'

Silence. Then the guy – looking a little surprised – clambered back to his feet and made a meal of brushing the powdery snow from his trousers and coat. Buying time for someone on the inside to rush to his rescue?

He took his hat off to reveal a shiny bald head, smacked the fabric against his coat to remove the white stuff, then pulled it back over his scalp.

'Ready now?' Ryker said to him.

'Follow me.'

They walked slowly, the man at the front, Ryker and Henrik a couple of steps behind. Every few yards the man glanced over his shoulder to them. Was he planning an attack? Ryker didn't think so. Whoever this guy was, he wasn't that well trained. Just a simple security guard. He'd wouldn't put his life on the line for his employer. His lacklustre efforts had already made that clear. Kind of like how those other two had run from conflict up in the mountains.

'Who's inside?' Ryker asked.

He got no response. Ryker looked about the grounds as they moved. Snow covered much of what he thought was a large lawn, flower beds too, perhaps, but all along the perimeter were a variety of trees – some evergreens, some deciduous, their twisting branches bare and forlorn.

Two cars sat parked up next to the house. Both rugged, off-road types. The house itself looked in good condition, even if it was obviously old-fashioned. No grand entrance, only an arched wooden door set back within the thick stone walls.

Movement there caught Ryker's attention. The front door opened.

Ryker whipped his hand to his side for one of the two guns he now carried.

'Don't,' he said, and Henrik, Baldy, and the wolf-killer all froze, as if they all thought the instruction was directed at them.

Ryker's hand remained in place, his fingers a couple of inches from the grip of the pilfered handgun. In front of him, at the door, the guard from the mountain mirrored Ryker's pose. A similar height to Ryker, the man was leaner, and also a good ten years younger. He had a full face, dense stubble rose up his cheekbones – the kind that would reappear only hours after a full shave.

'Bruno, it's okay,' the shorter guard said, holding his hand out to his friend, as if afraid of getting caught in the crossfire.

'Yeah, Bruno,' Ryker said. 'We're here to talk, that's all.'

Ryker slowly moved his hand away from his gun. Bruno hesitated, switching his gaze from Ryker to Henrik and back again.

'Anna is still in the hospital because of them,' Bruno said to his friend.

'That was all down to you,' Henrik said, the anger in his tone clear to all.

Another silence followed, the tension not easing at all. Ryker knew Henrik wanted nothing more than to race at Bruno and pummel him. Ryker, too, remained angry that for some reason this man, and the woman named Anna, had followed them to the mountain, armed, and intent on doing them harm. But most likely the answers lay with the employer of these two men. Other than satisfying a primal need for revenge, attacking Bruno now would achieve little.

'Just take us to your boss,' Ryker said. 'That's why we're here.'

'Their *boss*...' said a smooth female voice from behind Bruno. He looked aggrieved by the development, as though he now couldn't do whatever he'd been planning. He took a half-step to the side to reveal the woman. Late fifties, with thick, wiry hair, she had a lined face, and wore deft make-up, her lips blood-red. Together with the sequinned blouse, smart pressed trousers, and low heels, she didn't look like she belonged in a farmhouse in the snowy Alps. More like at a villa on the Med.

'I am their boss,' she said. Her English was good, though retained a soft French lilt.

'You must be Monique Thibaud,' Ryker said.

'I am.'

'I'm James Ryker. This is my son, Henrik.'

She looked Ryker up and down with disapproval, before setting her gaze on Henrik. No up and down look this time, just an all-out glare, her eyes narrowing.

Then she turned and walked away. After a couple of steps she called over her shoulder.

'Bruno, Jules, please invite our guests inside. Take them to the morning room.'

She moved out of sight.

'After you, gents,' Ryker said with a smile.

10

The morning room turned out to be a large square space at the back of the farmhouse, with low ceilings, thick wooden beams overhead, and a huge stone fireplace with remnants of a fire still in the grate. At the back of the room a set of patio doors looked out to the valley behind the house. East facing, Ryker thought, and he could imagine, on a clear morning, the sun blazing down at the glass, providing much needed warmth to the otherwise chilly interior. On a grey afternoon, with no heating on and the fire yet to be lit, the room felt frigid, as cold as the atmosphere between host and guests.

'My great-grandparents built this house, over a hundred years ago,' Monique said as she sat back in the floral armchair. She'd put on a thick cardigan – necessary given the cold room. Her natural elegance continued to shine through. Ryker and Henrik were seated on a worn leather sofa. Jules and Bruno stood either side of their boss, both now without their coats, both with their hands clasped in front of them.

'It's very... quaint,' Ryker said, looking about the room. Definitely tastefully decorated. The room, and the other parts of the house Ryker had glimpsed, were all full of character and traditional furniture and furnishings. His eyes rested on a picture above the fireplace – an oil painting of a smartly dressed man and woman. He guessed they were Thibaud's, but he didn't know which ones.

'You don't like it,' she said.

'The painting?'

Monique smiled. 'Not the painting. I *know* you don't like the painting. It's awful. It looks nothing like my great-grandparents, but it's... part of the family I guess. But I meant, you don't like my decorating. You'd prefer something more modern perhaps.'

'Honestly, I'm not that interested,' Ryker said and noted the look of offence in her eyes. Clearly, family painting aside, she had a sense of pride in her home.

'So what are you interested in? Me and my family, I think?'

'You could say that.'

Monique sniffed, a sign of disgruntlement. She glanced to the untouched coffees on the table separating them. Coffees brought to them by a suited butler who'd now disappeared. Other than him and the people in the room, Ryker hadn't seen or heard anyone.

'You're not married?' Ryker asked, looking around. A few photo frames, but nothing to suggest a husband or children.

'I never met the right person,' Monique responded. 'And I never wanted children.'

She looked to Henrik as she said that.

'Some people are better suited to parenting than others,' Ryker said.

No reaction on Monique's passive face. 'My great-grandmother was English,' she said, glancing to the blonde woman in the picture again. 'Did you know that?'

'No,' Ryker answered.

'She married my great-grandfather in a little town near Oxford. He was an interpreter for the British government. They moved here not long before the start of the Great War.'

She paused, as though waiting for some questions. None came.

'They had this house built for them. There was actually a farm here before, but the building was beyond repair. They knocked it down and used the stones from the original building and its barns to build this. It was one of the first houses in St Ricard.'

'It's... big,' Ryker said with a shrug.

'My grandfather and his brothers and sisters grew up here. Then when their parents died, my grandad, Albert, made this his home for a while. But he was an impatient man. He didn't like the rural life. You know about our family history?'

'Something to do with champagne?'

Monique laughed. 'Yes. Something to do with champagne. My grandfather wanted to make a name for himself. He had a friend who was close to the Pommery family in Reims. Our family was nothing like those big, well-known families then, but Albert was very persuasive and he agreed a deal with several vineyards to buy wine from them, and a deal with the Pommerys to use some of their cellars. Have you ever visited the champagne houses?'

'No,' Ryker said.

'You should. It's fascinating. Reims is built on chalk. The whole area around there is chalk, perfect for wine growing. It adds a distinctive taste you get nowhere else. But it's also a fantastic building material. The Romans were among the first people to dig there. They excavated huge pits, using the stone they took for their buildings all over France. Later, monks used those pits, connected them with tunnels, and started to keep wine there. It was monks who then first perfected what we now know as champagne. But they didn't commercialise it.'

'You did?' Ryker suggested.

'Not me. My grandfather. By that point the likes of Pommery and Taittinger and others were already huge, and very, very rich. But they'd had a head start. Once people realised the market for champagne, rich families flocked, trying to buy up land around Reims so they could exploit the ground beneath them. It wasn't really their ingenuity which made them into household names, it was their inherited wealth which gave them their advantage.'

'What about your grandfather?'

'He came from much more humble beginnings.'

Was a grand mock-farmhouse in the Alps really that humble?

'He had to work that little bit harder, and more smartly than the others. He started out by renting that land from Pommery. Then he set about making a champagne that was far superior. It was popular, so he needed more and more space to keep the bottles. So he took more and more space in other houses' cellars. Eventually the Franck Thibaud brand became so popular that competitors suffered. Albert bought a failed house that had the second highest cellar space under Reims, plus hectares and hectares of vineyards above it. He expanded rapidly to the point where other houses had to pay him a significant amount of money to vacate the land he'd previously rented from them, just so they could try and catch up, and to try and quell his growing appetite.'

She spoke with such fervour. Ryker wondered how many times she'd told this story. It wasn't as if she'd needed much of a push to dive in. Did she have a point to make at all or was she only showing off by telling the history of her family, and their wealth?

'I think, if it hadn't been for the war, we would have had the biggest champagne house the world has ever seen.'

'The Second World War?' Ryker asked.

Monique nodded. 'My grandfather didn't fight, but his three brothers did. They all went to war. They all died, on French soil. Two of them defending Reims from the Germans. One of them in a camp years later. Albert's sister died in a bombing raid. His wife was severely wounded, and he lost his baby son too. My mother, five years old when the war finished, survived. The war didn't just nearly destroy my grandfather's business, it almost entirely destroyed his family.'

'What happened to the business after the war?' Henrik asked, and Ryker was a little surprised he'd been so taken in by the story. Or maybe he hadn't. Maybe the question was the start of a ploy of some kind.

'My mother ran it for a few years after my grandfather passed. But she wasn't really a businesswoman, she didn't have the passion needed. So she took an offer, when I was a girl. A very good offer, actually, from an American businessman. She sold the entire stake the family had in the business. That man kept it for only a few years, built up the exports to America where the market was booming, then he sold the business for five times what he bought it for.'

She said that last part a little bitterly.

'But your family was still made very rich,' Henrik said.

'*Made* rich?' Monique said, a little put out. 'That deal my mother made didn't make us rich. The hard work of my family over many, many years did.'

'The hard work of your grandfather,' Henrik said, his tone flat. 'Not the hard work of your mother. And not you either. You just get to enjoy what's left.'

Monique opened her mouth to say something but then

didn't, though her aggravation was clear. She reached forward and took her coffee in her hand and took two sips before setting the cup back down again.

'My family is wealthy, yes. I didn't choose to be born into money. But I will do everything I can to protect my family members, my family's wealth, and the Thibaud reputation.'

'Only now?' Henrik asked. 'Or do you mean before your brother's death too?'

Her face...

The question was perhaps a little unfair, but perhaps not. Ryker was glad his young friend had asked it.

'Only, with him gone, you're now the head of the family,' Henrik said. 'Everything seems to have worked out well for you, I'd say.'

'Why did you break into my house?' Monique asked. 'I'm well used to people harassing my family. Even before my brother's murder. But since then... it's enough to send anyone crazy. The phone calls, unannounced visits to the house, people on the street. Journalists, a lot of the time, but often just nosey people with too much time and silly ideas of conspiracies.'

Perhaps the harassment she spoke of justified the need to have armed guards in her home?

'Where's Sophie?' Ryker asked, looking about the room, as though searching for her.

'You can't talk to her.'

'Because?'

'Because I say so.'

'You're her legal guardian now,' Ryker said.

'I am.'

'But who got your brother's money?' Henrik asked.

She set her beady eyes on him once more. She clearly didn't like the youngster, not least because of the break-in, but his questions were only adding to her dislike of him – deliberate on Henrik's part, Ryker thought.

'So?' Henrik said when Monique didn't answer. 'Was it you or Sophie who got the money? If her, is that why you keep her here, locked away, so she doesn't fritter away what you see as yours?'

'How dare you,' Monique said, and Ryker noticed Bruno shuffle, as if readying for a confrontation. 'I invited you into my home–'

'But why did you?' Ryker asked.

Silence as she now glared at him instead.

'Excuse me?'

'Why did you invite us into your home?' Ryker asked. 'You've just told us your family is well used to being harassed, and particularly since your brother's murder, which I'm guessing is the reason for these goons...' Ryker looked to Bruno and Jules in turn, noted the looks on both of their faces. Both were eager for some action. 'Yet when we turn up–'

'Let's backtrack from that,' Monique said. 'Because you didn't just turn up. Firstly, your son broke into my house in the night.'

'He did,' Ryker said. 'And he's very sorry, aren't you, Henrik?'

'Yeah. Very,' Henrik said with little conviction.

'And what were you looking for?' Monique asked.

'I just wanted to speak to Sophie,' he said.

'Because?'

'Because I think she's very pretty.'

Monique shook her head – disgust?

'The thing is,' Ryker said, 'after that we agreed with the gendarmerie to leave town–'

'But you didn't leave town, you went for a hike–'

'We did leave town,' Ryker said. 'And you sent Bruno here and that woman called Anna after us, with guns. Why?'

Monique sucked in air through her nostrils, causing them to flare.

'What? You wanted them to shoot us and bury us up there?' Ryker asked. 'All because of a simple break-in?'

'No,' Monique said. 'That's not it at all. But tell me truthfully this time. Why are you here?'

'To make sure Sophie is okay,' Henrik said. 'And to find out who really killed her family and why.'

A strange silence permeated the room. Ryker could practically see the cogs turning behind Monique's eyes.

'My brother and his family were killed because two greedy thugs lost control.'

Did she really believe that? Ryker honestly couldn't tell, the delivery in her words was so calm and passive, even if her body was stiff. A lie? Or simply a reaction to a painful subject?

'You might think I didn't work hard in my life,' Monique said after a contemplative sigh. 'And maybe in the traditional sense of employment, I didn't. But that doesn't mean I haven't always worked hard for my family, and what's right for us. And I'll always do that. The Thibaud name is everything to me.'

'That's very–'

'I'm not finished. I once read about a very powerful family...' Ryker sighed and relaxed in his seat, sensing Monique wanted some time for this one. She certainly liked to talk. 'The patriarch was a property magnate. He was one of the richest men in America. He'd built his empire from absolutely nothing, only hard work and determination. He had two sons who, naturally, both wanted to be part of the family business, so, when they were old enough, their father passed the reins to them. Only the brothers weren't like their father at all. They'd grown up with money, with entitlement, with greed. And they both wanted to be top dog. Neither could agree how to run the company together, and over the next decade the wealth of the business dropped significantly. Their father had retired, and unable to stop the collapse of what he'd built, he fell into ill health, traumatised by the thought that his life's work was being torn apart by his warring sons. The eldest son fell into alcoholism and died in his early forties. A heart attack. The father passed away not long after – perhaps the mental toll too much for him – leaving the other son to pick up the remains and try to regain what was lost.'

'You can't replace lost family members,' Henrik said.

'No. You can't. And I don't think this man wanted to. I think he only wanted power and money, he'd grown up knowing nothing else. So he used what was left of his father's business to try and become ever more successful.'

'And did he succeed?' Ryker asked.

'Yes and no. He remained rich, but, as I said, he wasn't his father. He was a megalomaniac, a narcissist, a liar, a cheat. He wormed his way through deal after deal, dirty money, backhanders. Many of the deals failed but he had enough money, enough appetite for corruption to make sure he carried on, despite a string of bankrupt businesses and partners behind him.'

Monique paused. The sourness in her tone was stark. Had she known the family she was talking about?

'You want to know what happened to him?' she asked with a strangely twisted look on her face.

'What?' Ryker asked.

'He became a politician.' Now she smiled. 'A very important one too. He used all of his cunning and lies to get himself to the top.' She shook her head in disgust. 'He sullied a once good name in the process. My family never saw our wealth in that way. Me and my brother, we appreciated what we had. We were grounded by it, rather than driven by it.'

'Is that the point of the story?' Ryker said.

'Almost. The point is, for me, the family money isn't my most important consideration. I knew my grandfather very well. He told me, every time a bottle of Franck Thibaud is sold it has to be perfect. It has to look perfect, it has to taste perfect. Even today, even when we don't own the company, that still holds true. The name on those champagne bottles still represents our family. And our family still represents the name on those bottles.'

'Except you can't control the quality of the product anymore,' Ryker said. 'Can you?'

She didn't answer straight away. Did that mean something? 'No. But I can, and I will, continue to control my family name. And I'll do absolutely anything to make sure that name is not tarnished. Do you understand me?'

Ryker wasn't really sure he did. 'Like I said, we only came here to speak to Sophie.'

'And I already told you, you can't.'

'Because you're worried of the damage it could do to your family name? That's very telling, don't you think? What secrets are you afraid she'll tell?'

'No. It's because she's seventeen years old, I'm her guardian, and her life is none of your business.'

Bruno and Jules both twitched when Henrik leaned forward in his seat.

'Sorry, do you think I could use your toilet?' he said, sweet as anything. Monique eyed him with the distrust he probably deserved. Ryker, too, wondered what he was up to.

Henrik stood up and squeezed his knees together.

'Please? I'm desperate.'

'Jules, keep an eye on him.'

Jules nodded and held Henrik under the arm to show him to the door. Ryker sucked in his annoyance at the unnecessary manhandling. Soon they were both out of sight.

'Is he really your son?' Monique asked.

'Why would you think otherwise?' Ryker answered.

'He doesn't look much like you.'

Ryker shrugged.

'And, no offence, you don't look like the father type.'

'What does a father type look like?'

'I see something in your eyes,' she said. 'Something that I don't like. It unnerves me. I think you probably know what I'm talking about.'

'Not really.'

'I don't know who you are, or why you decided to invade my family's life, but please, Mr Ryker, don't underestimate me. I may not look and act as tough as you do, but–'

A shout from out in the hall grabbed everyone's attention. A man's shout. Jules? A bang followed, then more shouting.

Definitely Jules.

Bruno reacted, racing for the door. Ryker bounced up from the sofa to block his path and used his arm like a clothesline move from the wrestling ring to send him sprawling onto the sofa. Bruno went for his gun. Ryker was about to as well...

'BOYS!' Monique shouted.

Ryker and Bruno both stared at her. She was on her feet, face full of determination.

She stormed for the door. Ryker and Bruno, both with their guns still yet to be drawn, followed a couple of steps behind her. Ryker spotted Jules along the hallway, clutching a hand to his bloodied face.

'He hit me.'

It wasn't clear with what. Not a fist. Henrik was too small for such an impact. The porcelain lid from the toilet cistern perhaps?

'He went that way,' Jules said, pointing to the stairs.

'Find him,' Monique said. Then she turned to Bruno.

'Keep *him* here.'

Bruno whipped his gun out and pointed it at Ryker, who didn't bother to react, because he didn't believe Bruno was really about to shoot him, there and then.

'If you hurt him...' he said to Monique.

She and Jules rushed off. Ryker heard banging upstairs. Footsteps. Voices. Shouting. Muffled at first. Then more heightened. Ryker kept his eyes on Bruno the whole time.

Moments later Ryker heard fast-moving footsteps approaching the head of the stairs. He looked that way to see Henrik's feet appear, and the boy bounded down.

Bruno was distracted too. Ryker made his move. He smacked one hand onto Bruno's gun arm, pushing the barrel away from him. He swiped his other hand in the opposite direction, grasping the barrel as he went, prising the gun from Bruno's grip. Simple physics to lever the gun free from the moving arm. Ryker grabbed the gun grip with his free hand and turned the weapon on Bruno, taking a step back so the guard couldn't repeat the same trick.

'Ah-ah,' Ryker said when Bruno twitched.

Henrik reached the bottom of the stairs. Out of breath. A kind of a smile on his face.

Jules rushed down behind him, Monique further back. Jules looked like he was about to pounce as Henrik slowed in the hall but when he looked up at Ryker he paused.

'What game are you two playing?' Monique blasted as she reached the bottom too, entirely unperturbed by Ryker pointing the gun at Bruno.

'Good question,' Ryker said, glancing to Henrik.

'I knew it,' Henrik said, fixing his gaze on Ryker. 'I knew she was lying.'

'What are you–'

Henrik cut Monique off without even looking at her. 'She's not here,' he said to Ryker. 'Sophie isn't here.'

Ryker looked to Monique.

'And judging by your charade,' he said, 'and the look on your face right now, you don't know where she is either.' All eyes turned to Monique. 'Do you?'

Monique said nothing. She didn't need to.

11

The mood in the hallway flattened. For the first time Ryker saw Monique Thibaud as a genuine threat, as though she was about to leap forward, teeth bared. Why the lie about Sophie?

'So if she's not here, where the hell is she?' Henrik said to Monique, perhaps misreading the mood, because there'd be no more questions and answers now. Ryker's only goal was to get out of the house without further conflict.

'Have you seen what he did to my face?' Jules complained to Monique, taking his hand away to reveal the gash above his badly swollen eye.

'It's an improvement,' Henrik responded.

The anger on Jules' face...

Monique didn't look at either of them, didn't respond to either, instead kept her focus wholly on Ryker.

At least her focus stayed on Ryker until she momentarily flicked her gaze over his left shoulder.

Ryker spun.

Anna. Three yards away, by the morning-room entrance, gun

pointed at him. Clever. So her injuries hadn't been too bad after all.

Ryker pulled his gun toward her. Fired. Knew the shot would miss – he'd fired too early – but also knew the pre-emptive move, and the commotion it caused, would give him an advantage.

Anna stooped and tried to move away. She fired, too, but Ryker was already on her. He spun again, on the move, and thundered an elbow into her head as he grabbed her gun arm. He pushed the gun up as she fired more shots. He prised the weapon away and it bounced along the floor, then, still holding her arm, he jolted forward and tossed her over his shoulder and to the ground with a thud.

Bruno rushed for him. Ryker ducked and missed the glancing blow. Further ahead Jules had pulled a gun. Henrik? Where was Henrik? Monique cowered by the stairs. None of that fighting look on her face now.

Ryker took a blow to his back from Bruno. Fired another shot that hit Jules in his foot and he hopped about then collapsed to the floor. Bruno had a gun in his hand now too. Anna's? He lifted it to fire at Ryker's chest...

Ryker leaped forward, wrapped his arms around Bruno's waist and sent them both flying. Bruno's back cracked against a side table and Ryker's weight pushed down on him as he let out a painful *oomph*. Ryker swiped the gun free and tossed it then smacked the butt of the gun he was holding in his other hand against the side of Bruno's face. His head lolled.

Ryker bounced to his feet. Anna had pulled herself up, knife in her hand. Jules remained on the floor, but he was still armed...

At least he was until Henrik rushed from out of a doorway and ran up to Jules and launched his foot into the guy's face. He flopped to the floor. Monique cowered, though her eyes flitted to the gun Ryker had tossed. Would she go for it?

'Come on, this way!' Henrik shouted, before turning and running in the opposite direction to Ryker.

Ryker faced Anna and held her eye as he back-stepped the way Henrik had gone. She got the point. If she launched herself at him, he'd shoot her, simple as that. She stayed where she was. After a couple more steps, Ryker turned and ran.

He moved through the hall into the large country-style kitchen. Spotted the open back door and felt the waft of cold air as he raced that way. He sensed the movement behind him. Only half-looked to see who had followed him as he fired a single warning shot that cracked into a cabinet and sent wood splinters flying.

Ryker rushed out into the open. A quick look around. No one in sight. At least, no armed guards, but he spotted Henrik standing by the open driver's door to one of the two cars outside – a mud-spattered Jeep.

'You drive,' Henrik shouted before running around the front of the car to the other side.

Ryker sprinted forward and jumped into the driver's seat. He pulled the door shut.

'Keyless ignition,' Henrik said, holding the fob in his hand.

Ryker pressed the brake and then the start/stop button and the diesel engine rumbled into life. Anna darted outside. Gun in hand. Bruno rushed out behind her, armed once more. No sign of Jules.

Ryker wound his window down as he selected reverse. He swung the car around. Fired off the remaining bullets in the gun still clutched in his left hand. The other gun, the one he'd taken from Anna the previous night, lay on his lap. The shots did enough to halt any immediate assault from Anna and Bruno. Ryker pushed the gearstick into drive and hit the accelerator.

Only a couple of seconds later he had to hit the brake again to come to a skidding stop at the closed gates.

'I've got it!' Henrik shouted as he rushed outside.

Ryker took the other gun from his lap and fired off more shots in the direction of Anna and Bruno. No hits – his intention, really – and Anna fired off several rounds in retaliation, causing both Ryker and Henrik to duck.

'Come on!' Ryker said to Henrik, his foot twitching on the accelerator.

Gates opened, the youngster dove back inside and was still in mid-air as Ryker slammed his foot on the accelerator once more. All four tyres skidded for a second, sending up plumes of snow spray before the rubber found traction on the icy surface and the Jeep shot forward.

Another couple of shots from Anna. One clunked into the back of the Jeep. But as Ryker looked in his mirror again he saw neither she nor Bruno were giving chase.

Ryker tossed both of the guns out of his window.

'What are you doing!' Henrik protested.

Ryker didn't respond, just kept on going until Monique Thibaud's home faded into the distance behind them.

They drove on for twenty minutes, initially heading back into town – the only way they could really get away from the farmhouse without moving off-road and toward the ski slopes. Once through the town they went north, until Ryker found a trail heading up into the mountains. He parked the car on a woodland track that – at least according to the Jeep's satnav – didn't go anywhere except further up.

'Why did you throw those guns away?'

Ryker looked at Henrik. 'That's really the most important question you have right now?'

Henrik didn't respond.

'I tossed them because we have no use for them. One of them was spent, the other one only had a few bullets. But more than that, we don't need them. For whatever reason, Monique Thibaud and her heavies are after us now, and the local police will side with them. If we're stopped, in a stolen car, having weapons will only make everything worse for us.'

'I thought you were a better shot than that,' Henrik said.

Ryker stared at him. 'I'm a very good shot.'

'They why didn't you get them?'

'Because I don't know if they deserved it.'

'After what they did on the mountain? And just now? That's twice they've shot at us.'

Henrik was right, yet Ryker still didn't know *why* Monique Thibaud and her guards saw him and Henrik as a threat.

Henrik glared at Ryker. 'You're angry at me,' he said.

Ryker was.

'For which part?' Henrik asked, sullen. 'Attacking that guy, Jules? Searching that house to discover *her* lie? Finding the key for this thing so we could escape?'

Ryker shook his head.

'What? You've nothing to say to me now?'

'You're a lousy team player,' Ryker said.

Henrik practically snarled. 'Take a look at yourself.'

'Oh, don't worry. I'm well aware that I work much better alone. I've always preferred it that way.'

He saw a flicker of hurt in Henrik's eyes.

'But at least when I'm teamed up, I understand the change in dynamics,' Ryker continued. 'I understand it's not just my ass on the line. I understand the need to communicate so we're all working together, rather than just running off doing our own thing.'

'Coming from you, that's the biggest load of bullshit I ever heard.'

'I might even have agreed with your approach. Sneaking off like that to the toilet. Attacking Jules so you could rush around the house. If you'd explained that's what you wanted to do, we could even have come up with something better.'

'No, we wouldn't have. Because I hadn't planned any of that. It was an impulsive decision because I knew she was lying to us. I took some initiative.'

'You were reckless. Again.'

'You just don't like that I take charge sometimes.'

Perhaps Henrik was right about that. But he was fifteen years old.

'We wouldn't have found out about Sophie if I hadn't done all that,' Henrik said. 'Monique would have kept on feeding us crap about her family until we were shown out of there. I've moved this thing on.'

'This thing? Which is what?'

'You know what. Helping a teenage girl whose family were murdered, and whose sole remaining relative is lying about her disappearance.'

Ryker took a long inhale then sighed.

'So what now?' Henrik said.

Ryker thought for a while. 'We have several choices.'

Henrik rolled his eyes. 'Please don't tell me one of those choices is we walk away, for good.'

It was. In fact it was Ryker's favoured choice in many ways. Certainly it was the choice that carried the least risk for them both.

'You're so obvious sometimes,' Henrik said with a grin now. 'So what else?'

Ryker tried not to return the look. He wanted to be angry but...

'I think it's too risky to stay in St Ricard. For now. We've just been involved in a shoot-out. We're in a stolen car. We already think the police and other locals are bowing down to Monique Thibaud for whatever reason. We'll find it difficult to move freely here.'

'But there are answers here,' Henrik said. 'She knows a lot more than she told us. Not just about that night but about what's happened to Sophie since. And like you said, other people are involved too. Yes, we'll be under watch here, but if we're careful...'

Ryker's brain whirred. Was there an ulterior reason for Henrik to be so keen to stay around St Ricard, despite the risks?

'Plus there's plenty still to figure out here,' Henrik added. 'We could go to Sophie's old home. It's empty now, there might be clues there as to what happened. And what about the dam project I told you about? Corinne Thibaud was opposed to that, big time. We could find out who the key players are who wanted to make sure that project went ahead, whatever the cost.'

'Or we could move away from St Ricard altogether for a while,' Ryker said.

Henrik slumped. 'I thought we took that option away.'

'No. I mean, we could go to Lyon. It's where the Thibauds' supposed killers came from, you said. We can track down their gangs. Find out what they know, see if we can find out who put them up to the murders.'

'Or find proof that they were never there at all.'

Did such proof exist?

Ryker mulled the options. Henrik watched him silently. For a while.

'What do you think happened to Sophie?' Henrik asked.

'She survived that attack,' Ryker said. 'She was taken in and sheltered by her aunt. Do we at least believe that?'

'I think so.'

'So at some point after she was rescued, she disappeared. Either of her own accord, or...'

Ryker dwelled on that.

'Or she was kidnapped,' Henrik said. 'It's possible she's being held hostage. That someone is ransoming her.'

It was possible.

'Another reason to stay in St Ricard then,' Henrik said. 'Those people weren't that scary. Bruno, Jules, Anna? We'd get the better of them again. We should go back and find out everything Monique Thibaud knows about her family's murder, and her niece's disappearance.'

Ryker smiled. He had to admire Henrik's confidence at least.

'What?' Henrik said, clearly agitated by Ryker's reaction.

'We will ask her. But you want to make sure Sophie is okay, don't you?'

He could see in Henrik's eyes that he really did. How had he become so infatuated with a young woman he'd never even met?

'Then we'll go back to confront Monique Thibaud another time,' Ryker said. 'If someone's taken Sophie, it makes sense that it's the same people who set up the initial attack on her family. Perhaps the intention was always to capture, not kill her.'

'Why?'

'Good question.'

'So we're going to Lyon to find out?'

Ryker started up the engine.

'Yes, we are.'

12

Gridlock. That alone told Ryker a lot about the city they were entering. Not a quiet or quaint place like St Ricard, but a sprawling urban centre. Ryker had never been to Lyon before, and he was sure there'd be plenty of tasteful, historical parts and famous sights here – and a lot of buzz. He could already see some modern glass-rich skyscrapers in the distance, most likely the business centre of the city, filled with offices and trendy bars and restaurants. A little unexpectedly, a large part of him wanted to be back in St Ricard.

They remained in the Jeep, although along the way they'd googled and found a metal scrapyard where they'd paid the night-time security guard there a hundred euros to let them take a look around, no questions asked. Henrik had found some licence plates from a ten-year-old Toyota Land Cruiser that they'd taken and quickly replaced for the ones on the stolen Jeep. Not a perfect ruse, but probably good enough in the short term. The plates at least nearly matched the age of the car.

'Lyon is the second biggest urban centre in France,' Henrik said, reading from his phone, as Ryker stared frustratedly at the sea of brake lights in front of them. 'It was the capital of the

Gauls during the Roman Empire. There are quite a lot of Roman remains still. Amphitheatres and things.'

'You want to do some sightseeing?'

Henrik glared at Ryker, enough to cause Ryker to retract his smile.

'The headquarters of Interpol are located here too.'

Ryker's face fell a little further. He really hoped that fact wouldn't come back to bite them at any point.

Finally the traffic in front moved and Ryker rolled the Jeep forward then looked to the satnav screen. Their turn was coming up.

'What do you think we'll find here?' Henrik asked.

A good question. And one which Ryker initially answered with a contemplative sigh.

'Trouble, most likely,' he said.

'Without a doubt, I'd say,' Henrik added with a curious smile.

The area they parked up in, on the edge of the areas of Perrache and Ainay, was dominated by nineteenth and early twentieth century apartment blocks, six to twelve storeys tall. The buildings, mainly stone blocks of varying shades of grey and dirty brown, ranged from the overly plain to the intricate, the latter with ornate iron-edged balconies and decorative stonework around doorways and windows, looking even more quaint with the orange street lighting at night. That said, judging by the level of upkeep, and the quality of the pavements and parked cars outside, the area wasn't hugely affluent, though Ryker was sure it was far from the poorest. Simply a typical inner city residential street that could be found in pretty much any city in the Western world.

'Not what you expected?' Ryker said to Henrik as they stepped from the car, noting his nonplussed look.

'A lot nicer than I expected... I don't know why.'

Perhaps because he wasn't used to bigger cities, and the size of the buildings made them appear more impressive than they were. Or because he'd expected less of the common criminal, Didier Lenglet?

'We're looking for 218,' Henrik said. 'Apartment 306.'

Ryker had already memorised the information which Henrik had uncovered on the journey from St Ricard – a sneaky combination of basic internet search and a call/fishing exercise to a utility company and the building's supervisor. All of it without action or advice from Ryker. The fifteen-year-old's 'skills' continued to impress and surprise and in some ways horrify him.

'Here it is,' Ryker said, looking up to the double doors of the apartment building. The doors had a traditional lock but the fact the left-hand door sat an inch forward of its twin showed it wasn't being used – perhaps didn't work at all – and so they both slipped inside without bothering with the intercom.

'Easier than expected,' Henrik said as they ascended the stairs.

Ryker didn't respond. He didn't want to jinx it.

They reached the door to 306 without seeing anyone, though various sounds drifted from behind the doors of neighbouring homes.

Ryker knocked then waited. He heard footsteps on the other side of the wood. A TV too. A cooing baby.

'What do you want?' said a female voice, in French, from the other side.

'We're here to sort out your heating,' Ryker said, trying his best to avoid any trace of Anglicisation in his words.

Silence. Then locks unclicked, and the door edged open before catching on a chain.

'Liar,' she said, looking up to Ryker. 'Our floor was fixed last week.'

So Henrik's digging had only partially worked.

'So who are you?' the woman asked.

'Me and my son travelled from St Ricard,' Ryker said, stepping out of the way to show Henrik's puppy-dog face. 'We're... we're hoping you can help us.'

The woman's smile dropped. Her eyes pinched.

'St Ricard?'

'We're in trouble with the Thibauds. We wanted to talk to you about Didier. We think what happened to him might–'

The door slammed shut. Ryker and Henrik looked at each other. Then the door reopened, more fully this time. The heavyset young woman glared at Ryker. All of five foot two, she wore leggings that seemed at least a size too small and a tank top that revealed a mass of tattoos that swirled up her arms. She held on to a baby that clung to her chest, and behind her another child toddled into view, crisp packet in hand.

The woman stuck her head out of the door, looked both ways along the corridor.

'You're not journalists?' she said.

Ryker shook his head.

'You don't look like you are.'

'We're not.'

'Come in,' she said, stepping aside to let Ryker and Henrik through.

The apartment was cramped. One open living space, a bathroom, two bedrooms, although one was barely big enough to fit a single bed. The decor was plain and tired – probably the landlord's choice and the residents hadn't bothered – or weren't allowed – to make it any more homely or personal.

A pan bubbled away on the stove in the kitchen area. A meaty stew of some kind, Ryker thought from the smell.

'Sit down,' the lady said as she put the baby into a high chair. The toddler placed himself a foot away from the TV screen.

'You must be Didier's wife,' Ryker said. 'Valerie?'

She didn't answer as she took a seat on the edge of an armchair. Ryker sat on the sofa opposite. Henrik remained hovering.

'You knew Didier?' the woman – Ryker assumed Valerie – asked. 'Actually, you don't need to answer that. I know you didn't.'

As instructed, Ryker said nothing.

'You're not French, are you?'

'English,' Ryker said.

'And him?'

'My son.'

No response.

'Why are you here?'

'Because we're looking for Sophie Thibaud.'

Valerie glanced to Henrik whose face remained passive. Then she looked to her own kids before back to Ryker.

'I don't know her. I don't know any of the Thibauds.'

'But you know of them.'

'Nearly everyone knows of them. And what happened in St Ricard.'

'Then that saves us some time.'

'But you said you're looking for her. Like she's missing. But she's right there, in St Ricard, with her aunt.'

'But she isn't,' Henrik said. 'You won't get the family admitting that, but Sophie is missing.'

A dubious, but also slightly wary look from Valerie, who fidgeted, looking at her kids again.

'I already said, I don't know those people. And I don't know why you're interested either.'

'You might not know them. But your husband did.'

'My husband. My dead husband. Who you never met.'

'How long were you together?' Ryker asked.

'You really care?'

Ryker held his tongue.

'Five years.'

'They must miss their dad?' Henrik said, indicating the kids.

'You're going to bring him back from the dead for me?'

'No,' Ryker said. 'But if you help us, then perhaps we can find out exactly why he *is* dead.'

Valerie didn't respond, but then she smiled, then she laughed, catching the attention of the two children. The baby in the high chair smiled and cackled to see his mother apparently so happy. The toddler stared at her like she was mad.

'Didier is dead because he was an idiot. I knew that for a long time, but I loved him anyway. But I always told him what would happen. And he always promised me he'd change. But do you know how hard it is for a man with his background to get a real job here?'

'I can imagine,' Ryker said.

'Can you? Because looking at you, I'm not sure you can. Didier did what he had to do to support this family. I didn't like it, I didn't agree with it, but we needed money.'

'What did he tell you about that night?'

'Which night?'

'St Ricard.'

'He didn't tell me anything. He never did, and I never asked. He only said he would see me in the morning. That either meant he was stealing something or partying.'

'And when he came home?'

Her face twitched. Her frustration, agitation, even anger, dissipated, and for the first time Ryker saw some sadness behind her dark eyes.

'He was scared. I think... he was ashamed.'

'You believe he really did do it?' Henrik asked. 'That he really went to St Ricard and killed those people?'

No words but a slight nod in response. The answer wasn't what Ryker had expected – hoped for? – at all.

'Why?' Ryker asked. 'Why would he be involved in something like that?'

'I told you already. Because he was stupid.'

'Who did he work for? The other man, Ramiz Touba?'

A flicker of anger in her features. She knew the name. She didn't think much of it.

'No. Not him. He was an animal but Didier wouldn't have followed him there.'

'You don't think Touba was involved?' Henrik asked.

'I didn't say that. I said Didier wouldn't have worked for Touba.'

'Then who?'

Valerie glared at Henrik but she didn't answer the question.

'Valerie, who paid Didier for that job?'

'You think I'd tell you, even if I knew?'

'You think it was a set-up?' Ryker suggested.

'The robbery at the Thibaud's? Probably. Didier was not a killer. I'm not saying he wasn't there, but he didn't go there for that.'

She sounded positive enough about her belief.

'But afterward...'

'Afterward what?' Ryker prompted.

'*That* was the set-up,' Valerie said.

'What was?' Henrik asked.

'The night the police came here,' she said, as though Ryker and Henrik were being dense. 'I already knew something was wrong by then. Didier hadn't spoken to me properly for days. He was moping, on edge. I still didn't know about him being in St Ricard then. I didn't know that until after the police shot him. When it was on the news the next day. But before that, I'd never seen him so... scared. If you'd ever met him, you'd know what I mean. He was tough. Tougher than anyone I know.'

'Who was he scared of?' Ryker asked. 'The police? Touba? The Thibauds?'

She shook her head. 'All I know is, the police arrived at our door that night. Six of them. And they had no intention of taking my husband with them. They launched in here, took one look and fired.'

'You think the police came here intending to kill him?' Henrik asked.

'Kill him?' Valerie said with a sneer. 'The police didn't kill Didier. They executed him.'

Valerie's chilling words reverberated in Ryker's mind.

'Why would the police do that?' Henrik asked.

Valerie looked put out by the question, and not for the first time when he'd addressed her, as if she didn't like the teenager questioning her, or perhaps it was only because of the sore subject.

'Because they're corrupt,' she said, more to Ryker than to Henrik.

'Who've you told about this?' Ryker asked.

'Who would I tell?'

'You didn't make a complaint to the police?' Henrik suggested.

'To the people who killed my husband? Do you think I'm a fool?'

'We don't think you're a fool,' Ryker said.

'I didn't tell the police. I knew it would make no difference.'

'We want to help you,' Ryker said. 'We want to find out what really happened in St Ricard. What really happened to Didier. If you–'

Ryker paused when he noticed Valerie's phone screen light up. She flicked her eyes to the device on the table, not the first time she'd done so, then got to her feet. Ryker sighed and looked up at her.

'So what now?' he asked her.

She looked at him questioningly.

'They're at the door already, aren't they?'

He'd heard the footsteps. Soft, but deliberate. He'd wondered whether it was simply a light-footed neighbour coming home, but now he knew otherwise – he'd guessed as much as he'd watched her fiddle with her phone, discreetly, but not discreetly enough. He'd also wondered why she'd invited them into her home so readily – perhaps she was under instruction to do so if anyone came asking about Didier.

'You hadn't thought this bit through though, had you?' Ryker said.

Valerie looked frightened now. She glanced from Ryker and to the front door along the short hall behind him.

'Who is it?' Ryker asked, trying to sound as calm as possible.

Valerie stepped away from her chair now. Not toward the door and the new arrivals, but toward her children. Ryker got up from the sofa, looked to Henrik.

A thud on the door.

'Valerie!'

She quivered with fear as she picked the now startled-looking baby from the high chair. The toddler in front of the TV stared at his mother too.

Then Valerie squealed and cowered as the front door blasted open.

13

Despite the commotion, Ryker gave Henrik a calm nod and the two of them huddled together in the open space. The toddler jumped to his feet and rushed to hide behind his mother's legs as two men barrelled into the apartment. Dark clothing, big puffa jackets that made them look like the Michelin man. Gloves. Hoods over their heads. Thuggish looks, and they were both young, probably early twenties.

They came to an abrupt stop when they clocked Ryker and Henrik.

'You okay?' the taller and skinnier of the two said to Valerie.

She nodded in response.

'You're coming with us,' the other one said to Ryker with a snarl that revealed a mouth of mismatched teeth, some of them metal-plated, like a bad take on the classic James Bond villain. Probably a designer statement rather than a dental requirement.

'We are?' Ryker said. 'To where?'

'Out of here. No one wants to get hurt.' Jaws pulled his coat apart to reveal a more than foot long machete strapped to his side.

'You'd really use that thing?' Ryker said. 'In here? In front of children?'

Jaws' eyes flickered.

Ryker looked to Henrik, then to Valerie. No need to cause a scene.

'We'll leave,' Ryker said. 'But if you touch my son, I'll shove that thing down your throat.'

Jaws glared, the other one cackled, as though teasing his friend for taking the insult. Egging him on.

Ryker held his hands up. 'Come on then,' he said.

Jaws held his ground as Ryker and Henrik moved forward. His companion turned for the door, taking the lead. Valerie said and did nothing as the group filed out. Ryker didn't begrudge her, not really. She'd likely only done what she felt she had to, and if she really didn't have any answers about Didier, these men more likely would.

They walked in a line down the stairs, Jaws bringing up the rear with a hand inside his coat. As they moved out onto the street Ryker spotted the van, a few cars down. Perhaps these guys weren't as clueless as he thought. Two more men, almost carbon copies, stood by the van, another couple in the opposite direction from the building, perhaps there to grab Ryker and Henrik if they decided to run.

'Just stay calm,' Ryker whispered to Henrik. 'We're not their enemies.'

'Are you sure about that?' Henrik responded, his louder and less calm response drawing a glare from the man in front.

'Into the van,' he said.

'My son is fifteen years old,' Ryker said. 'Do you really think–'

The man turned and delivered a pretty hefty slap to Ryker's face. He moved away from the blow, but chose to take it rather than fully defend, or to attack. They were outnumbered, and Ryker really didn't want to shed blood unnecessarily, or so openly on a city street. But if they carried on provoking him…

One of the men slid open the side door of the van. Ryker peered inside. Dark and empty. The man who'd opened the door jumped in. Ryker and Henrik were patted down. They had only their phones and penknives on them, plus the car key; they'd left everything else in the Jeep. The men took their things and Ryker indicated to Henrik, who moved into the van, then Ryker stepped in too, followed by three more men, including Jaws.

Cramped. They lined themselves up on the bare metal benches. Ryker and Henrik next to each other. One man either side, shoulders and arms and legs all squeezed together. The two others opposite had a bit more space. Enough for Jaws to pull out his weapon. He held it pointed down, the tip of the curved blade resting on the floor of the van. He gave Ryker a crooked smile before the van door slid shut with a thunk. No doubt the other men all had weapons too, but it was already clear Jaws was the leader here.

Not complete darkness. There was no divider to the front seats and orange street light filtered through. The remaining two men got into the front and with a cough and a splutter the van got moving.

'Nice and cosy in here,' Ryker said, switching to English for the first time. A test.

'Shut up,' the man next to Ryker said – French still – digging him in the ribs to emphasise the point.

'Not so cosy where we're going,' Jaws said in English. As Ryker had expected, the man's accent had a heavy African twang.

'I don't know where we're going, but remember our deal,' Ryker said. 'You hurt my son…'

Ryker didn't finish the threat. Instead he held Jaws' eye, as a smirk spread up the man's ugly face.

The journey didn't last long. Less than ten minutes before the van jolted and jostled over what Ryker imagined to be horribly pockmarked tarmac, then it eventually came to a stop.

No one in the back moved. The two up front got out. The side door opened again. Soon all eight bodies stood out in the cold and dark. An industrial area. The grounds of a warehouse or a small factory. Whichever, it was a big, corrugated-steel block. Hard to tell in the darkness whether it was in use and closed down for the night, or simply derelict.

'Come on,' Jaws said.

Four of the men this time to chaperone, while two waited by the van. When they reached a padlocked door, one of the men stepped forward to unlock it before they all moved inside, into the darkness, one after another.

No lights on inside. No one made an attempt to turn any on either.

'You know what this place is?' Jaws said. Ryker could see him just well enough, with the sparse street lighting seeping in through the open door, to realise the question was directed at him.

Ryker had already inhaled as he stepped through the door, and the acrid smell gave him an idea of the building's main use.

'Meat processing,' he said.

Another of those cackles from Jaws' friend.

'Very good,' Jaws said. '*Meat processing.*' He mimicked Ryker's accent. 'Chopping, dicing, mincing,' he added, swooshing the machete through the air for effect.

Silence.

'Sorry,' Ryker said. 'Is that supposed to scare me? Are you suggesting you're going to mince me up? A lot of dicing needed with that one knife.'

Behind Ryker, one of the men flicked a light switch. A buzzing sound followed, then one after another the strip lights high above blipped and flickered into life.

Not exactly ultra-modern, but the large space was bright and clean. Gleaming metal apparatus, conveyor belts, storage bins.

'Take him.'

Rough hands grabbed Ryker. He squirmed. But only a little. Jaws wandered up to Ryker, his chin held high. He pushed the blade onto Ryker's neck. Not quite enough to draw blood, but not far off.

'You think you're brave?' Jaws said.

Ryker didn't answer.

'Take the boy.'

Henrik squirmed as Jaws' remaining accomplice grabbed him. The boy struggled. Ryker did too, but not as much as he wanted. With the blade so close to his neck, the men holding him, he had little choice.

'Lock him in the old freezer,' Jaws said, before turning back to Ryker as the man dragged Henrik away. 'Don't worry. It's not turned on. Yet.'

Ryker – the blade still pressed to his neck – watched Henrik, writhing, tugging against the man's hold. He looked over his shoulder to Ryker, pleading.

'Remember what I told you,' Ryker said to Jaws again. 'If you hurt him–'

'It'll be because of you.'

Jaws looked over Ryker's shoulder. Nodded. One of the men behind Ryker let go. No chance to attack. A split second later and a thudding crack to the back of Ryker's head sent his brain spinning. The men took Ryker off his feet and forced him to the ground, left cheek to the floor. One man pushed his weight down onto Ryker's back, dug a knee into his neck. Another man held his head and one arm, twisting it at the wrist to push it to breaking point. Ryker winced. He still had one free arm to work with...

'Hold it out,' Jaws said.

Ryker squirmed and grimaced. His lack of appropriate response resulted in his face being ground further into the rough floor.

'Hold out your arm,' Jaws said.

Beyond Jaws, Ryker spotted the man who'd taken Henrik away. No sign of the teenager now. Had they underestimated him? Would Henrik find a way out?

Ryker slowly stretched out his arm at a right angle to his pinned body.

'Good,' Jaws said.

Then he lifted the machete into the air and swiped it down, like a lumberjack chopping wood. A powerful move, further emphasised by the malice on Jaws' face. Ryker closed his eyes as the blade bore down on his forearm...

He whipped his hand away at the last second and the blade crashed into the concrete floor, sending up a spray of sparks. Jaws straightened up. Looked angry, but then laughed.

'That was close,' he said. 'But I knew you'd get scared. Mr Tough Guy, huh?'

The fourth man arrived by Ryker's side and sank to his knees and Ryker wrestled to keep his remaining arm free. A further turn of his other wrist, and a dig into his neck, put paid to that, and moments later Ryker's arm was spread out on the concrete once more.

'Let's try that again,' Jaws said with his crooked smile.

The machete went up into the air. Swooshed downward...

Ryker flinched, tensed, shut his eyes...

He jumped as the blade cracked into the concrete a second time. Opened his eyes to see the front edge of the machete rested on the floor, the back portion of the metal less than an inch from his wrist.

Jaws laughed. His friends followed suit. An uproar.

'Close?' Jaws said as he crouched down by Ryker's face. 'Do you think that was an accident?'

Ryker said nothing.

'You asked me at Didier's apartment if I'd use this thing on you. What do you think now?'

Still Ryker didn't answer.

'Do you think I can get any closer next time?'

'I've never seen you get closer,' said the man on Ryker's neck.

'It's true,' Jaws said. 'But we'll wait a moment. We'll talk a moment.'

Silence. Ryker listened intently. For what? Any indication of Henrik? He heard nothing but the breaths of the men holding him, and the ever so distant sounds of the city at night.

'Who are you?' Jaws asked.

'James Ryker.'

A slight pause before, 'So that's your name,' Jaws said. 'But *who* are you?'

'No one important.'

'Why were you asking about Didier?'

'Because of what happened in St Ricard.'

Jaws didn't respond.

'He was set up, wasn't he?' Ryker said.

Jaws' face took on a far more contemplative look.

'The police executed him,' Ryker said. 'That's what Valerie told me.'

Apparently Jaws didn't like the idea of that at all. His face twisted with bitterness. At the thought that Valerie had said too much?

Ryker thought quickly. The response here... This was Didier's gang. He was gone. Murdered, by the police, but perhaps only because they'd been paid off? Too late for these guys to protect Didier now. They were protecting themselves. From who?

Ryker sighed.

'I know why they killed him,' he said.

No response.

'Didier was set up. And I know by who.'

'Go on,' Jaws said when it was clear Ryker was drawing out his revelation.

'In my pocket. There's a paper. An email. It's a message from Monique Thibaud. You know her?'

'A message to who? About what?'

'Best you see for yourself.'

Jaws looked as confused as he did angry by Ryker's revelation.

'Which pocket?' he asked.

'Coat. Inside left.'

Jaws didn't even need to say anything, or do anything. The intrigue, the mere idea, planted into the heads of the men holding Ryker, that they'd need to somehow flip him over to find the mysterious letter, was all the distraction Ryker needed.

Ignoring the risk to his wrist, Ryker wrestled free his other hand with a quick snap, then jolted up, arching his back. Whipped his other hand free. Burst backward, eventually planting his feet onto the ground to send the man on top of him flying.

The machete swiped toward Ryker. He sidestepped, ducked and came around Jaws' side, grabbed his arm and swung him around. The blade glanced across the shoulder of one of the other men, who screamed and reeled away.

A fist coming for Ryker. It smacked into his jaw. A horrible crack, probably a broken tooth or two. Ryker sent a blistering uppercut back in return. The man crumpled.

The man he'd tossed remained on the floor, about to get up. A kick to the face and a heel to the side of the head kept him on the ground.

Jaws...

Still armed, he raced for Ryker with a war cry spitting from his lips.

Ryker waited then cut him off, rushing forward and ducking and taking Jaws around the knees. Ryker heaved and groaned with effort and pulled Jaws from the ground, took two steps and smashed him against the metal wall of a storage bin with a booming thud. The reverberation shuddered through Ryker. The machete fell from Jaws' limp grip.

Ryker glanced around at the four fallen men, then to the closed door. Had the two outside heard?

He waited a moment. No response.

Of the four men, Jaws remained the one most with it. Then the one with the bleeding shoulder. The two Ryker had felled with headshots were out for the count.

Ryker grabbed the machete from the floor. He pulled up Jaws by the scruff of his neck and smacked the handle of the machete against his head. Did it again. Then let go and Jaws flopped back down. Ryker looked around. Spotted the freezer doors. Three of them. All were closed.

Ryker grabbed the man with the bleeding shoulder – the one who'd taken Henrik. He squeezed the wound. The man groaned in pain, trying to be strong, but the look on his face said it all.

'Which one?' Ryker said.

The man gave no response.

Ryker squeezed harder then took hold of the neck of the man's coat and dragged him to the freezer doors. Only a few yards, but when he reached the doors Ryker was out of breath, his skin clammy from exertion and adrenaline.

'Which one?'

'Left.'

Ryker looked to that door and moved to it. He pulled the lever to release the lock.

'Whoah!' he said as Henrik raced toward him, a meat hook in his hand.

Henrik paused, then walked forward.

'Took your time,' he said.

Ryker noted his swollen eye. He stopped Henrik with a hand to the shoulder.

'I tried to fight him off,' Henrik said.

Ryker grit his teeth in anger. He pulled the man into the freezer. Looked back across the room.

'We'll get the two others in. Jaws is coming with us.'

They rushed back to the three men, who were stirring. Within a couple of minutes they had Jaws' wrists tied up with a metal chain, and three groaning, sullen men inside the disused freezer.

'See you later,' Ryker said, before closing the door with a thunk and pulling the lever to lock it.

'How much air do you reckon they have in there?'

'Enough,' Ryker said.

He took another look at Henrik's swollen face. The teenager glanced to the control panel on the wall. The switches that'd turn the men's confinement into a frozen grave.

'No,' Ryker said, even if a large part of him wanted to dish out further punishment. But not that. 'Come on.'

Henrik didn't move. Ryker trusted him to make the right choice. He turned and moved back over to Jaws. He'd propped himself up against the bin. Blood wormed down his face from where Ryker had cracked him with the machete handle. He looked just about with it, and angry.

Ryker grabbed hold of his thick hair and yanked his head back.

'What about the other two?' Henrik said, breaking Ryker's concentration.

'Good point,' Ryker said. 'Go and fetch them, will you?'

Henrik looked at Ryker curiously. Then apparently realised what he meant.

Ryker hauled Jaws up as Henrik moved to the door. He opened it, then called out jovially, 'Psst, over here!'

Then he slowly backtracked.

Moments later the two men appeared, rushing in at first. They slowed almost to a stop when they spotted Ryker and Jaws, the machete up to Jaws' neck, one hand behind him, pushed up toward his shoulder blade.

'This way,' Ryker said, edging back to the freezer.

Not long after and the number of men in the freezer had increased by two thirds.

'Still think there's enough air for them in there?' Henrik said.

Ryker looked up to the large clock on the wall.

'As long as this place is open in the morning.'

Jaws muttered under his breath. Ryker took the blade away from his neck then kicked him in the back to propel him forward. Jaws hadn't expected the move and his face smacked into the freezer door with a thud.

He rolled on the ground to face Ryker. He looked defeated, even if he was trying to stay strong. Ryker smiled down at him.

'Now it's my turn to ask some questions.'

14

Henrik didn't know the man at Ryker's feet. He didn't know his name, his history, what good or bad he'd done in life, only that he'd been prepared to use that weapon in the most grievous way. On Ryker. On Henrik too? Or had they planned to leave Henrik in that freezer?

Henrik was raging. His legs shook as he tried to control it. One push of the button next to him and those men beyond would get what they deserved. Wouldn't they?

Yet once again Ryker was letting off people who'd tried to kill them. Why? First, Bruno, Jules, Anna, now this gang. These people wouldn't have had the same sympathies, so why did Ryker?

It wasn't that Henrik was ruthless or sadistic even, simply that... why did Ryker always have the final say? In fact, most of the messes he and Ryker ended up in were because of Ryker. If they did things Henrik's way more often, perhaps the end results would be different.

Now they were standing in a meat factory with five men locked in a freezer and one on the floor to be interrogated, who likely wouldn't give up anything useful without force.

How far was Ryker prepared to go? Far enough?

'Some advice for you,' Ryker said, kneeling down, and pushing his face close to the man that Ryker had called Jaws. 'Now you talk. Whatever you would have done to me, imagine that but worse. And believe me when I say I've delivered before.'

Jaws didn't respond. Henrik considered the words. Perhaps he'd misread Ryker this time. He sounded angry. Really angry.

'You're Didier's friend,' Ryker said.

A slight nod.

'Who's in charge,' Ryker said. 'Of your gang.'

'I am.'

'No. You're not. Look at you.' Henrik noted the offence in the man's eyes. 'At most you're in charge of some poxy street crew. Guys who've listened to too much gangsta rap, and watched too much TV. But you're not in charge of anything that anyone gives a crap about.'

Nothing from Jaws.

'I know guys like you. There's always someone above. They work you. Or, perhaps, they allow you to work. So who calls the shots? Who gives you work? Who pays you?'

Jaws didn't answer.

Ryker sighed. 'Did you know about the job in St Ricard? Before it happened.'

'No.'

'Is that unusual? That Didier would have work that you knew nothing about?'

'It would never happen.'

'What about the other man, Ramiz Touba?'

'I don't even know him.'

'Never met him, or heard of him?'

'Heard of him.'

'What did you hear?'

'That he was a psycho.'

'He work for the same boss as you?'

'In this city we all do, one way or another.'

Interesting. Henrik wanted to ask more about that, but Ryker spoke again before he could.

'Why would Didier take a job with Touba, without you knowing?'

No answer. Had Ryker missed the point?

'You think he got a promotion above you?'

A snarl on Jaws' face. He didn't like the idea of that. 'I think the story you heard about St Ricard is bullshit,' he said.

'You don't think Didier was there?' Ryker asked.

'If he was, he was played.'

'Played how?'

'The news said it was a robbery. Gems, diamonds, jewellery. Didier never saw any of that. I would have known.'

'And the police–'

'Like Valerie told you, they killed him. Easier to keep the story straight that way.'

'The police. They work for the same man as you?'

'Some of them.'

'And those that don't?'

'You'd have to ask them.'

'So for all you know, it could be your boss who set this all up. For money, pure and simple. Then he had Didier killed to keep him quiet.'

'I don't believe that. And neither do you.'

'I don't?'

Jaws smiled his crooked smile. 'You wouldn't be here if you did.'

He glanced from Ryker to Henrik. The look in his eyes caused Henrik's heart to thud a little harder.

'You're not here for Didier,' Jaws said. 'You didn't even know him. You're here for something else. The Thibauds perhaps.'

A devilish grin now on his face, as though he'd cottoned onto a secret that Ryker and Henrik held close.

'Okay,' Ryker said. 'Time to go.'

Jaws clenched his mouth closed and shook his head.

'You're taking me to the man at the top,' Ryker said.

'He'll kill me.'

'You don't think I will?'

Jaws kept his mouth shut.

Ryker sighed. Then he grasped the man's hair and dragged him kicking and screaming out of there. To the van. Henrik slid open the side door.

'Get in,' Ryker said to Henrik.

He jumped inside.

'Take his hand.'

Ryker thrust out Jaws' arm and Henrik grabbed hold. Jaws tried to wrestle free but Ryker sent a punishing shot into his kidney with his boot. Then he grabbed the handle and yanked and slid the door closed with force. Henrik jerked in shock as the metal crashed against Jaws' arm. He screamed in pain as the door clattered backward, the lock unable to take hold with the foreign object in the way.

Ryker ducked down. Grabbed Jaws' arm. Turned it over as the guy writhed. Then Ryker looked up at Henrik. Something in his eyes...

Henrik had wanted this man punished, but now it was happening, now he was right there, next to it, witnessing it...

'Still intact,' Ryker said. 'I'm surprised. Let's try higher up.'

He shoved Jaws further forward then slammed the door shut again. Another harrowing cry erupted and Henrik winced, imagining the pain.

Ryker inspected the arm again.

'Would you believe it?' he said. 'Still no break. Third time lucky, I guess. Kind of like you with that machete earlier, right?'

When Jaws tried to snatch his arm free from Henrik's grip, Ryker stooped down behind him, ran an arm around his neck to choke him and keep him in place.

He grabbed hold of the door handle.

'More force needed,' Ryker said. 'Definitely a break this time. But how many times until it comes off completely?'

'No!' Jaws screamed as Ryker got ready with the door.

He paused. Caught Henrik's eye. Henrik froze. Did he want this? Did Ryker?

'Okay!' Jaws shouted. 'Okay. I'll take you to him.'

'Good decision,' Ryker said as Henrik hung his head. Relief, or disappointment, he wasn't quite sure.

Henrik remained on edge, alert, as they travelled through the unfamiliar night-time streets of central Lyon. Jaws hadn't explained anything about who they were going to see, or what to expect when they arrived. He simply gave directions, mainly through gritted teeth as he battled through the pain in his arm. No obvious snapped bones there, Ryker said, but perhaps a stress fracture, certainly significant soft tissue damage. Now the brutality was over, Henrik didn't really care.

The viciousness of the response to him and Ryker turning up at Didier Lenglet's apartment dominated his thoughts. Six men had come for them. Men who'd been prepared to seriously hurt, brutalise, him and Ryker? For what? Asking Valerie Lenglet a few questions about her husband's death at the hands of the police?

It wasn't only the reasons why he and Ryker had been in harm's way like that which he thought about, it was the fact it had happened at all. By Ryker's side, by the side of someone as strong-willed and unrelenting as him, how many more times would Henrik's life be in such danger? There had to be another way. On his own, would Henrik have found answers in Lyon without the aggravation?

He'd continue to mull over that. Regardless, what about the answer as to why Jaws' gang had reacted so aggressively? The explanation that Henrik came back to over and over was that Jaws and his crew, everyone who knew Didier Lenglet, was scared. On high alert. They didn't understand how their friend – an everyday criminal, a tough-guy wannabe gang member – had become involved in the murderous events in St Ricard. They didn't fully understand why the police had – allegedly – executed him. They didn't know who they could trust. Everyone outside their inner circle – especially strangers like Ryker and Henrik – were an enemy, a threat.

'Turn right here,' Jaws croaked next to Henrik. They'd chained him to the metal bench in the back, but Henrik, in the back, too, while Ryker drove, had the machete in his grip, just in case.

Ryker followed the instruction. They turned onto a street of high-rise buildings. For the last half mile they'd steadily moved toward the dazzling lights of the city's skyscrapers.

'Take the next left, it goes to the service entrance.'

Ryker did so, moving onto a narrow road that served as the back entrance to several tall buildings, driving a bit more cautiously as though a sudden ambush was a real possibility on the less busy street.

'Down the ramp on the right.'

Ryker took it, heading toward the barrier for an underground car park.

'What is this place?' Ryker asked, sounding confused.

Henrik thought he knew why. When Ryker had asked to be

taken to see the boss, for some reason he hadn't pictured a gleaming city-centre office block as the destination. He'd expected some massive out-of-town villa, perhaps? Ultra-modern and sleek, like criminal kingpins had on TV shows. The everyday setting felt... wrong.

Ryker pulled the van to a stop at the barrier. Henrik noted the CCTV cameras up ahead, one to the right too, pointing at the driver's window. An intercom sat beneath it.

'And?' Ryker said.

'The cameras will read the licence plate.'

Sure enough, a moment later the barrier swung up and Ryker rolled the van forward and inside.

'There's an elevator bank in the far left corner.'

Which wasn't where Henrik would have gone, because the overhead signage suggested the main stairwell and elevator bank was off to the right, toward the centre of the building.

Ryker parked the van in the near-empty far corner, then turned around.

'Why are we here?' he asked.

'Why do you think?'

'Okay, so *who's* here?'

'*The boss.*' Jaws smirked.

'And his name is?'

Jaws shook his head. 'He'll tell you if he wants to.'

Fighting the growing doubt in his stomach, Henrik glanced out of the windscreen to the closed doors. Another camera there. No guards or anything as overt as that.

'Let's go then,' Ryker said, opening his door. Henrik reached for the side door then stopped when Jaws spoke.

'It's not too late. We could go now. He wouldn't know.'

Ryker paused but then carried on to the side and opened the door. Henrik noted the uncertainty on his face. Was he having the same doubts?

'Get out,' Ryker said.

Jaws looked from Ryker to Henrik then back again as Henrik unknotted the chain.

'God help us all,' Jaws said with genuine sombreness, as Ryker pulled him out of the van.

15

The three of them moved up to the doors, Ryker staring at the camera above. Jaws' desperate, haunted words echoed in his mind. Who the hell were they meeting here? But he wasn't about to turn and walk away now.

'Press the button,' Jaws said.

A button. That was all. No speaker, no PIN pad to input a code. Just a simple chrome button in the middle of a simple, square chrome surround.

Ryker pressed. Nothing. He glanced from the button to the camera to the doors.

Then he heard locks release. He tensed, at the ready...

The doors opened. Beyond, inside a small entranceway, stood a man and a woman. Not what Ryker had expected at all, appearance-wise. Both wore smart, formal clothes. Black suit for the man, tie neatly knotted around his neck. The woman wore a navy suit, cream blouse underneath. Neither was particularly intimidating in size or stature.

'You can leave the knife there,' the woman said to Ryker, no hint of emotion in her voice or on her face.

Jaws and Henrik both stared at Ryker, as though unsure how Ryker would react.

'Fair enough,' he said.

He propped the machete by a bollard, then the suited pair moved aside and Ryker, Jaws and Henrik headed through onto the plush carpet. The doors closed behind them. With no fuss, no words spoken, the man and woman patted down the new arrivals. All very formal, but relaxed. Ryker was certain he could quite easily tackle these two if he wanted.

Why didn't he?

He did notice that both had sidearms, in holsters strapped inside their jackets.

Henrik and Ryker lost their phones and their penknives and car key once again, the woman taking the lot. Apparently satisfied they had no other weapons or contraband, the man pressed the up button for the single lift. The shiny doors opened straight away.

'After you,' he said.

Ryker stepped in first. Then Henrik. Jaws shuffled in a little more reluctantly, head down. He'd given no hint that he knew the two chaperones, nor had they indicated in any way they knew him. The man and woman got into the lift. The doors closed. Buttons for only three floors. S/S for the basement, or *sous-sol*, plus 20 and 25.

The woman pressed 20.

The lift moved. Moments later they were heading up the outside of the building, floor-to-ceiling glass on two sides of the lift to give an unobstructed view of the Lyon cityscape with all its twinkling lights.

'Wow,' Henrik said, gazing out.

Ryker remained more interested in the man and woman.

'So what are your names?' he asked, looking from one to the other.

The man didn't react. The woman caught Ryker's eye. Almost a flicker of something – a smile? – on her otherwise expressionless face. Almost.

'Whatever you want,' she said.

Ryker shrugged. 'Dumb and Dumber it is then,' he said, to the woman and the man in turn.

Neither showed any reaction to that.

'It's Vaz and Layla,' Jaws said, prompting a glare from Vaz. Ryker wondered whether Jaws had just opened himself up for even more punishment at some point.

The lift came to a stop and the doors opened to reveal a luxurious corridor, thick carpet, gold trappings here and there. A chandelier overhead. Another two suits, standing to attention.

Layla stepped out of the lift. Then Henrik. Then Jaws.

'No, not you,' Vaz said to him. No physical attempt to stop him, but Jaws turned and looked at him and slumped before moving back inside.

Ryker watched them both for a moment, then moved around Jaws and into the corridor. As the lift doors closed, he caught Jaws' eye, noted the devastation on his face, and felt the smallest bit of guilt rise within. A feeling he didn't like at all, and one which he'd never expected to feel about a runt like that.

'This way,' Layla said as she strode down the corridor, hips swaying, her two-inch heels leaving neat impressions in the thick pile.

The two sentries stayed in place. Ryker and Henrik set off. They passed closed doors. A big set of double doors on the right. Ryker heard music and chatter beyond. Not boisterous, but a big event. A formal event.

'Party night in the office?' Ryker said to Layla. She didn't respond in any way.

They reached another set of double doors at the far end of

the corridor. Layla knocked, then opened them and peeked inside.

'You can wait in there. He'll be with you shortly.'

She stood by the open doors. Both Ryker and Henrik hesitated a moment before Ryker took the lead and moved on in.

A conference room. Of sorts. Along one wall hung thick maroon curtains, floor to ceiling. Not covering the windows. Those, similarly floor to ceiling, took up the adjacent wall at the far side. A round meeting table – dark, beautifully embellished wood – with eight chairs stood at the near side. At the far side three leather sofas arranged as three sides of a square looked to the windows, a sculpture-cum-coffee table between them – a surrealist impression of a naked man, holding up the glass tabletop on his back.

The doors banged closed. Ryker glanced to them. Layla had gone. He tried the handle. Locked.

'Not what I expected,' Henrik said.

'Not even close,' Ryker responded.

He looked over to the wall on the right where a long storage cabinet took up most of the space. A wine fridge sat there, a couple of dozen bottles chilling behind the glass door. A similarly sized normal fridge next to it, with soft drinks. An expensive-looking coffee machine sat on top.

Ryker's eyes settled on the ceiling. Two cameras up there, in opposite corners.

'Drink?' Ryker asked Henrik.

The teenager shook his head. Ryker shrugged. May as well pass the time.

Quite a lot of time. More than half an hour passed. Ryker helped himself to two super-strong and delicious espressos. Henrik lounged on one of the sofas. Ryker mainly stood by the tall windows, looking to the city below, watching the moving lights of cars and buses, snaking through the night-time streets.

Finally a noise outside the room. Ryker turned as the doors opened. Layla and a man stood there. Ryker was a little surprised – he'd expected a heavy entourage. Some serious muscle. The doors closed behind the arrivals. The man was short and slight and wore a black tie. His angular face was dominated by silvery stubble, which matched the nearly shaved silver hair on his head. Distinguished was the first word that came to Ryker's mind.

Rich and arrogant too. The way he walked. The way he held his head high. The slight pinch – disdain? – to his eyes.

'I hope you've been making yourselves comfortable,' the man said, his English good, but not perfect. He looked to the cup in Ryker's hand.

'Good coffee,' Ryker said with a nod.

'I know.'

Ryker put the cup down on the coffee table. Layla held back while the man came over. He placed Ryker's and Henrik's phones on the table, the car key too, but not the knife, then sat down on the sofa next to Henrik and folded his legs. Ryker wondered about the gesture of returning their phones. Most likely his underlings had tried to glean some information on who Henrik and Ryker were from the devices. They wouldn't be able to. The phones were hardly used – Henrik's virtually brand new.

'You don't know who I am, do you?' the man said.

'Not yet,' Ryker said. 'But I can imagine the type.'

No show on the man's face as to whether he was offended by Ryker's insinuation.

'I understand your name is James Ryker. And this is your son?'

'Henrik,' the teenager said.

Did he only know Ryker's name because Jaws had told him, or from some other means?

'And you are?' Ryker prompted.

'Aziz.'

Ryker waited for more.

'That's it?'

'For you, yes.'

Ryker looked about the room. 'Where are we?'

'What does it look like?'

'An office. Plain and boring.'

Again, no tell on the man's face as to his emotion. He was as cool as Layla and Vaz and the other guards outside.

'Busy night?' Ryker asked, indicating the suit.

'Not as busy as it's going to get now. But yes, I was hosting a banquet. You've spoiled that. I've made my excuses to leave, but I've let a lot of people down. You may have cost me a lot of money in the process too.'

Ryker rolled his eyes. 'Of course, the most heinous crime. Can never have too much money, right? Greed knows no bounds.'

Still no reaction on Aziz's face.

'I understand you're interested in St Ricard. In the murders that took place. The Thibaud family.'

'I am,' Ryker said. 'You know about that?'

'I think everyone in this part of France knows *something* about it.'

'Two men who worked for you were the culprits,' Ryker said.

Aziz shook his head. 'No, that's not right.'

'It's not?'

'Didier Lenglet didn't work for me.'

'Not what I heard.'

'And what do you know? My business interests are spread all over this city. This region. I can't be responsible for every man who benefits from association. Do I look like the type of man who'd have a low life such as that close to me?'

'Yes,' Ryker said. 'You can put on whatever fancy clothes you want, surround yourself with shiny, material things. But a well-dressed piece of shit is still a piece of shit, and it still reeks.'

Just the tiniest flicker of annoyance this time.

'Plus, I wouldn't be here if you didn't know Didier Lenglet.'

'Ah, because of Jambo?'

Jambo? Jaws, Ryker presumed.

'Another low life who doesn't work for you?' Ryker said.

'A middleman, you could say. At least he was.'

Ryker's brain whirred as to the connotations of that. Was Jambo already dead?

'And the other dead man from St Ricard?' Ryker said. 'Ramiz Touba?'

Nothing in response now.

'He was Algerian,' Ryker said. 'You look like you could be. Your name too–'

'I'm curious as to why you're so interested in what happened in St Ricard? What is it to you?'

'Call it an urge for rooting out injustice.'

'You care about the victims in the Thibaud family? Or the two men who lost their lives for their involvement?'

'Apparent involvement.'

'So you're a justice warrior?'

'I am?'

'You don't know any of these people.'

'I'm beginning to.'

'I don't see how what happened there had anything to do with you.'

'Did it have anything to do with you?'

A pause as Aziz glared at Ryker. Slowly, but surely, he was

becoming riled, despite his best intentions – training, even perhaps – to appear supremely in control.

'Seems to fit to me,' Ryker said. 'The Thibauds are a rich family. The police say the attack on them was a robbery gone wrong. Several million euros' worth of goods stolen.'

'You think I'm sitting here today from stealing jewellery from other rich people?'

'Or how about because Corinne Thibaud was intent on scuppering your business plans.'

'Now you've lost me,' Aziz said, and he genuinely did seem puzzled by Ryker's statement. He'd taken a leap there, hinting to the dam development that Henrik had mentioned before. Was Aziz involved in that at all? Ryker would look into it. If he got the chance.

'Ramiz Touba,' Ryker said. 'So did you know him or not?'

Aziz glanced at his watch with a sigh.

'Am I keeping you from something?' Ryker asked.

'I already told you the answer to that. But I'm also waiting. Not long to go now.'

He attempted a smile. It didn't work on his face at all, made him look constipated.

'Twice now I've mentioned Touba's name,' Ryker said. 'Twice now you've avoided telling me if and how you knew him.'

Aziz held Ryker's eye. 'I knew him.'

'Good start. He worked for you?'

'Actually he did.'

'Doing what?'

'Did you read the news articles?'

'A hitman?'

'That's what they said.'

'And what do you say?'

'Depends who asks me.'

'I'm asking you.'

'I told you. Touba worked for me.'

'Killing people.'

'If that's what you want to believe.'

'He worked only for you.'

'Yes.'

'So why was he in St Ricard if you had nothing to do with the events there?'

'Who said he was in St Ricard?'

Ryker paused. 'So he wasn't?'

'No. He wasn't.'

'You know that for sure?'

'Yes.'

'How?'

'Because he was working for me that night. Nowhere near the Alps.'

'Where?'

'Nowhere near the Alps. I already said.'

'Doing what.'

'His job.'

'Killing someone.'

'I didn't say that.'

'You have proof? Of him not killing someone, or otherwise, nowhere near the Alps that night?'

'The question is irrelevant to the fact. There's no one I need to prove this to.'

'You didn't bother telling the police your man was nowhere near St Ricard that night?'

'You're assuming the police have spoken to me at all.'

Ryker rolled his eyes. The clipped, circular answers were becoming irritating.

'Touba was killed awaiting trial,' Ryker said.

'Of course he was. The police couldn't afford to put an

obviously innocent man on trial for murder, could they? Especially in a case so public.'

'So you think the police had him killed.'

'I didn't say that.'

Ryker sighed. He'd never get a straight answer from this guy. Not without coercion. But then, the fact this apparent kingpin was speaking to Ryker at all was something of a surprise. And in such calm and comfortable surroundings. What was Aziz's endgame here?

Ryker heard an almost imperceptible buzz and Aziz looked at his watch once more.

'Ah. Finally. The wait is over. Time to get things moving.'

He looked across to the closed curtains. Ryker turned that way too. Layla moved to the end of the curtains, by the door, reached around the fabric. Pressed a button?

A moment later a mechanical whir sounded and the curtains slowly drew open, as they would on a theatre stage. Except there was no stage beyond them. Only a wall of black glass, which Ryker had found earlier, but still didn't fully understand its purpose, although he wasn't sure he liked where the situation was headed.

'You were waiting for this?' Ryker asked.

Then Ryker twitched when lights beyond the glass flickered on to reveal a room. Brightly lit. Plain. Several people inside.

Henrik gasped in shock. Ryker tried his best to hold in his reaction but his stomach curdled in horror at the sight.

'This, is what we're waiting for,' Aziz said, a sickening grin spreading across his face.

16

Jaws sat on a chair, no clothes on his youthful, muscular body except for a pair of white boxers that were streaked with blood. *His* blood, judging by how much of it also covered his skin, seeping from the several gashes to the flesh on his torso and face and arms and legs. Largely superficial, but painful cuts. His remaining friends from the meat factory stood around him. Dressed, but also bloodied, and with their heads down, unable to look at each other. At the left side of the room stood two suited men, standing to attention, arms clasped in front of them as they stared blankly toward the glass. On the right of the captives a man and woman. The man was Vaz, from the lift, the woman may well have been Layla's sister, she looked so similar in stature and appearance and attire. As though Aziz had a production line of carbon copy suited henchmen and henchwomen.

'What is this?' Ryker said, looking from the grim sight and to Aziz whose eyes remained fixed on the sorry figures beyond the glass.

He said nothing, but nodded, though it wasn't clear who he nodded to.

Ryker's eyes whipped to the doors to the conference room when he heard the lock releasing and in strode another three suited guards. One stood by the door. The other two came over to Ryker and Henrik. Ryker stood from his chair, so too did Henrik. As they did so, the men both pulled a handgun.

'Sit back down,' Aziz said, no hint of anything really in his tone.

Ryker stared at the guns. The men were three yards away. A risky move to try and tackle them. Ryker slowly lowered himself back into his seat, looked back to Henrik who did the same. The teenager looked terrified, none of that youthful confidence remaining. Perhaps this was one violent scrape too many.

'You know that power is all about control,' Aziz said, fixing his emotionless stare on Ryker. 'When you control people, you can trust them.' He paused, holding Ryker's eye. 'Do you know much about my country, James Ryker?'

Ryker felt he probably did, but he didn't bother to respond.

'Algeria has a rich, but complicated history. A history of warfare and rule by different powers with various cultures and religions. You can imagine, over the centuries, with so many different people fighting each other for conflicting causes, that there has been significant bloodshed, so much anger, and revenge too, and with all that come many stories of a truly horrific nature.'

'Humans have done shitty things to each other throughout history,' Ryker said. 'Is that your point?'

'Did you know Algeria was once part of the Ottoman Empire?'

'I did.'

'Did you also know Hungary was?'

'Is any of this relevant?'

Aziz paused again. 'I've always been fascinated by how modern-day countries have developed from those empires that used to control them,' he said. 'Fascinated by the individuals too, who became famous, and infamous. Noblemen, warriors, martyrs.'

'I'll ask again,' Ryker said. 'What's your point?'

'Oh, nothing really to do with politics or religion or anything serious like that, this is more of an explanation for the position that you, and the men in that next room, find themselves in.'

'I'm not sure I understand your explanation at all.'

Aziz glanced from Ryker to Henrik and back again. As passive as his face remained, Ryker sensed he was enjoying this moment. Sensed... a strange air of pride.

'Have you heard of György Dózsa?' Aziz asked.

'No,' Ryker said.

'I have,' Henrik said.

Aziz smiled his ghastly smile at that. 'Can you tell us what you know?' he asked.

'He started a rebellion against the rulers in Hungary in the sixteenth century. He came from Transylvania, I think. The damage he caused, and the mess he left in Hungary, and parts of Romania, helped the Ottomans take over.'

'A nice summary,' Aziz said, nodding in appreciation. 'I'm surprised you know this. You're not Hungarian?'

'No,' Henrik said. 'I read.'

'Very good. But it's Dózsa's death rather than his life I'm more interested in. Do you know the details?'

'Yes,' Henrik said, hanging his head.

'But not you?' Aziz said to Ryker, who only shook his head. 'Then let me explain. Dózsa, who himself had severely punished his enemies, was eventually captured, and as punishment before his execution, was made to sit on a smouldering iron throne.' Aziz became more animated as he spoke now. 'He was forced to wear a red-hot iron crown, to hold a red-hot iron sceptre, mocking his ambition to be king. Can you imagine even that part of the story? The pain and injuries that hot metal would cause to the skin and flesh on his head and hands?'

Unfortunately Ryker could, though he'd never had to witness or experience something so horrible.

'Yet that wasn't the worst part, or even the most relevant part for me telling you this story. Next, the guards pulled at his flesh with hot pliers, tearing at it, before, one after another, his closest allies were brought to him, on their hands and knees. The captors forced them to bite off and eat chunks of his mangled flesh. Those who did so were spared. Those who refused were executed on the spot.'

Ryker felt sick at the images in his head. Aziz looked seriously pleased with himself.

'Dózsa, of course, was condemned, his crimes too severe for him to find forgiveness, and he died the most grim and painful death. But the men who worked for him... they were given a choice. A chance.'

Finally Aziz gave his attention to the men in the next room once more. Beyond the glass, Vaz now had the machete in his hands. Blood streaked the metal. He moved up to one of Jaws' crew. No words were spoken as he stretched out his hand, the machete dangling from his grip. Jaws' friend took the machete. He glanced to the glass, then looked down to Jaws. The hand holding the machete trembled. Vaz spoke, though the soundproofing of the glass was so strong that Ryker heard nothing at all, only the slow, controlled breaths of the robotic guards in the room with him.

The man slowly brought the machete up above his head, as though ready to swipe down and kill – or at least horribly injure – his friend. But he was shaking too much. He was terrified. He wasn't going to do it.

'You don't have to do this to them,' Ryker said to Aziz. 'Please.'

The next moment the man with the machete flinched, but rather than swipe down on his friend, he turned as though about to attack Vaz.

Too obvious.

Vaz whipped a knife from nowhere, lunged forward, avoiding the blow with the machete. He drove his blade into the man's side. The guy's eyes went wide with shock. His friends all cowered or quivered. Vaz grabbed the machete, spun the man around, pushed him to his knees and brought the blade of the machete up to his neck.

Vaz glanced to the glass, directly at Aziz.

A nod from Aziz. Then Vaz swiped the blade across and a gash opened up in the man's neck, blood pouring. Ryker grimaced, looked away. To Henrik, who was looking at the floor, his face white. A fifteen-year-old boy. He'd already witnessed so much of humankind's barbaric nature, but this horrific, planned violence was something else.

'Please,' Ryker said to Aziz. 'All they did was bring us to you.'

'*All they did*. No. They broke a very clear rule. I only work with people I can trust.'

'People you can control.'

Aziz smiled once more. 'You're picking up my way of thinking quickly.'

Ryker went to stand up. Several sets of eyes turned to him, Aziz included. The man behind Ryker took a step forward. Closer. That was good. Ryker paused, half sitting, half standing.

'Please don't,' Aziz said. 'Let's wait until this show is over before we decide what to do with you and your son.'

Ryker already knew. Aziz had no intention of letting Ryker and Henrik leave the building alive. They were only still breathing for Aziz's amusement, and for him to show his power.

Ryker slowly lowered himself back down, but remained perched, trying to calculate his move, trying to calculate how he could tackle the man behind him. He was confident he could, but what about Henrik? Would he end up with a bullet in the back of his head the moment Ryker went for it? Plus, even after dealing with the first man, what about everyone else?

Back in the other room, the machete was now in the hands of one of Jaws' other crew members. He looked a little more confident than his dead friend, but not much. With a silent cry of desperation – silent to Ryker at least – he slashed down on Jaws with the machete. Hit him over and over on his shoulders, torso, arms, moving in a frenzy as though consumed by... Ryker guessed it was nothing but a primal survival instinct.

Ryker winced. Jaws shook and jolted, blood pouring everywhere. His left arm was nearly cleaved off when his friend finally stopped. The blood-dripping blade was taken from him as he panted heavy breaths. He stared through the glass to Aziz, seeking approval.

'He made a good choice,' Aziz said.

Another nod from the boss and one of the suited men grabbed the man and led him off.

'Now do you understand?' Aziz said to Ryker.

Ryker didn't answer, but he couldn't sit and watch any more, even with a gun pointed to his head. He'd rather die trying than do nothing.

'Why are you doing this?' Henrik asked, still staring at the floor. Not looking as scared now. Angry. Determined.

'Because he can,' Ryker said.

A simple answer for something so horrible.

Ryker bounced to his feet. But he didn't attempt to swipe the gun from the man behind him. Instead, he lunged right, toward Henrik. More specifically, to the man behind Henrik. A surprise move. One which likely saved the teenager's life, at least in the short term, because the man there had no choice but to turn his weapon onto Ryker.

Before the first bullet was fired, Ryker flung the coffee cup he'd grabbed – a minor distraction that he hoped would make the difference. He collided with the gunman as a shot boomed. The round hit the glass screen which blistered but didn't shatter. Ryker thundered his fist into the man's neck as they fell. A horrible crunch as the man's windpipe collapsed. He'd take his last, choked breaths soon enough.

A shot from behind Ryker as he headed for the floor. The bullet grazed Ryker's left shoulder. He ignored the shock of pain, smacked into the floor, took the gun from the dying man's grip, righted the aim and fired two shots at the guard who'd stood behind him.

Shoulder, chest. He went down.

Ryker glanced to Henrik, hiding in cover himself behind the sofa. Then he looked to the glass. Chaos in there, Jaws' remaining friends had started a battle for survival – perhaps encouraged by Ryker's attempt at freedom.

Aziz. Ryker's eyes rested there. Layla and the remaining male guard covered the boss as they moved him to the door. Ryker aimed. So too did Layla, right back at him. Neither fired. At least not straight away, because the next moment a siren sounded – an ear-piercing shriek. Then water cascaded down from two sprinklers in the ceiling.

The doors to the conference room burst open. Another guard.

'It's a raid!' he shouted. 'Let's go!'

Ryker ducked behind the sofa a split second before Layla fired a shot. It hit the coffee table, shattering the glass top. He fired off a warning shot in return, but when he bobbed his head up, the room was empty. As was the space next door, except for four corpses in there: Jaws, two of his friends, and one of the guards, who had the machete wedged in his skull.

'You okay?' Ryker asked Henrik. Shouted really, to be heard above the din.

Henrik looked anything but okay, yet he nodded.

'Come on,' Ryker said, pulling Henrik up.

Ryker grabbed their things from the table, handed Henrik his phone. With the gun at the ready, Ryker jogged to the door as water poured onto and off him. No one in sight immediately outside the room, but as he glanced further along the corridor... a stampede of shouting, rushing people. Men in black tie and women in ball gowns darted about, soaked through from the sprinklers. Heavily geared police swarmed, corralling the partygoers away.

Ryker ducked back into the conference room when an officer turned his way.

'Why are the police here?' Henrik asked.

A good question. As was, who'd set off the fire alarm?

Not questions to dwell on right now.

'Aziz didn't go into the crowd,' Ryker said, looking directly across the corridor to the other doors there. 'He must have another way out.'

Ryker thought for a moment. Tried to picture the basement car park. The main lifts were surely out of order if the police had planned this properly. So what were their options for escaping? The lift they'd come up in didn't have a stairwell by it. They couldn't use the main one either, which was where all the action was centred.

'We should go out with the crowds,' Henrik said, breaking Ryker's concentration.

He had to admit, it wasn't a bad suggestion. Even if Aziz and his gang had been intent on horribly murdering Ryker and Henrik, the safest action now wasn't finding the guy and seeking immediate revenge, but trying to blend and escape the building with the crowd. The police were surely only there for Aziz, weren't they?

Except Ryker and Henrik didn't blend with the formally dressed guests at all.

Footsteps in the corridor. Ryker looked up to the ceiling and closed his eyes a moment as he waited and prepared himself.

Then he leaped out into the open. Spotted the two officers, skulking toward him, powerful carbines in their hands. Not ordinary police officers but an elite firearms unit. Ryker fired a shot into the Kevlar of one of the men, kicked out at the knee of the other then hammered the back of his neck with the butt of the gun to send him down.

'Come on!' Henrik shouted, rushing along the corridor to the crowds.

Ryker went to go after him, was about to toss the gun...

One of the felled officers grabbed Ryker's ankle and he tumbled to the carpet. Ryker kicked him off. Smacked him in the head with the heel of his boot. Enough to subdue him.

When he looked back across the corridor Henrik had already disappeared into the melee of people. Ryker took a step that way, then another kitted-out officer came into view from the crowd. He spotted Ryker, and his felled colleagues. He lifted his weapon as he shouted out...

Ryker had no choice. He turned and ran. Banged through a door into the room opposite. A smaller conference room. There was another door at the far end. Had Aziz come this way?

He raced across the room, through the door. Found himself in a plain, concrete-walled corridor.

Ryker rushed along, and soon came to a similarly plain, concrete-walled stairway. Up, or down?

Ryker looked over the banister. A long way down. But no suggestion any police were coming up that way. Only a few floors up, but surely no escape there, unless a helipad or similar sat on the roof, craft ready and waiting. Yet it wouldn't be ready and waiting for Ryker, but for Aziz. Perhaps he'd already left that way.

Noise below. Ryker glanced over the edge again. Footsteps. Several sets. Definitely heading down, rather than up.

Then noise behind him too. Again, more than one set of feet. The police, coming for Ryker.

He darted down the stairs, taking them two at a time, his left hand on the gun, his right hand on the banister to help stop him from stumbling and falling.

Shouting above him. The police telling him to stop. Ryker moved from the banister, making sure he wasn't in view from above, stopping any potshots.

He passed floor after floor of nothing, counting the flights as he went. Two turns per storey. Soon he neared the ground floor and was sure he'd edged away from the police above him.

Ground floor. But there wasn't a doorway out. There hadn't been since floor twelve, as though this stairwell was a private entrance and exit for Aziz, much like the lift at the other side of the building.

Ryker carried on down, to the basement level. Slowed up a little as he moved to the closed door. No glass to see through to whatever – whoever – lay on the other side.

But he couldn't afford to hesitate. Within seconds the police would have him in their sights. Gun at the ready, Ryker pushed down on the handle then kicked the door open.

A car park, as he'd expected. But it was tiny. Not the same car park he'd entered into, but a closed-off space with markings for only a dozen or so vehicles. Only three in sight. One to his left – a silver Mercedes. No one there. Two more cars right in front of him. A black BMW SUV, and a navy Volvo SUV.

The lights of the BMW were on. The lights to the Volvo came on as Ryker moved into the open, heading for a pillar for cover as the passenger front and side doors to the Volvo opened. Two of Aziz's guards stepped out, firing as they moved. Ryker pressed himself up against the concrete strut as bullets blasted into the thick material, sending a cloud of dust into the air.

Two powerful engines roared into life. The BMW sped across Ryker's line of sight. He fired four shots. Two hit metalwork. Two hit tyres which spat out hissing air. The driver swerved, or perhaps simply lost control of the beast and the BMW smashed into a concrete pillar.

Ryker burst from his position. Spotted movement. Fired a shot that way. No hit, but he knew where one of the shooters lay hidden at least. The Volvo jolted forward. The front passenger door was still open. Ryker fired off another shot which hit the driver in his shoulder and he, too, lost control. The Volvo clipped the back end of the BMW and spun to a stop.

Ryker slid behind the Mercedes as the second of the gunmen opened fire on him. Bullets raked the metalwork but Ryker scooted to the far side and pressed up against the wheel for cover.

Heightened shouting. More footsteps. Gunshots boomed. Not handguns but the rat-a-tat of rapid-fire weapons. The police. Taking out Aziz's crew. Good for Ryker? Except as far as the police were concerned, Ryker was probably one of them too. Or at least as much a target as they were.

Ryker stole a glance over the bonnet of the Mercedes. No attention his way as the police and Aziz's crew fired back and forth at each other.

Five yards of open space between the Mercedes and the BMW. Had Aziz been in there? Beyond the BMW, the exit ramp.

Ryker took his chance. He darted away from the Mercedes. Flung himself forward, rolling to a stop by the crumpled front end of the BMW. A bullet dinged the body. He'd been spotted. He moved further around. The driver's door was open. The driver remained strapped in, his bloodied face resting on the airbag. Alive, but seriously drowsy.

A shuffling noise right by Ryker.

Aziz. Clutching his shoulder as he cowered at the back end of the BMW.

Ryker, crouching low, moved to him. But then caught sight of a figure in the corner of his eye. Moving fast, from the Volvo?

Layla.

She wasn't armed. Blood wormed down the side of her face. She dodged left, then right as she closed in. Ryker went to attack but she feinted, moving more quickly than Ryker could, and she snapped at his gun arm causing the weapon to spill loose. Ryker went for a counterstrike but she feinted again, got hold of his other wrist as she ducked and came up behind him. Arm bar. Holding Ryker's hand above his head, Layla twisted, causing Ryker to turn and fold to the ground as she pushed down. Slick moves. She was trying to use her speed and skill to overcome Ryker's superior strength. But Ryker had come across capable adversaries plenty of times before.

He reached out with his other hand. Grabbed her ankle and yanked. She tried to twist Ryker's arm further, completing the threat of a broken arm, but his countermove caused her momentum to shift the other way. He spun out from her hold and reached up and grabbed her by the neck and lifted her off her feet and tossed her away. She clattered across the top of the BMW's bonnet. Gunfire boomed. Bullets pinged. Layla took a bullet, possibly two. Not fatal shots and she shouted in pain as she slid off the car to the floor. Ryker looked back to Aziz.

He had Ryker's gun. Pointed at Ryker's head.

'You brought them,' Aziz said.

Ryker shook his head. 'I can help you,' he said. 'I'll get us out of here.'

Aziz's lined face showed his distrust.

'I think you know more about St Ricard,' Ryker said. 'I'll help you get out of here, you'll tell me all about it.'

Aziz didn't respond, but the proposition had distracted him. Ryker shot forward and easily took the gun. He turned it on Aziz, who couldn't hide his anger.

'Come on,' Ryker said, ignoring the roaring doubts in his mind.

He darted for the exit ramp, Aziz close behind him.

A single gunshot and Aziz crumpled. Ryker ducked and looked down. Aziz clutched the back of his leg.

'Help me up!' he shouted to Ryker, desperation in his voice.

Beyond him, the police officers closed in.

The doubts won out. Aziz may have been useful, but Ryker owed him nothing.

He turned and rushed for the exit.

17

Ryker moved quickly away from the office block and hid in an alley a hundred yards down the road, away from the swarming police presence. The officers had rolled out tape, blocking the street in both directions across a thirty-yard square. Ever so slowly the guests from Aziz's private gathering were released, one or two at a time. No sign of the man himself, though Ryker had no view of the private entrance from his lookout point. He presumed the police had captured Aziz – and any of his crew who remained alive – but had they in fact killed the kingpin?

No sign of Henrik either. Ryker sent a couple of texts to his phone but received no response. Once the crowds had died down, and the police vehicles started to filter away, Ryker decided to move. He slinked through the dark and quiet streets, hiding in alleys, behind cars and vans every time he heard a siren or sensed people approaching. After a mile or so he relaxed a little more, deciding no one was on his tail, and sped up his pace as he retraced the route from earlier in the night to take him back to the street where Valerie Lenglet lived.

The Jeep was still there. No sign of Henrik.

His worry growing, Ryker sent another text as he stood by the Jeep, then looked up the street, up at the Lenglets' building, to the window of their apartment. No lights on. Ryker thought about going up there. With Jaws and his crew all dead or in police custody, Valerie likely wouldn't have any more tricks up her sleeve, but would she really have any useful information for Ryker either? Certainly she wouldn't know where Henrik was, which was Ryker's most immediate concern.

Did the police have him? Or some remnant of Aziz's crew?

But why had the police showed up at all?

Ryker sighed and unlocked the Jeep and sat down in the driver's seat, brain still on overdrive. His phone weighed heavy in his hand as he stared at the screen, at the three unread text messages he'd sent. His options were limited. He could wait a little longer, then head back to Aziz's tower block to search for Henrik there. But even if the police had fully cleared out, what would he find? There was no reason why Henrik would have stuck around if he had a chance to leave, was there? Alternatively he could rest up in the Jeep, catch some sleep, hope Henrik turned up, safe and sound. Or he could–

The phone buzzed in his hand with an incoming message. Henrik.

I'm fine. I got away.

Ryker typed out a couple of words in response, then deleted them and hit the call button instead. No answer. Another message came through.

Can't talk. I found something.

Ryker waited for more. Nothing came. So he sent a message back.

I'm at the Jeep. Where are you?

He stared at the screen, awaiting the response.

I had to run. I'm hiding at Rue de Ville, opposite the fire station. Pick me up?

Ryker typed the address into the Jeep's satnav. A couple of miles away. The opposite direction from Aziz's place to where he was. With a sigh, Ryker turned the engine on and set off. He took a circuitous route, never getting too close to Aziz's building, just to be safe, and arrived on Rue de Ville some twenty minutes later. The fire station looked dead. Obviously a quiet night for them. Either side of the fire station, and all along the street opposite, were apartment blocks, similar in style and age to the street where Valerie Lenglet lived, though judging by the cars parked here, the homes were a little more upmarket.

He found a spot to park the Jeep then stepped out to surveil the street. No sign of anyone. A couple of alleys, or at least narrow roads leading between apartment blocks. Decent enough hiding spots.

Ryker called Henrik. No answer. Sent a text.

I'm here.

No response.

So Ryker tentatively walked toward the nearest of the alleys. He was a couple of yards from it when the lights on an Audi A8, a couple of cars in front of him, blinked on. Ryker squinted from the glare. He hesitantly stepped toward the car. The rear window wound down. A familiar face peered out.

Monique Thibaud.

'Busy night?' she asked Ryker.

'I'd say I'm surprised to see you, but I'm really not.'

The whole text message thing had stank from the start.

'Where's Henrik?' Ryker asked.

Monique held up the phone.

'Sorry. I don't have him. Only his phone.'

Ryker closed his eyes and sighed.

'Why don't you get in so we can talk?' she added.

The front passenger window wound down. Anna was there. She tapped a handgun on the dashboard. Not with an intent to use it, simply showing Ryker she was armed. Bruno was in the driver's seat. Jules was most likely in the hospital still having his shot foot tended to.

'You're running low on muscle,' Ryker said to Monique. 'At least ones without injuries.'

'I think tonight there are a lot of people down on numbers.'

Ryker didn't flinch as Anna stepped out from the car. She glared at Ryker. Real hatred. She opened the back door and Monique slid across to the other side.

'Please?' Monique said.

Ryker winked at Anna, then sank into the plush leather seat. The interior of the top-of-the-range Audi carried an equally luxurious odour. Anna climbed back into the front. The engine remained off.

'So let me guess,' Ryker said, fixing his stare on Monique, whose face showed satisfaction – with what? 'You followed me and Henrik here to Lyon. Or, at least, you figured we'd come here, because we didn't have a tail.'

He paused, waiting for a response, but Monique said nothing as she smiled at him.

'You also organised that police raid.'

She still didn't respond. Was that confirmation? The events surely couldn't just be coincidence.

'You've got control of the gendarmerie in St Ricard, but the police here too? I have to say, I'm surprised at your reach.'

'Surprised or impressed?'

'I don't find corruption impressive at all.'

That took away some of her satisfied look.

'Do you know who Aziz is?' Ryker asked.

She shook her head. 'No. Not really. I've never met him. And I'm not like him. You must realise that. I'm not a gangster. I have no involvement in organised crime.'

'You're just a very rich woman who pulls the strings of various authorities.'

She didn't say anything to that, but he did get her point. She was not like Aziz. Not at all. He didn't trust her, he didn't believe she acted wholly above board. For one, she had the questionable characters in the front of the car working for her. But her activities were on a different level to the madman Aziz, and her hired muscle was all the less intimidating for it. And he felt comfortable sitting in the car with her, on her own terms, because of it.

'How did you get Henrik's phone?' Ryker asked.

'Luck, mostly.'

'Is he in police custody?'

'Not that I'm aware of.'

'But you knew that was his phone?'

She shrugged. He didn't like her nonchalance.

'What–'

'Let me explain it for you,' Monique said. 'Because I sense your tired little brain is struggling.'

Ryker bit his tongue.

'My Sophie has gone. I don't know where to, but believe me when I say I am very protective of her. I want to find her. I'll do pretty much anything to achieve that.'

She paused and looked away from Ryker, as though deep in thought.

'I'm suspicious of anyone coming to our town asking questions about my family,' she continued, still looking out of her window. 'We've already been through so much. When you and your son arrived... how could I possibly trust that your interests were aligned with mine? You're so... you're not exactly normal, are you?'

Ryker really didn't know how to take that, so he said nothing. He caught sight of Bruno in the rear-view mirror. The big man smirked, obviously having taken Monique's words as an insult to Ryker. When he looked back to Monique she had her gaze on him once more.

'So naturally I was suspicious of you, your motives. And yes, I made sure we followed your movements. Both when you went for that strange hike in the mountains, and when you came here. I realised who you were meeting, first with Didier Lenglet's family, and then Aziz Doukha. And, the more I thought about it, the more I realised perhaps... our interests are more aligned than I at first thought.'

Ryker still said nothing when Monique once again paused.

'Was Aziz involved in the attack on my family?' Monique asked.

He'd considered asking her the same thing.

'I honestly don't know,' Ryker said. 'But he was definitely connected to the two dead men. Didier Lenglet and Ramiz Touba.'

'You didn't ask him about what happened in St Ricard?'

'Of course I did.'

'And?'

'He said Didier Lenglet didn't work for him. Not directly anyway. Lenglet was too lowly, in Aziz's eyes.'

'What about Touba?'

'Ramiz Touba wasn't in St Ricard that night.'

A flicker of surprise on Monique's face.

'He said that?'

Ryker nodded. 'Touba, by all accounts, was a hitman for Aziz. But Aziz claims Touba was working a different job that night. That's all I know. I have no information on where he really was. And I don't even know if Aziz was really telling me the truth.'

She looked disappointed. Or perhaps worried about something.

'I still don't understand you,' she said after a drawn-out silence. 'I don't understand why you came to our village at all. But I am starting to think that perhaps you're more ally than enemy to me. And you've shown that you're very... resourceful.'

'What are you saying?'

She held Ryker's eye then sighed, as though building up for a difficult announcement.

'I'll get the police in St Ricard to back off from you. You'll have no problem in the town as long as you don't cause me any problems.'

'No more breaking into your house?'

'Please don't.'

'And no more tussles with your friends?'

He looked at Bruno and Anna.

'No. I don't think any of us need that. But I'm not doing this because I like you. I'm doing it because I think, with your unorthodox techniques, you might actually help me to find Sophie, one way or another.'

'Why have you kept it a secret that she's missing?'

She shook her head, making it clear that she wasn't going to reveal anything more.

'When we first met,' she said, 'you mentioned the work Corinne was involved in, related to the Villeneuve dam project.'

'I did.'

'If you want to find out more, I suggest you begin with a man named Julian Hofman.'

'Who's he?'

'I'm sure you'll figure it out. And... if you do find that Aziz is involved, in either that dam project, or in the attacks on my family, you'll let me know straight away.'

Ryker nodded. 'Aziz is still alive?' he asked.

'He is.'

'Be careful,' Ryker said.

Monique stared, eyebrow slightly raised in question.

'I'm just saying. You may have had enough sway to organise that raid tonight, and to have Aziz arrested, and I'm sure in a normal situation the police would have enough evidence purely on what they find up in that tower to keep Aziz behind bars for good. But... Aziz is not normal. What I'm saying is, don't underestimate him.'

'Thanks for the advice,' Monique said, sounding anything but thankful.

'And if you–'

'Yes. If I find any information about your son, I'll let you know.' She waved the phone in the air. 'I have your number.'

The inside of the car fell silent. The conversation was over. Ryker opened his door and stepped out. The engine roared into life, and moments later the Audi swung out and took off down the street.

Ryker took his phone out and looked at the messages again. He'd suspected not all was as it seemed with the texts, apparently from Henrik. Following that bizarre conversation he certainly didn't fully trust Monique Thibaud, but he did trust that she didn't have Henrik.

The big question then, was where on earth was he?

18

The stolen motorbike Henrik rode out of Lyon was powerful enough, though hardly the best vehicle for the wintry terrain – at least without specialist clothing. He had a helmet, but only his normal clothes and winter coat, and the wind blasted against him as he travelled along the snaking, mountainous roads back toward St Ricard.

Why was he there and not in Lyon?

Having persuaded the police – who corralled everyone inside that building to the lobby for 'sorting' – that he was in the wrong place at the wrong time, and gave them his best innocent child look, he'd initially headed back to the Jeep, but Ryker hadn't been there. He waited. But nerves got the better of him.

He'd left the Jeep and hidden. He'd seen Ryker arrive back there. He'd kind of known Ryker would be okay. The man had a knack for survival, that was for sure. But Henrik hadn't showed himself. Instead, satisfied that Ryker was safe, he'd left Lyon altogether. For more than one reason.

He liked Ryker. He respected him. He looked up to him. In many ways, Henrik *needed* Ryker, who'd protected him from harm time and time again. But James Ryker also attracted trouble. It's how the two of them had met in the first place. And what Henrik had witnessed tonight in that tower block...

He didn't want to think about that. Ever.

He liked Ryker. He hadn't abandoned him for good. He'd find him, when he needed to. Eventually he hoped they'd ride away from this place together. But for now, he'd carry on alone. For his own safety, and hopefully for Ryker's too. As a child, an unassuming one too, Henrik knew he could move more easily, more freely than Ryker. People were less suspicious of him, they noticed him less.

And, honestly, he liked the idea of not having to answer to anyone.

Sunrise remained a couple of hours away as Henrik arrived on the outskirts of St Ricard. The streets were deathly quiet, most of the usually twinkling string lights turned off for the night. Henrik parked the motorbike and trekked up the frozen path into the mountain, shivering badly. Using nothing but the moonlight in the clear sky above, he eventually found the spot in the woods where he and Ryker had left their backpacks... when was that? Not even twenty-four hours ago. He could scarcely believe how much they'd been through in such a short space of time. How many people they'd aggravated and now wanted to do them harm.

Would all that have been avoided if Henrik had done everything his way from the start?

He moved further up the mountain. Not as far as the ridge, but far enough to be well away from the town. He set up a fire, got it going. Didn't bother to pitch his tent. Instead, he climbed into his sleeping bag right next to the warm flames.

It took a while for his shivering to wane. His eyes remained open. He was tired. About as tired as he could ever remember being in his life. But, as he lay there in the dark, frozen forest, the wind gently whistling around him, branches creaking and cracking, he realised he was also very, very alone.

Despite himself, regret bubbled away in his gut now as he thought about Ryker, and wondered where his friend was.

As he struggled to find sleep, he really wished he had Ryker – his protector – by his side after all.

Two, maybe three hours of shut-eye. Not much really, but certainly better than nothing. Henrik didn't wake with the sunrise feeling refreshed, but he was at least warmer than he'd been after that frigid journey from Lyon. And he was safe, despite the feeling of loneliness which somehow hadn't left him even when he'd drifted off.

Still, that feeling dissipated with daylight, and as he stretched and then packed up his belongings, he pushed thoughts of Ryker to the back of his mind once more. He had work to do.

He tucked his backpack in the hiding place next to Ryker's. The spot was easy enough to find again, and, as they'd decided the very first time they put their things there, it was easier to move around the town without the bulk.

Next stop was a patisserie in the town. The first shop that opened. His belly growled viciously as he paid for the pastries. The young shop assistant – well, older than him, but probably only mid-twenties – gave him a warm and welcoming smile. No hint that she had any clue who Henrik was. No hint that she saw any kind of threat in him whatsoever, despite the fact the police had run him and Ryker out of town not long ago.

He stepped out of the shop feeling ever more sure of his decision to come back here alone.

He only took one more step before he stopped and dove into

the paper bag and took out the still warm pain au chocolat. He devoured it in four hungry but satisfying bites. He ate the next two pastries on the move, his belly overly full by the time he'd finished. Perhaps he'd overdone it, but he'd been so hungry...

He spotted the gendarmerie patrol car turn into the street ahead. He scrunched the empty paper bag in his hand and tossed it into a bin as he walked. Kept his eyes straight ahead, but watched the car with his peripheral vision. He didn't let up his pace. Didn't deviate. Just kept on going. As did the patrol car. Soon it passed him without incident. Henrik smiled to himself.

The walk from there took him forty-five minutes. More secluded even than Monique Thibaud's grand home, the house where her brother and his family had lived was nearly a mile along a twisting private road that rose high into the hills surrounding St Ricard. Tyre marks had created wide gouges in the snow on the road, no signs of footprints, though the heavily compacted snow, which had obviously iced over several times during cold nights, was too hard for Henrik's modest weight to leave an impression. Had other people walked up here?

He rounded a bend and the stone-built villa came into view. Handsome, but not as big as Monique's. There was no perimeter wall here, only a set of wrought-iron gates, hedges either side. The gates had no locks and Henrik opened them and slipped through the gap then paused as he looked over the house.

Clearly abandoned. The front door still had police tape splashed across it, though the tape was torn where the door had since been reopened. The windows were all boarded up – to prevent squatters, Henrik presumed, though he didn't imagine there were many of those around here.

As he looked on, he wondered why the house had been left like this. Months had passed since the murders. The house wasn't for sale, and Henrik really didn't know how many people would want a house where such a brutal crime had taken place anyway, but why hadn't Sophie Thibaud come back here after she'd been rescued? Had she wanted to but her aunt had forbidden it?

He didn't trust Monique Thibaud at all. She was hiding something. Not only did she know more about the attacks than she'd told him and Ryker, but she knew more about Sophie's disappearance too.

Perhaps he'd make her farmhouse his next stop today?

Maybe. There was also one other person he wanted to see.

He carried on toward the house, his eyes busy as he moved. To his right the snow-covered field rolled out and down into a valley, giving a far-reaching view over the Alps. Behind the house and to his left the frozen gardens were surrounded by dense pine forest. Within those forests – about a mile away – lay the spot where Sophie and her family had been taken to. Where Sophie's parents and brother had been executed. Where Sophie had fled. Perhaps he'd trek out that way.

He reached the front door. Tried the handle with his gloved hand. Locked.

He moved around the side of the house. Boards were nailed and screwed in place over every window. Secure. He kept going, past a side door that was similarly boarded, to the back of the house where he found boarded-over patio doors. A couple of windows too.

Wait. The patio doors. They were boarded over, but the bottom of the two boards fixed over the right-hand door sat proud of the wood above it ever so slightly. Misalignment or...

He pulled at the corner of the wood. The screws remained in place in the board, but they were loose in the door. The board had been prised off, then simply pushed back into place.

Henrik took the wood with both hands and pulled if off and set it to the side. He tried the door handle. Locked. And no sign of forced entry. The rectangular panes of the glass were all intact.

Henrik sighed as he thought. Then he strode across the snow to the trees. Grabbed the first thick branch he found on the ground. Strode back. He paused a few steps from the house and looked over the snow-covered lawn. Plenty of little indentations there from birds, foxes perhaps. Plenty of remnants of footprints too. Even though this place was boarded up now, there'd no doubt been plenty of people here over the last few weeks – police, family, reporters – roaming around. He looked behind him at the two neat trails of prints he'd left – by far the freshest he could see.

Whatever.

He walked back up to the patio doors and crouched down. He swung the log back and smacked it against the glass. Nothing. He tried again with more vigour. The glass cracked but remained in place. He hit it again, again, again. Finally the glass gave way and he used the log to clear the remains away from the edges. Then, hands first, Henrik pulled himself through the small gap. Small, but easily big enough to accommodate his frame.

Ryker's? Probably not, Henrik thought with a smile.

He rose up inside the house. It was cold, dark and smelled damp. He flicked on the torch he'd brought with him. Furniture remained in place in the room, uncovered. The room he stood in, a lounge of some sort, still had sofas, side tables, a rug, TV, stereo. Even magazines still lay in a pile on top of a coffee table. The whole place was like a scene-of-crime museum.

Henrik moved on through, not exactly sure what he was looking for, but determined to search the place from top to bottom anyway. He started downstairs. Had finished there within a few minutes. Nothing stuck out to him, except for the mess of white-and-brown footprints – a combination of wet snow, dirt and perhaps salt – that concentrated around the front door and spread out across the wood floor like tentacles. Further evidence of the presence of police and others in the days after the murders.

Henrik headed upstairs. He found Sophie's room first. What he expected a typical teenage girl's bedroom to look like. Pop star and movie posters adorned the walls, along with a collage of photos. Make-up was strewn on a nightstand. A wardrobe and drawers brimmed with clothes. A clutter of schoolbooks sat on a desk... but no computer. Perhaps the police had taken that away.

He moved to the photo wall, scanned over the pictures. A few shots of Sophie with her girlfriends. Some smiling, some pouting, some posing in funny or acrobatic poses. He smiled when his eyes rested on one of Sophie swinging one-handed from a tree in the middle of the forest. An autumn shot, judging by the brown hues. Her smile was infectious.

As he looked more closely he saw the same few male faces too. Her father, brother, but also teenagers. One he recognised from the bar, but another–

Noise.

Outside.

Not a car engine. Too quiet. Not the wind. Something else. The crunch of snow from footsteps? He stood and waited. Heard nothing more.

Just his imagination.

He spent a couple more minutes rifling through drawers, but other than finding out more about Sophie's taste in fashion, he didn't come away with any new information – nothing to help solve the puzzle of her near death and subsequent disappearance. No secret diary. No phone or tablet or computer that might hold private messages or anything like that.

He moved out of her room, across the landing, to a bigger and grander room with a king-sized bed and a roll-top bath sitting in a bay window. Probably, the bath had a fabulous view of the valley, though with the window boarded the fixture looked ridiculously out of place in the room, rather than the bathroom.

Henrik turned and spotted a small doorway, next to a chest of drawers that stood at a diagonal to the wall – shifted aside? The doorway was three or four feet high and wide. A cut-out in the wall. He moved over and crouched and looked inside the panic room. The screens on the wall were all turned off now. He thought for a moment as he stared into the cramped space, twisting his torch left and right.

According to what he'd read, the police believed Sophie had been inside the panic room at some point during the ordeal. He'd noticed various cameras in the house – had they recorded her movements? The moments the attackers had arrived and captured her family? The local police would have those records. He wondered if he could get hold of them too. What else did the police know that he didn't?

But if Sophie had been in the panic room, safe, then why had she come out at all?

Noise. Again. Outside.

Henrik stood and strode to the door. He looked over the landing to the hallway below and held his breath as he listened.

Nothing once more.

Rats, perhaps? Or some other animal that had found its way into the abandoned house for shelter?

A wolf?

Crunch.

The sound was definitely outside.

Henrik crept down the stairs and looked to the front door. Why? He could see nothing there. He moved even more slowly to the patio doors at the back, and the broken window where he'd come inside. The log he'd used to smash the glass was right there. He reached forward quickly and grabbed the wood and pulled back inside and pressed his back to the wall as he listened.

Nothing inside. Nothing outside now either. His heart drummed in his chest.

Think.

What would Ryker do?

He crouched low, looking out. Then he ducked outside and straightened up against the wall.

The sound of crunching snow to his left, then, from much closer, '*Fils de pute!*'

He didn't understand the French, but the angry tone made clear the words were an insult.

The man grabbed Henrik by the back of his coat. Henrik spun around and swiped across and the log splatted against the side of the man's head. The force in the shot wasn't enough to fell him, but enough to get him to let Henrik go, and he stumbled back, clutching his face. But then the man came at him again, spewing expletives. He grabbed for Henrik, who snapped away from his grip and swooshed the log at him once more. No contact, but the man slid on the icy surface. Not flat on his face, but enough to give Henrik a chance.

Without another thought, Henrik hurled the log at the guy, then turned and sprinted for the woods.

19

After catching nothing more than an hour's shut-eye in the Jeep, when morning came Ryker first headed to a pharmacy to get some basic first aid supplies to tend to the graze on his shoulder. The bullet had only nicked him, leaving a two-inch line where skin and the top layer of flesh had been blasted away. No stitches needed – antiseptic and a simple gauze dressing was sufficient.

He found the offices of Hofman Rheinhard in the central business district of Lyon, all of a couple of hundred yards from the tower block where the police arrested Aziz the previous night. But before he made his approach, one more task.

Ryker headed to a department store where he purchased some new clothes to make himself look a little more presentable – dark jeans, a white polo shirt and maroon jumper, laceless black shoes, smart herringbone coat. Not exactly formal office wear, but at least passable in the modern age of dress down. Over his years working as a government agent he'd had to play many different roles when working undercover. Back then he'd easily assimilated into whatever character he needed to be. Diplomat, suave businessman, drug dealer, hitman, whatever.

Acting had become second nature to him, and he'd been damn good at it, but ever since he'd left that world behind him, it felt as if he'd left that part of him behind too. Now he hated trying to be anything he wasn't.

Yet what *was* he?

Certainly not a smartly dressed businessman.

But he'd try and pretend at least.

He walked confidently up to the revolving doors and into the lofty lobby. At a little after 10am the area had a few people dotted about, but it wasn't particularly busy, most workers likely already at their desks or in meeting rooms. The large security desk off to the right had three stern-looking guards in blue uniforms sitting behind it. Above them a board displayed the building's occupants. Of the fifteen storeys, Hofman Rheinhard took up the top four.

Ryker headed to the desk. Only one of the guards was free – the oldest and grumpiest-looking of them.

'I'm here to see Julian Hofman,' Ryker said, deciding on English.

The guard glared at him and reached out and took a small plastic card from a tray.

'Name?'

'James Ryker.'

'Look at the camera please.'

He tapped the camera attached to the top of his screen and Ryker stared for a couple of seconds. The guard put the card into a printer and moments later it popped out with Ryker's name and picture on it, and indicated that he was a visitor of Hofman Rheinhard.

'My colleague will let you through the gates. Their reception is on the fourteenth floor.'

Ryker thanked him and headed away, through the glass security gates that otherwise needed a key card to open them, and to the lifts. He watched the other people waiting. Whichever company the staff worked for, they all wore lanyards around their necks. Name, picture, company. The cards worked the gates at the entrance, and most likely the doors for the relevant floors.

Before he left, Ryker would get himself one of those key cards. Perhaps from one of the security guards as theirs would most likely work on every floor.

Ryker stepped out of the lift on the fourteenth floor. The reception area of Hofman Rheinhard was large, with designer sofas and coffee tables and armchairs and a shining wooden reception desk where two ladies worked. The large windows gave unobstructed views of the city, and as Ryker moved for the reception desk, he spotted Aziz's building. He tried to work out which windows belonged to the room he'd been in last night, even though the distance was too far to make out anything that lay beyond the glass.

Had the police cleaned up the horrific mess in there by now?

Ryker quickly pushed those thoughts away when he reached the desk and the bespectacled woman in front of him gave him a slightly suspicious smile.

'*Bonjour*,' the woman said.

Ryker smiled. 'I'm here to see Mr Hofman,' he said, again choosing English.

Why? He was looking for any advantage he could. If the staff here, possibly even Hofman himself, thought Ryker was a typical Brit who had nothing but the absolute basic commands of any other language but English, they were more likely to let their guard down when speaking to each other in French. Perhaps he'd learn something, hear something they really didn't want him to.

'Do you have an appointment?'

'No, but I'm sure he'll want to speak to me. And I don't mind waiting.'

The woman's older colleague looked over now too, equally dubious.

'He's normally very busy,' the woman in front of Ryker said.

'He is in today,' her colleague said to her – in French of course. Ryker didn't react. 'I saw him earlier with those ridiculous chequered trousers.'

'What's your name?' the first woman asked Ryker.

He told her. Then added, 'Monique Thibaud asked me to come here.'

That got the attention of both of them. They both clearly knew the name. The woman with the glasses was soon on her phone, though she bent down and covered the receiver with her other hand so as to not let Ryker hear. When she straightened back up she gave Ryker a forced smile.

'He's not available until 11am. You're welcome to wait, but he won't have more than a few minutes for you.'

'I'll wait,' Ryker said.

And he did. Despite himself, because he was tempted to simply sneak – barge? – through the security doors at the first opportunity and head through onto the office floor and find Hofman. Building security would descend but he'd persuade Hofman to call them off.

Instead, he did as he was told, and at one minute past eleven a young woman stepped out from the office doors, glanced to Ryker, then moved to the reception desk. The women there pointed her in Ryker's direction. Moments later Ryker and the woman were on the inside of a sprawling but bland office. Weren't all offices bland? About half the terminals in the open-plan area were taken. Private offices – or were they only meeting rooms? – lined some of the outside wall, but they took up only a small proportion of the space.

'You came from England?' the woman asked as they walked across.

'Not today,' Ryker said.

The woman smiled, entirely uninterested, her question simply meant to pass the time until Ryker was handed over. Ryker thought they were heading to the closed door in the far corner, but instead, the woman detoured left to the desk by the window. A large, but horrendously cluttered desk at which sat a balding man with rounded glasses, his face a couple of inches from a computer screen.

He stood up as Ryker approached. Middle height, pudgy. Open-necked white shirt. Brown-and-yellow chequered trousers. Definitely Hofman then.

'You must be James Ryker?' Hofman said, English, but a Germanic edge to it.

'I am.'

'Should we speak somewhere private?'

'Perhaps,' Ryker said, looking around the room. None of the desks immediately by Hofman were occupied.

'Meeting room five is free until twelve,' the woman – his assistant or just an underling? – said.

'This way,' Hofman said to Ryker.

Ryker nodded, his eyes flitting over Hofman's desk before he moved. Laptop. Phone. Tablet. Briefcase. Could he get his hands on any of that?

He followed Hofman to the meeting room that was equally as bland as the rest of the office. Table, a few chairs. Whiteboard. An abstract picture on one wall which was likely intended to provide warmth and interest to the space but was so generic it added nothing. Nice view though.

Ryker turned down the offer of a drink. Hofman looked disappointed and did the same.

'I'm sorry, I don't have long.'

'Should be fine.'

'It's very unusual to turn up unannounced,' Hofman said as they took seats opposite each other. Hofman tapped on his phone then placed it in front of him on the desk. An indication that Ryker had his attention, but only so long as the phone screen didn't light up. 'Why do you want to see me?'

'So, Hofman Rheinhard. You're Hofman. Where's Rheinhard?'

Hofman glowered. 'My partner is on a sabbatical. He... health reasons.'

'So you're the top dog now. Nice.'

Hofman didn't respond to the taunt.

'You don't have a private office though,' Ryker said. 'You work on the main floor with everyone else instead.'

'It's the modern way. I think it makes for a more productive team.'

'Treating everyone as equals?'

'Exactly.'

'I get you. Except you still get the biggest desk, in the nicest position.'

Hofman shuffled as if irritated – perhaps because of Ryker's snide tone as much as his words.

'Do you pay everyone the same as you too then?' Ryker asked.

'Is any of this relev–'

'It's not really any kind of equality then, is it?' Ryker said. 'Just a token gesture. Perhaps to appease your overworked and underpaid staff.'

'Mr Ryker, I–'

'Where are you from?' Ryker asked.

Hofman paused and frowned at the unexpected question. 'A village near Strasbourg. But my family are mostly German. Is that important to you?'

'Not really.'

'And you?'

'Thanks for asking. London. But you could say I'm well travelled.'

'And how do you know Monique Thibaud?'

'Actually, I have to confess, I don't know her that well really.'

'But you–'

'Do you know Monique Thibaud?' Ryker asked.

Hofman winced, as though riled at Ryker continually cutting him off.

'I know who she is,' Hofman said. 'I've never met her. I've heard... things.'

'Yeah?'

Hofman said nothing more. Ryker would come back to that.

'Why did me mentioning her name get you to agree to speak to me?'

Hofman frowned and opened his mouth to say something but then didn't.

'You've never met me before,' Ryker said. 'I've never met you. I understand you're a very busy man. You told me so. As did the receptionists. They also complimented your trousers.'

'They... I–'

'But that's besides the point. The point is... you've never met Monique Thibaud before, apparently, but by me mentioning her name, I managed to get time with you.'

The room fell silent. Hofman fidgeted, trying to find a response.

'Have you ever been to St Ricard?' Ryker asked.

'I have. But... sorry, Mr Ryker. You've come here to see me. I've been kind enough to offer my time. I did so because you claimed Monique Thibaud sent you here. I haven't met her, but I was intrigued. She's a prominent person and–'

'I've been to St Ricard,' Ryker said, then paused, inviting

Hofman to respond. He didn't. 'My son wanted us to go there. I'm no skier though. Do you know what we did there instead?'

'I haven't a clue.'

'The other day we broke into Ms Thibaud's house.'

Hofman looked beyond Ryker to the door, as though wondering if he could jump up and rush there before Ryker attacked him. Or perhaps hoping someone would come in to interrupt them.

'You... why are you telling me this?'

'To explain why I'm here.'

Hofman squirmed again.

'You heard about what happened to the Thibauds?' Ryker asked.

'Of course I did.'

'I'm trying to find out why. Monique Thibaud suggested I ask you.'

Hofman shook his head, looked as confused as he was wary.

'Tell me about your work,' Ryker said.

Hofman looked at his watch, then reached for his phone.

'Leave it,' Ryker said, just enough threat in his voice to get Hofman to comply. 'Tell me about what you do.'

'We're... we're a real estate company. Mostly we buy and sell commercial properties. We rent office space too. We work with developers, providing or organising funding to build or renovate commercial property.'

'Just property, or infrastructure too?'

Hofman's eyes narrowed. 'Yes, infrastructure too, but it's not our main area of focus.'

'What about the Villeneuve dam near St Ricard?'

'How...'

'How what? How do I know you're involved in that?'

'Actually I'm not involved in that.'

'You're sure?'

'I think I'd know.'

'You're not a very good liar.'

Hofman's face turned angry for the first time. 'I'm not lying.' He went to get up. 'I think–'

'Sit. Down.'

Ryker glared. Hofman tried his best tough-guy look too but it fell way short. He eventually lowered himself back into his chair.

'Monique Thibaud told me you know about the dam project–'

'Know about it? Yes. Okay. Years ago we helped the main developer acquire some of the land but–'

'You just told me you had no involvement.'

'We don't! Not now. Not in the plans or the build. It was a simple land purchase.'

'So the success or not of the project is of no concern to you?'

Hofman held Ryker's eye. 'No.'

Ryker didn't believe him, despite the conviction in the single word response.

'What do you know of Aziz Doukha?' Ryker asked.

'Who?' Hofman said, confusion, but then anger. 'Look, I've been accommodating to you so far, but you really are starting to annoy me now. I don't like the insinuations in your questions.'

'The truth can be uncomfortable,' Ryker said with a shrug.

'Why do you think I know about what happened to the Thibauds? Why do you think I have any ongoing involvement in building a dam in the Alps?'

Ryker stared but didn't answer. He was asking the questions, not Hofman.

'You said you've heard about Monique. What have you heard?'

'What...? I...'

'You know about her family?'

'I know they're into champagne. Franck Thibaud. Kind of obvious, isn't it?' Hofman laughed nervously.

'Actually, the champagne has their family name, but they have nothing to do with it anymore. So what else.'

'Erm...'

'What?'

He looked really unsure of something. Like he didn't know if he should speak or not.

'Tell me,' Ryker said.

'I heard a rumour. That's all. I have no idea if there's any truth.'

'Go on.'

'Monique Thibaud *does* have an interest in the champagne business still, is what I heard. For the last few years she's been secretly reacquiring a stake in the business.'

'How would you hear a rumour like that? Someone who's never met her or had anything to do with her.'

'They're a famous family, and...' Hofman paused, then sighed. 'A friend of a friend knows an accountant who helped her to set up some offshore shell companies to buy the shares. So that what she was doing wouldn't be public.'

Ryker chewed on that for a few moments.

'Why would she do that?'

Hofman frowned and shook his head. 'How should I know? I told you I've never met her. But... have you heard about the rumours of her house in St Ricard?'

'No?'

'You said you'd been there. If you have, perhaps you would have seen what's *under* it.'

'No. You're going to have to explain that one to me.'

Hofman looked at Ryker like he was an idiot.

'Tunnels. Caves. Built by Franck Thibaud himself. He was a

lion of a businessman. Apparently. People say all sorts of secrets are buried under that house.'

Ryker glared as he thought.

'You really do know this family after all, eh?'

Hofman looked away, a little embarrassed. 'No. I don't.'

His phone lit up and he glanced at it.

'I have to get that,' he said, shoulders slumping when the screen went black again.

'I'll not take up much more of your time. If you tell me the truth. Why did Monique Thibaud tell me to see you? About the Villeneuve dam. Tell me the truth this time.'

'I don't know!' Hofman protested.

Ryker sighed. 'I tell you what,' he said. 'Why don't I tell you a story instead?'

Hofman shook his head. 'I don't believe this.'

'Don't believe it? But's it's a true story, so sit and listen. Have you ever heard of British Hydro Investments Ltd?'

A pause, as though Hofman was deciding whether or not to sit and listen, then, 'No.'

'No. You haven't. Because the entity doesn't exist. But about ten years ago I pretended to be a consultant for British Hydro. I had a business card, email address, postal address, phone number manned during office hours by a pleasant-sounding secretary. It was all bogus, all of it set up by my employer.'

Hofman's eyes narrowed as he took that in. 'Your employer?'

Ryker waved the question away. 'Politics. I don't work for them anymore. The point is, I represented British Hydro. I was sent to Abu Dhabi. The emir's cousin there had been handed a key role in promoting the emirate's renewable energy projects. You know, eventually all that oil will run out and those guys need to find a way to make sure they keep on being stinking rich. Have you ever met any of those families?'

Hofman didn't answer. Ryker thought that perhaps meant yes.

'So I travelled to Abu Dhabi and this guy had a beautiful office. I mean, think your building here, but five times higher, wider, more plush. Extravagances everywhere. I had a meeting with the cousin... Hassan, was his name. We talked and talked and I pretended to be interested in helping him to develop a hydro-electric plant on the coast, and I told him the British government were considering making a multi-billion pound investment. Anyway, to cut to the important point, my reason for being there wasn't for investment. It was to find a way to steal information from Hassan. We believed, using his facade as this infrastructure guy, he was taking money from the Russians – investments, if you will – but passing some of that money to terrorist groups. The Russians, as they still do now, were sneakily assisting in destabilising Western relations in the Middle East, while the emir's cousin got richer and richer.'

'I don't have time for this.'

Hofman again flinched as though about to get up.

'You do. Because you really need to hear how this story ends.'

Hofman stayed in place. Looked just a little bit scared.

'My aim was to identify the Russians, but also find evidence of the money going to the terrorist groups. Anyway, we started off all nicely, nicely. Dinners, office meetings. Trips to horse-race meets. A boxing bout. But late in the evenings I'd break into his home or office and steal information from his computers and the like, but, quite honestly, I was getting nowhere fast. You want to know how I speeded things up?'

Hofman didn't answer.

'We were sitting in a meeting room, kind of like this. And I just came out and told him. Like I've told you. I explained why I was really there, got rid of all the pretences, and just said to him, *tell me the truth.* Do that and I'll be gone, and you won't get horribly hurt in the process.'

Ryker paused, trying to gauge how interested Hofman was in what came next.

'And?'

Ryker smiled. 'He didn't like me coming clean as much as I thought he would. And rather than telling me the truth, he stormed out of that room, called his security team, and had me thrown out of his office. Or that was his plan anyway. But as we reached the ground floor, I tackled each of his security team in turn, dragged Hassan to his car, drove him to his house. I tied him up on a chair and I... have you ever been tortured, Julian?'

Hofman quivered but didn't answer.

'It's hard for me to say out loud some of the things I've done, but... let's just say I wasn't very nice to Hassan. He didn't like our alone time together. At. All. But, within an hour, he did tell me everything I needed to know. He even gave me his phone, laptop, access to emails and everything to give me the proof I needed. I left Abu Dhabi that same day.'

Silence in the room.

'What happened to Hassan?' Hofman said. 'I mean... afterward.'

'The emir had him executed.' Ryker held his hands up. 'Hassan's fault, really, if you think about it.'

Hofman shook his head, disbelief. His face had drained of colour.

'To bring this story back to today though,' Ryker said, 'I'll give you one more chance. Tell me exactly what your involvement is in the Villeneuve dam. And tell me everything you know about the Thibaud family, and the murders.'

But perhaps the story hadn't struck enough of a chord with him, because the next moment Hofman grabbed his phone and darted for the door. Ryker leaped up, took hold of Hofman's arm and twisted it into a hammerlock then slammed him face down onto the table.

'Help!' Hofman shouted.

'You idiot,' Ryker said.

'Help!' Hofman shouted again, even more loudly.

Ryker let go, stepped back. Glanced to the door. Hofman turned himself over.

The door opened. A man. Not a security guard. Just an office worker. Beyond him half a dozen others were up from their desk chairs staring over.

'It's okay,' Ryker said to the man. 'He fell and hurt his wrist.' He glared at Hofman.

'Yes,' Hofman said, nodding, clutching his wrist.

Good choice.

The man rushed to his boss's aid.

'See you soon, Julian,' Ryker said before he brushed past Hofman's colleague, out into the office space. Three others darted toward the meeting room, but no one went toward Ryker. He was a little surprised Hofman kept his mouth shut.

Ryker snaked around the desks, out of the doors and to the lifts, unchallenged. He smiled as he headed down, put his hands in his pockets. His right hand curled around Hofman's phone.

No solid answers yet, but plenty to work with at least.

20

Henrik walked back along the streets of St Ricard. The man hadn't chased him through the woods from the Thibaud house. At least, he'd not seen or sensed him at all, but then for a good twenty minutes after rushing from the house he'd darted and weaved through the trees at full pace – perhaps the man had simply realised he couldn't keep up with him.

Despite the brush with the unknown man, Henrik still decided it best to head back into the town rather than to hide. Even as an outsider, in the town he felt a relative safety among other people. The streets were much more busy than earlier in the day, with groups of people – mostly skiers – either heading for breakfast or the slopes.

For most of the walk back, thoughts of the man he'd tackled dominated his mind. Who was he? A police officer? Certainly not a uniformed one. A squatter? One of Monique Thibaud's men? Not a very old man, that was for sure. Even though his face had been partially obscured by his hat, and the fur of his coat, the vision Henrik had in his mind was of a young man.

Shit.

All thoughts of the house and the man were pushed aside

when Henrik spotted the uniform on the other side of the street. Not just a gendarme, but one Henrik recognised. The big guy, Coupet. He was talking to a group of men... Coupet looked over. Henrik turned his head away, sank his chin down into his coat and walked at pace. A yard away from a left turn he looked over his shoulder...

Coupet hadn't moved and remained talking to the men.

Henrik sighed in relief then carried on his way. He slowed up a little as he approached the steps to Fabrique, the bar he and Ryker had gone to on their first night in St Ricard. It was open. Every bar in the small town opened early it seemed, keen to take advantage of the many tourists staying in self-catered accommodation looking for early morning food, perhaps too hung-over to sort it out themselves. Or those who'd come to the Alps more for boozing and atmosphere than skiing.

He looked around him then walked up the steps and inside. Quiet. A quick glance around confirmed none of the main characters from the previous fight were inside. If they had been, Henrik would have made a quick exit. But he did spot a couple of the teenagers from that night over by a pinball machine.

Henrik walked up to them, the boy keenly watching the girl as she slammed the sides of the pinball machine. She shouted in anger and smacked the glass top and the boy laughed at her misfortune, then both turned as they sensed Henrik approaching.

The girl's face was sour, but perhaps more because of the game. The boy's smile remained for a second until a spark of recognition took it away.

'You?' the boy said.

'I'm not here for trouble,' Henrik said, holding his hands up.

The girl and boy looked at each other.

'Please. The other night was a mistake. But... I wanted to find Ella. Do you know where she is?'

No answer for a few seconds. Then, 'She works at the Grimaldi Lodge in the mornings, cooking breakfast,' the girl said. She looked at her watch.

Henrik sensed movement to his side. He glanced that way. No one nearby but the barman – same one as the previous night – was standing at the end of the bar glaring over.

'Thanks,' Henrik said to the boy and girl, then he spun around and quickly headed for the door.

Grimaldi Lodge. He'd spotted the sign before. A log cabin-type structure that sat near the base of one of the ski lifts. He turned right, away from the bar, thinking about what he'd say to her...

Smack.

He walked straight into the man. Well, it was hard to miss him really, he was massive. And wearing a not particularly inconspicuous uniform.

Coupet.

Henrik thought about bolting.

'I thought it was you,' Coupet said, looking down on Henrik with something approaching a snarl on his face.

Henrik took a step back but Coupet reached forward with a long arm and rested his meaty hand on Henrik's shoulder.

'Where's your dad?'

Henrik looked around him. He spotted a number of pedestrians. A few looked over, perhaps wondering what he'd done wrong to be accosted by the officer. Should he shout for help before running? Would anyone come to his aid?

'He'll be right here,' Henrik said. 'Any second.'

Coupet's eyes flickered. Anticipation? Doubt?

'Yeah? So you know, I'm not happy about you two coming back here.'

Henrik didn't say anything. Perhaps the lie, the threat of Ryker, was enough to keep Coupet at bay.

'Just make sure you both stay out of trouble. Or your deal with Ms Thibaud is off.'

With that Coupet took his hand away and sauntered down the street, leaving Henrik brimming with relief, but equally confused as to what the hell had just happened.

What deal with Thibaud?

He watched Coupet for a few seconds, glanced across at the other passers-by too, all now minding their own business. Then Henrik walked off, bemused.

Less than five minutes later he climbed the steep steps to the entrance of Grimaldi Lodge, his feet crunching on the freshly laid grit-salt. A smell of fried meat wafted as he headed inside. A plump middle-aged man sat behind a worn-looking wooden reception desk. He looked up at Henrik who simply nodded as he carried on, following his nose. All he had to do was appear confident, he'd learned, and people assumed he belonged.

He headed along a corridor, past the not very busy dining room, through a swing door and into the chrome-rich kitchen that was filled with smoke and steam. Four workers. Not exactly rushed off their feet. A grumpy-looking man with a dirty apron and bright-red cheeks, checking a clipboard, noticed Henrik first. Glared at him. Henrik spotted Ella, taking a pile of plates from a dishwasher. She flinched when she saw Henrik, almost dropped the pile.

'This isn't the dining room,' the red-cheeked man bellowed and looked like he was about to come over to stop Henrik going any further into his space.

'It's okay,' Ella said, darting forward. She spun Henrik around. 'You shouldn't be here.'

'I came to see you.'

'I'm working.'

She pushed him out the door. He turned and looked at her.

'Until when?' he asked.

She didn't answer straight away. Then sighed. 'Eleven.'

'I'll wait.'

'Not in here you won't.' She looked back to her boss, who continued glaring, then pushed Henrik further away. 'I'll meet you outside.'

Ella came out of the doors of Grimaldi Lodge at five past eleven. The snow had started twenty minutes before that and Henrik had shaken himself down several times to stop the accumulation on his head and clothes. Hairnet and apron gone, Ella's light-brown hair spilled out from beneath her woolly bobble hat, and draped down the front of her winter coat, framing her freckled face. He wanted to grab her and squeeze her, she looked so good. Even if she didn't exactly look pleased to see him.

'I wished you hadn't done that,' she said to him, taking away some of his smile.

'What?'

'Barged into the kitchen like that. Olivier doesn't like me anyway, I didn't need any more reasons for him to be angry with me.'

'Sorry, I–'

'Why are you here? I mean, I'm surprised you're here. I thought after...'

'After?'

She didn't say anything.

'You thought after your friends and those men tried to beat up me and my dad that we'd run off?'

'Yeah... I think so. Except... they didn't beat you up, did they? Your dad...'

She didn't finish the sentence, but something about the way

she spoke suggested she was in awe of Ryker, perhaps with the way he'd handled the scuffle while so outnumbered. She'd probably be horrified if she knew exactly what Ryker was capable of, and what he and Henrik had already been through together.

'And most of those people aren't my friends,' she added. 'I know them, but that's not the same thing.'

'You look gorgeous,' Henrik said. Kind of blurted really.

She smiled meekly. 'With my boots and big winter coat and hat? Yeah, really glamorous.'

At least his compliment had softened her mood a little.

'It's freezing out here,' Henrik said. 'Could we go somewhere warmer?'

'Somewhere? To do what?'

'Talk.'

She held his eye a few beats, as though trying to read his mind. But as attracted to her as he was, he really had no ulterior motive. He did want to talk.

'I live a few minutes away. My parents are at work.'

Henrik smiled. 'Let's go.'

Ella's home was small but quaint. One of several apartments in a stone-built complex. The type of place tourists visiting the area would love, with a wood-panelled open living space taking up the top floor, overlooking the ski slopes, while the bedrooms were all downstairs. Henrik sat back in a sofa as Ella brought the hot chocolates over. Outdoor gear stripped off, her tight jeans and roll-neck jumper showed off her svelte frame.

'Where's your dad today?' she asked.

'Skiing.'

She didn't look convinced by that. She sat down next to him, curled her feet under her, holding her mug in both hands.

'What did you want to talk about?' she asked.

'You,' he said, receiving a coy smile in return.

'Go on then. Ask away.'

And for the next ten minutes he did ask all about her. He got her talking freely about her parents, her younger brother who annoyed the hell out of her, her plans for next year when she wanted to go to university, though she was torn as to whether to defer and work a ski season or two and travel first. Henrik was genuinely interested, but he was also looking for the moment to divert the conversation.

'What about you?' Ella asked.

'Me?'

'You said you're from Norway.'

'Originally.'

'But your dad is English.'

'Yeah.'

'And you're here for how long?'

'We haven't decided yet. We're both... we don't like to plan too much. The thing is...' Henrik thought and sighed. May as well just move things on. 'The other night, you know why I got into trouble, don't you?'

'I think because you were looking for it,' Ella said. 'Though I'm not sure why.'

A fair summation?

'Because I was asking questions about Sophie Thibaud.'

She held his eye. 'Yes. You were. So who are you more interested in, Sophie or me?'

'No, that's not it at all.'

'It isn't?'

'I'm sitting here with you, aren't I?'

'But you're talking about her. Again.'

'Why does talking about her get you beaten up in this town?'

'Some people are very protective of their privacy.'

'No. Something else.'

'Then what do you think?'

'That some people know things that they want kept secret. About Sophie, and what happened to her family.'

Ella sighed and put her cup down on the table in front of them.

'You really want to talk about her?'

Henrik nodded.

'I think... you're nice, Henrik, even if you do look like you're only fifteen.' She laughed; he did too, even though he felt a little bad for her. He'd told her he was eighteen. She'd turn eighteen in a few months too. He certainly didn't look old for his age, but he guessed he acted more maturely than most fifteen-year-olds did, given everything he'd been through, and he was sure if he'd been honest she wouldn't have invited him over to her house. 'You're funny too. And... I've always tried to ignore the tourists who come here looking for flings, but... I like you.'

'I like you.'

'But you're not winning any favours with me by always wanting to talk about someone else.'

'Can't I be interested in more than one thing?'

'Two different girls? Not with me, no.'

'That's not what I meant.'

He put his cup down next to hers and leaned forward. She didn't move as he reached out and kissed her lightly on the neck, then as he moved in closer, she ducked down a little so his lips met hers. They both stayed there a few moments. Then he pulled away.

'Better?' he asked.

'I don't know,' she said.

'Can I be truthful with you?'

'You haven't been already?'

'There's a reason I'm asking about Sophie.'

Ella grumbled and looked away.

'Please, just listen. You can't tell anyone this. Do you promise?'

The suspicion in her face gave away her thoughts but she still said, 'Yes.'

'Me and my dad... we're not really here for a holiday.' That grabbed her interest, though the suspicion remained. 'I can't say who we work for, but... it's important. We're investigating what happened to the Thibauds. We think they weren't really killed in a robbery. We're not even sure the men the police blamed are even responsible.'

'But... they're...'

'They're both dead. They can hardly clear their names now, can they?'

'So your dad is an investigator?'

'Kind of.'

'Who hired him?'

'I can't say any more.'

'Why are you telling me this?'

He reached out and put his hand over hers. Felt a little bit bad for his manipulation – is that what it was? – but only a little bit. Is this how it felt to be Ryker? 'Because I like you, and I trust you.'

Ella didn't respond. She didn't move at all. Henrik left his hand on hers.

'You and Sophie were friends,' he said.

'We...'

'I've seen photos of the two of you together.'

'When? What photos?'

'I'm not trying to trick you. I just want to know about her. What was she like? Were there any problems at home? Or with anyone else in town? Boys?'

Her face twitched at that last word.

'She had a boyfriend?'

Ella shook her head and looked away and took her hand out from underneath Henrik's.

'Not a boyfriend. Not really. I think... I think she liked him more than he liked her.'

She flicked a glare at Henrik, as though insinuating the same with the two of them.

'What's his name?'

She sighed. 'I shouldn't...'

'You should, Ella. This could be really important. And the police must have asked you about this already?'

'The police?'

She looked really worried.

'The police never spoke to you about Sophie?'

'No. Never.'

'See? You don't think that's odd?'

'You think the police...'

'Are hiding something? Yes, I do.'

She seemed to think about that for a few moments, the worry on her face growing all the time. Gone now were the questions over whether Henrik was interested in her or not.

'Have you seen Sophie since she was rescued?' Henrik asked.

'No. No one has.'

'And you haven't spoken to her on the phone? Messaged her? Anything?'

'I did message her. But her aunt... she's really protective.'

'When was the last time you heard from her?'

'Weeks ago.'

'You don't think that's odd?'

'Of course it's odd. But everything about St Ricard is odd. Take away the tourists and we're like this little inbred town. And the Thibauds run it. They always have done. They own most of the homes, the hotels, bars, restaurants, the ski slopes even. Me and my friends used to joke it should be called St Thibaud.'

'They own everything?' Henrik said, sounding more surprised than he'd intended.

'You didn't know? The town was basically started by them. They owned all the land. Still own most of it now. Most of the buildings here were built by stone they mined from their land or from the wood from their trees. They own *this* building. My parents pay rent for this house every month. Of course, it doesn't go directly to the Thibauds but it's a company controlled by them. Same for virtually everyone here. And many people rely on them for jobs too. Why do you think those men in the bar got so angry when you started asking questions? Everyone has to bow down to them or they have no job, no home.'

Henrik mulled that over for a few moments. He picked up his hot chocolate and took a large mouthful. Only lukewarm now.

'What about her boyfriend? Has he seen her?'

'I said, he's not her boyfriend.'

'So who is he?'

She seemed reluctant, but then said, 'Michel Lemerre.'

'Do you have a picture of him?'

Reluctance again, but then Ella took out her phone and scrolled through the pictures before turning the screen Henrik's way. He'd seen the same photo on Sophie's wall, a sunny picture in the mountains with Ella, Sophie, another girl, two boys, one of which was the guy who Henrik had punched in the bar.

'Him,' Henrik said, feeling anger rise as he pointed to that guy.

'No. The other one.'

Henrik looked again in silence for a few moments.

'He looks older,' he said.

'He's twenty.'

'He lives here?'

'Not anymore. He's at university in Marseille. He went back in September.'

'You haven't seen him since?'

'And I wouldn't expect to. His parents left the area in October, so he won't be coming back.'

Henrik considered her words. Had he stumbled over something key? He realised Ella was glaring.

'That's really helpful,' he said. He shuffled closer to her, and reached out to take her hand again, but she whipped it away.

'No,' she said, moving back. 'You've already got what you came here for.'

'But, I–'

'Sorry, Henrik, but it's time for you to leave.'

21

Julian Hofman's home on the outskirts of Lyon was pretty much what Ryker expected of a rich executive. Large, detached, with sprawling gardens surrounding it. Big wooden gates, dense hedges and tall trees closed off the view of the house from the road.

Not massively secure though.

Having easily scaled the wall that ran a few yards either side of the gates, Ryker took his time to sneak closer to the house, being careful not to be seen by anyone at the windows.

In the intervening hours since meeting Hofman at his offices, Ryker had carried out further research on the man and his family, gathering as much information as he could before he made this next move. Hofman lived with his wife, Anya, and sixteen-year-old son, Jean. As far as Ryker could tell, Anya didn't work, so he had to expect that one or both of Hofman's family members could be home.

Hired help too? Possibly. Though he'd spotted no cars by the grand double garage.

Ryker pulled up against the back wall of the house. At the front he'd seen no signs of life, no noticeable lights on despite the fading daytime. The back was a different story. Right by him, through the windows of the kitchen, lights were on, though no one was inside. But he could hear music. Not from the kitchen. More distant.

Ryker ducked and moved under the kitchen windows and further along the back wall to a set of patio doors for the dining area adjacent to the kitchen. He tried the handle. Locked. He could pick the lock, but he was sure the music was coming from somewhere nearby. He looked up. Plenty of windows up there. At the far side of the back of the house stood an elegant extension with arched timber windows, a flat roof, and two big skylights sticking upward. Windows up there too, for the top floor. Closed, but...

He moved quickly that way and used a drainpipe to scramble to the top of the extension. Two wooden sash windows in front of him. He stared beyond the glass. A landing, several doorways off it. Light spilled out of one of the rooms, though the music he'd heard before had faded – just as he'd thought, whoever was home was downstairs.

Ryker moved to the other window which served a little-used guest bedroom, he presumed, given the relatively small size and the spotless appearance. Certainly not the master, or a room belonging to a teenager.

He took out his pocket multitool and selected the penknife and wedged the blade under the window. No. It was clasped shut, so he couldn't prise it easily, at least not without making noise. The fixture wasn't exactly old, and was in good condition, but timber-built windows, even modern ones, were generally a straightforward construction. Ryker used the knife and quickly but carefully prised the wooden beading from the corners of the inner frame, exposing the edges of the double-glazed glass unit for the bottom of the sash. He cut all around the edge, breaking the glue bonding, then used the knife as a lever to snap the glass out of the frame. He carefully put the glass down on the flat roof.

Job done. He climbed inside and moved to the door and peered onto the landing. No one in sight. As he stepped out, he pulled the door closed to hide the deconstructed window from view.

Keeping his steps light, Ryker silently headed across the landing. Master bedroom, empty. Office, empty. But that was the room Ryker wanted to be in, so his gamble of entering on the top rather than ground floor had paid off. Still, he kept on going, to the room with the light on, and pulled up outside the open door. Quiet in there, but even the glimpse he could see of the room from his hiding spot – dark-blue walls, the edge of a poster, underwear and other clothes on the carpet – gave away that it was Jean's room.

Most likely it was the teenager downstairs too, listening to the raucous rock music on his dad's no doubt fancy stereo.

Satisfied that he could get to work, Ryker crept back to the office, pushed the door to then sat down on the comfy leather swivel chair. So Hofman hadn't rushed home after the incident in the office. Had he called the police? Certainly there was no indication at his home that he'd sent out an alert to his family members. Had he not taken Ryker's threat seriously? Perhaps he felt he couldn't raise the alarm with the police because doing so might expose what he'd done

Now Ryker just needed to find out what that was.

He looked over the space in front of him. A few drawers. Desktop. He powered it on. The screen came to life. Password needed. Not to worry. Ryker worked around the system's security, going into the core programming to create a new admin account for himself. Within a few minutes he was inside. Time to copy. He inserted the USB thumb drive that'd take a full copy of the desktop's hard drive.

While he waited, he went to the desk drawers. Not locked. Ryker quickly searched through. Bills. A clutter of stationery. A couple of old phones. Ryker pocketed those for later research, in case Hofman hadn't already erased the contents. He found some bank statements. Interesting. Ryker scanned through. A joint account with his wife. Probably not the place to find any criminal activity, though Ryker took pictures of each of the statements going back six months, which covered the period before and after the attack in St Ricard.

Nothing else of interest, so he went back to the computer. He clicked on the email icon. It opened Hofman's personal Gmail account, rather than his work account. Perhaps more useful anyway, as he was hardly likely to use a business account for nefarious activity.

Ryker performed a search. Aziz Doukha. Nothing. Just Aziz. Nothing. He tried Lenglet and Touba too. Still nothing. Thibaud. Nothing. Villeneuve. A lot.

He took a few minutes to scan the emails in turn, noting the senders, anyone else copied in, the contents too. The same four email addresses came up again, and again, though the handles were anonymised, and the emails never had full names in the sign-offs, only initials at most.

Ryker performed a further search for all activity with those four email addresses. Nearly a hundred results. He paused on one of the email chains. The subject read LVH LLC – the latter three letters likely being the common designation used by companies in numerous different countries. But what did LVH stand for? The original email, from Hofman to the other four, was short and sweet.

LVH is up and running. When is completion
expected?

Several responses came after that.

```
Problems  on  the  ground.  Funds  delayed
until resolved.
```

```
We've  come  too  far  for  problems  on  the
ground. TK, you need to sort.
```

```
I  have  a  solution  in  progress.  I'll  let
you know.
```

That was the end of the chain, a little over four months ago, but not the end of the communications. Ryker found a later email chain, started by 'TK'.

```
I need more time.
```

The responses to that weren't kind. Indirect threats. Reminders of 'who we're dealing with'. Questions over 'compensation' if the original deal wasn't upheld. Everyone quite non-specific about what the problems were, which was only natural if the five of them were up to no good.

Ryker's thought?

Most likely Hofman had been truthful about his company's early involvement in the dam project. Hofman Rheinhard had taken a commission for the land purchase. But he hadn't been truthful about that being his only involvement. There was dirty money involved somewhere, or perhaps just a fraud of some sort – skimming? Hence the need for the secretive exchanges. Perhaps Hofman and others were due backhanders, contingent on success of the project, or some other factor. But clearly there'd been issues in getting that money.

Problems that had caused Hofman, or his associates, to organise the multiple murder of the Thibaud family?

Ryker looked up from the screen with a jolt when he heard a creak out on the landing.

He didn't move as the door edged open and a startled teenage boy stared over at him.

'Jean?' Ryker said, standing up from the chair.

'What are you doing in my house?' he asked in French, his fear obvious.

'I'm from your dad's office,' Ryker said, taking hold of the security card dangling from the lanyard around his neck. The card that stated Ryker was a visitor, rather than employee, if anyone looked closely enough, and the colour of the lanyard further gave away Ryker's status, but would the sixteen-year-old Jean have any clue how security at his dad's office worked?

'I'm from the IT team.'

Jean said nothing.

'There was a security issue at the office earlier. Your dad asked me to check the home computer, to make sure nothing's wrong here. You haven't noticed anything weird? Slow processing times, anything like that?'

Jean frowned, as though thinking, but his wariness and suspicion remained.

'No... I don't think so, but... how did you get in here?'

Ryker smiled and laughed. 'Your dad let me in.' He wiped away the smile, as though surprised by Jean's concern. 'He was here with me, only a few minutes ago. You didn't see him?'

'I didn't see him. Or hear him.'

'Not with that loud music.'

He still didn't look convinced.

'He got an urgent call. He had to rush off. You really didn't know we'd come in?'

Nothing from the boy. Ryker's own look of concern deepened. He held his hands up.

'Jean, call your dad. Check with him. I don't want to worry you.'

A pause, then, 'No point, is there? He probably won't answer anyway.'

'Probably not,' Ryker said, his face brightening a little. He looked down to the thumb drive, the green light indicating the copying was complete. 'You know what, I'm done here now anyway.'

'I'll show you out,' Jean said.

Ryker pulled the thumb drive out and closed the email window.

'Yeah, sure. Thank you.'

22

Ryker didn't go far. Only back to the Jeep, parked a couple of streets away, on a side road that was right off the most obvious route to Hofman's home from the city.

With darkness on the horizon he made a phone call as he sat in the cold interior, the engine off to make him less conspicuous. The call went to voicemail. Perhaps because the recipient was busy, or perhaps because of her natural wariness, and the fact she didn't recognise Ryker's number. He didn't leave a message, simply called again.

Answered on the third ring.

'Who is this?' said the familiar voice of Jen Worthington. Familiar, though he'd not spoken to her for more than three years, and not seen her face to face for closer to five.

'It's Ryker,' he said.

A pause, before, 'James. This is a surprise.'

Apparently not a pleasant surprise, given her tone.

'Can you talk?' he asked.

Another pause. As though she was weighing up how to answer. Or was there another reason? He'd called her on her office number. He did remember a private number for her, but had no clue whether she still used that or not.

'You need my help, I assume.'

Which, really, was plainly obvious given he'd called her at work.

'I'd call it an offer,' he said. 'Mutual benefit.'

She laughed. Definitely sarcastic. 'Sorry. You said this was James Ryker, but you must be an imposter as that doesn't sound like him at all.'

He wasn't sure whether to be offended by that or not.

'So how are you, James? Retirement treating you well?'

She really wanted to chat?

'I've been worse.'

She laughed again. 'Retirement, eh? Except you're calling me, so clearly you haven't got your feet up by a pool somewhere sipping a cocktail.'

'Oh, I still find plenty of time for that. But not right now.'

'Where are you these days?'

'Nowhere in particular. Lyon right now.'

'Should I be expecting to see chaos and destruction from the Rhône on my TV sometime soon?'

Images of the police raid at Aziz's offices flashed in Ryker's mind. Details of that were already in the news, though it seemed it hadn't reached Jen's radar. And technically, although he'd been there, none of that was really his doing. Was it?

'You never know,' he said.

She sighed. 'Not exactly the best answer you could have given me.'

'Probably not. So this is the deal. I have four email addresses I need some help with. An offshore company too.' She sighed but didn't counter, so he carried on. 'I need to know everything you can find about them. IP addresses for the emails, any details on identities, anything you can find on ownership for the company. Financials would be a huge bonus.'

'And what's in it for me?'

'Is Aziz Doukha on any of your watchlists?'

Silence. Jen didn't say anything at least, but Ryker could hear her typing away. Then the typing stopped but she still didn't speak.

'I'll take your lack of answer as a yes,' he said.

Most likely she was staring at a profile of Doukha as he spoke.

'I see here that Doukha was taken into police custody in Lyon last night,' Jen said. 'That have anything to do with you?'

'Not really.'

'I find that hard to believe. And if the French authorities have him, I'm not sure I'm really that interested. One bad apple already off the street. And it's not even my street anyway. I know a few people in France but it's hardly an area I'm hot for.'

He'd expected her to be like this. And not just because of her bullish personality, but because they'd never been that close. In a way that was why Ryker felt more comfortable calling her rather than other old acquaintances. Their paths had crossed a few times over the years, when he'd worked as an operative for the secretive JIA, and she'd worked as a field agent for the slightly less secret MI6, but they'd never carried out any shared missions together. An intelligence gatherer, more than anything, Jen had worked across various territories, but particularly countries in the Middle East and Africa, and as far as he knew, those parts of the world remained her main focus. She was decent enough at her job, but her life had changed when the safe house that she and several other agents were staying at in Mogadishu was targeted by a car bomb attack. Two of her colleagues lost their lives. Jen lost her left leg, her left hand, and was blinded in her left eye. She'd remained with MI6, but moved to an office function. An analyst, of sorts.

But, she was still dedicated to her job. Which meant she would be interested in intelligence on a person who was already on MI6's radar, whether as a suspected terrorist or criminal kingpin or whatever, even if that person wasn't her immediate concern.

'I think one of the email addresses could be Aziz,' Ryker said. 'He's Algerian.' Thrown in as a sweetener given her previous African experience. 'We're looking at potential embezzlement, money laundering. Depending on the identities of the others, possibly even terror funding.'

That last one was perhaps wishful thinking, but he had to put it out there – another carrot to dangle.

'Give me the details. I'll see what I can do.'

Ryker smiled. 'You're a star.'

He gave her the details then ended the call. Then sank down a little in the driver's seat and sighed. Would Jen keep the call to her secret? Most likely not. Would alerting her to where he was, and who he was investigating, have repercussions for him? Very possibly. But he felt the risk was worth it. Worst case, if there was something in it for them, MI6 would send their own people to Lyon to dig further into Aziz, if they chose not to simply pass the buck to the French intelligence services. Neither of those outcomes would result in direct threat to Ryker, but too much heat could hinder him finding any answers as to where Sophie Thibaud was, and why her family were executed.

A police car blasted past, siren wailing, snapping Ryker from his thoughts. He sat up in the seat, craned his neck to follow the car's path, but it was already out of sight. He fired up the engine and pulled out and drove slowly toward Hofman's home. Sure enough, as he passed the gates, he spotted the police car's flashing lights by the house.

He'd wondered how long it'd be before Jean noticed the broken window in the spare bedroom. Honestly, Ryker had expected it to take longer, as he couldn't see what would cause the teenager to bother to look in there. Perhaps he'd felt the cold as he walked across the landing. Or perhaps Anya or Julian had arrived home, and Ryker simply hadn't spotted them driving past.

He turned the car around, did another drive-by, then parked back up in the same spot as before.

Minutes later he was on foot once more as he crept through the Hofmans' garden, much like he had earlier in the day, edging closer to the house where the police car remained. No one in sight outside. Ryker stopped at the back of the garage, from where he could peer toward the front of the house and also had a clear view of the driveway, all the way to the gates by the road.

After a couple of minutes of near silence he heard a raucous engine, high revs of a big diesel, approaching fast. The big BMW rocked as it careened off the road and onto the drive, racing for the house. Tyres skidded as the brakes were hit. The driver's door opened...

Not Julian Hofman but his wife. She darted to the front door. Ryker heard her call out. Shouting. Then much calmer male voices. The police, Ryker presumed.

For a short while after that he didn't hear much more, and he thought about moving around the garage and exploring at the back of the house where he presumed the police would concentrate any efforts to take forensic evidence of the intruder – finger and shoe prints and the like. The idea didn't particularly concern him – they wouldn't get far with that evidence. Anyway, no sign of a forensic technician yet. No sign of Julian Hofman either.

Then out of the front door came the two policemen. Anya

Hofman too. Ryker pulled back a little, trying to stay out of view, but also keen to see as much as he could. At least with the ever fading daylight he could remain in the shadows by the dark corner of the garage.

Sounds of their muted conversation drifted over though Ryker struggled to make out the words. He thought Anya was asking the officers not to leave. Asking for someone to keep watch on the house until her husband came home. He couldn't hear the officers' excuses for not doing so, but soon they were in their car and on their way.

So where the hell was Hofman?

Ryker waited more than two hours, by which point the temperature had dropped significantly with night-time. No more police arrived – either to stand guard for the Hofmans, or to take scene-of-crime evidence. Apparently break-ins by mystery intruders weren't given much of a priority by the local police, though Ryker could see why, given no one had been hurt, and nothing had been stolen – except data, but did the Hofmans even know that?

He'd intended on waiting for Hofman to arrive home. Despite the story he'd relayed earlier, he didn't plan to torture the man – not without further cause, at least – but he did want to put further pressure on. Which was one reason why he'd broken into Hofman's home in the first place. A reason why he'd left obvious evidence of his presence.

And a reason why he remained at the house. He'd expected Hofman to rush home, and had planned, as soon as the police left, to confront the man a second time. With less witnesses.

But he was freezing just standing out in the cold. Time to take a more direct approach once more.

Ryker retreated to the Jeep and headed back into the city. The main evening exodus from the many office buildings had already finished, though at a little after 7pm the streets were far from deserted. Ryker parked in the same spot as earlier in the day then walked back toward Hofman Rheinhard. Of course, there was the chance that Hofman had left the office hours ago, or even while Ryker was coming over, and they'd passed each other going in opposite directions, but if Hofman wasn't here, Ryker would still make good use of his time.

He headed through the revolving doors. Glanced to the security desk. Only one guy working there now. He'd been there earlier too, but it wasn't the one who Ryker had spoken to. Ryker nodded then confidently carried on his way to the security barriers. He held the card up to the reader. Not his visitor card, but one he'd easily pilfered from a man in the ground-floor canteen earlier, before he'd left the building after his confrontation with Hofman. Of course there was a chance the 'lost' card had been disabled...

Green light and the glass barriers slid aside and Ryker slipped through.

He headed up in the lift alone and came out on the fourteenth floor. To his left lay the double doors that led to the reception area, but to his right another set of double doors that provided direct access to the office floor. The card once again worked and Ryker stepped inside. Not empty, but only a few heads were visible above the desk dividers. Ryker moved purposefully across the space, heading for Hofman's desk. No sign of the man himself. No sign of anyone within four or five desks.

Ryker strode over and sat down at Hofman's chair as he glanced back across the office. No one paid him any attention.

Ryker looked to the desk. No laptop or tablet now. No coat, briefcase, or anything like that.

So had he headed home after all? Ryker was more than a little disappointed at the thought, but he'd go back across the city once more if necessary.

Or had Hofman run? To where?

Ryker tried the desk drawers. Unlocked. But he couldn't see anything of interest in there. A few files and folders on the desk itself, but again nothing that stuck out to Ryker.

A little reluctantly he got to his feet and walked toward the doors. He was halfway there when he spotted a computer screen on. Not locked. A handbag on the floor. A coat on the back of the chair. No sign of the owner though. Toilet? Meeting?

Ryker sat down, keeping his head low so as to not be visible above the divider. He dove straight in. Headed into the company's server area where various folders contained open-access client data. He searched for Thibaud. A few hits. Searched for Villeneuve. More hits. Doukha. Nothing. A few minutes later and all the relevant files were copied to his thumb drive.

Ryker stood from the chair. A head bobbed up from one of the desks nearby. A young man with a telephone pressed to his ear. He clocked Ryker, his face flickered with suspicion. Ryker had seen the same face earlier in the day, one of the many who'd stared on as Ryker came out of the meeting room.

'*Bonsoir*,' Ryker said, nodding over.

The man nodded back and Ryker carried on without waiting for any further response or questioning. Would the guy call security? Possibly.

Once back inside the lift, Ryker hit the button for the basement, rather than the ground floor. Both so he'd avoid passing by the security desk, but also because he wanted to check the car park.

The basement was big and dark, each section lighting up only when sensors detected movement. Less than twenty cars remained in the sprawling space, dotted about, most of them big and expensive. Ryker spotted Hofman's. Even if he hadn't known the vehicle already, the nameplate on the wall behind it gave away who it belonged to.

So where was Hofman?

Looking around him first, Ryker walked over, feeling a little more nervous than before. The black paintwork of the Mercedes GLC gleamed in the artificial light. Ryker reached it and peered in through the driver's window. Nothing in there.

He looked around him again, thinking, then spotted that the boot lid was ever so slightly ajar. On a plush model like this, most likely the boot lid was automatic. Had it caught on something as it tried to close?

Ryker stepped to the back of the car. He reached into the gap under the boot lid and provided gentle pressure and with a mechanical whir the lid lifted up into the air.

As Ryker stared at the unmoving, bloodied face inside, he finally had the answer as to where the hell Julian Hofman was.

23

Henrik had no qualms about stealing things, about breaking into buildings, if it helped a just cause. Even at his young age he'd broken into offices, factories, shops, homes. Sometimes to steal essentials. Sometimes for shelter. Always for a legitimate reason, as far as he was concerned.

He'd never before broken into a police station.

Although, technically was this breaking in? Or simply hiding?

The station for the gendarmerie in St Ricard was small, functional. A little bit touristy, almost, from the outside at least, as though they wanted the building – which blended with those surrounding it – to appear quaint and charming rather than ominous.

Having kept watch on the outside for a while after darkness had first arrived, Henrik strolled inside early in the evening, moving in behind a female officer – who he didn't recognise – and a group of three tourists. At least he thought they were tourists. The man and two women were all dressed in ski gear anyway.

They ended up in a small waiting area. Not much to wait for in a police station. A desk sergeant, or whatever they were called, sat in position, and a conversation started with his newly arrived colleague and one of the women from the group. The other man and woman stood behind. No one paid Henrik any attention.

He moved closer to the group. Anyone looking on would probably assume he was with the adults. The conversation between the officers and the woman carried on in stilted French, and a little bit of English. The group were from Estonia, and didn't have a very good grasp of any other language. The gist appeared to be that jewellery belonging to one of the women had been stolen, though when and from where, Henrik – and the officers – had a hard time understanding. The tourists struggled to explain exactly what had happened, and the gendarmes struggled to explain exactly what they could and couldn't do to help.

Henrik looked about the place. Apart from the exit, the waiting area had three doors leading off from it. On the far side, the door led to a visitor toilet. To Henrik's nearside, two doors with glazing in the top half revealed corridors beyond. One, on the left, held cells, the other, office space, interview rooms perhaps.

'Wait here a moment,' the female gendarme said, and she rushed off to the right-hand door. No lock. She simply opened the door and disappeared out of sight.

Moments later she reappeared with papers in her hand – a form? – as the male officer's and woman's conversation became more and more heated.

The man in front of Henrik said something to his other friend, as though they too were agitated and on the brink of joining the debate. The guy turned to Henrik, glared. Henrik froze. Should he leave? Say something? But then the man looked away and took two steps to the female gendarme and starting shouting at her. Gesticulating with his finger. All attention turned that way. The second female tourist tried to calm him down. Pulled at his shoulder. But his sudden outburst only spurred on the other woman from the group whose voice raised further as angry Estonian spewed from her mouth.

The officers tried to stay calm, tried to control the situation. The desk guy came around the side, into the open. He and his colleague stood by each other, as if for safety, but still intent on trying to calm the situation with words.

Henrik sidestepped. Again. Again. Edging closer to the door.

The man snatched the papers from the officer's grip. Desk Guy didn't like that. He grabbed his arm, twisted it around. Shouting from all involved. Pushing, shoving...

Henrik made his move. He darted for the door. Pulled it open. Sneaked inside. Ducked down as he closed the door as quietly as he could. He waited a second. No one coming. He looked around. Six doors off the corridor in front. Three to the left, two to the right. A fire exit at the far end.

He remained low as he moved forward. First on the left was a small kitchen. Then a toilet. On the right an empty meeting room. Then an office space. He spotted a head beyond, behind a desk, and stooped lower still as he moved on. Coupet or Renaud in there perhaps?

Whoever it was, they hadn't spotted him, nor had they been alerted to the commotion in the waiting area.

Henrik carried on to the final door. A storage cupboard with cleaning equipment, boxes of stationery and other office equipment. Henrik pulled a couple of boxes aside in the corner, squeezed into the small space behind, then waited.

Three hours passed, then four. Despite trying to stay alert, Henrik's eyes slid closed more than once during that time, though he never dozed for long, his brain quickly pulling him back to reality. He spent a lot of time thinking about Ryker. Thinking once more about whether he'd made the right choice in leaving him. Wondering where he now was. Still in Lyon? In St Ricard, but their paths simply hadn't crossed? Was Ryker worried, looking for Henrik, or simply carrying on what they'd started without him?

Or had he simply taken off and headed away altogether?

That last option left Henrik feeling a little empty inside, even if it'd been his decision to carry out these next steps alone.

He also spent time thinking about Ella. The time in her house. Some of it beyond good, some of it strained. But that kiss with her...

They'd hardly parted on the most positive of terms. Still, he'd seek her out again.

Noise outside the closed door. The first time he'd heard any hint of action for some time. Nearly 11pm, so the station would be operating only a skeleton crew by now, wouldn't they? Just enough people to respond to emergencies. Or drunken brawls, or whatever it was that occupied the St Ricard gendarmes through the night.

Heavy footsteps moving away. Banging doors, then... silence.

Henrik waited a couple minutes longer before finally slipping out from his hiding spot. His body ached and he stretched up, having to shake his legs a few times to get blood moving back through them properly again. He stepped to the door. Pulled it open slowly before peeking out.

No one in sight.

He moved along the corridor. No sign of anyone in the waiting area beyond the door at the far end, though presumably

Desk Guy – or his replacement – was still there. So Henrik stayed low as he neared the door for the office.

Empty. He remained crouched as he tiptoed inside. Not a big office. Six desks. Each had various states of clutter on top, and all around the room sat boxes filled with files, the cabinets lining two walls also crammed. The blinds to the windows were closed. Good, so he'd remain out of sight to anyone on the street.

He began his search. He wanted to find anything and everything he could related to the Thibauds. There had to be case files related to the murders, even if the main investigation had likely been taken out of the hands of the gendarmerie at some point.

But he couldn't find anything, and found no obvious system or order to the clutter. Case files all had designated numbers and letters but recent ones were placed right next to older ones. No sense that they were organised by crime type either.

Henrik's eyes settled on the large corkboard along one wall. The kind of board that he'd seen on TV, used by police investigation teams when mapping out related crimes, or gang hierarchy. Except this one had taken on a far less serious use, it seemed. A shift rota took up a lot of the space. A few business cards for local bars and restaurants were pinned too – perhaps for late-night food deliveries. Hand-drawn caricatures of the staff too. He smiled at Coupet's. Whoever the artist was, he or she was good.

But nothing really of interest on the board. Except...

Behind one edge of the large rota sheet lay another piece of paper. Henrik moved over and removed the pin from that corner of the rota. The one from the bottom corner too. He peeled back the larger paper. Huffed as he stared at the A4 poster below. A missing person poster. Not very recent. A quite grainy image of a woman, the quality of the printing poor. Thirty-six years old, according to the text. Italian. Missing since... more than three years. He wondered how long ago the rota sheet had been placed over the top.

Had she been found?

That wasn't the only piece of paper behind there. Henrik took the whole rota sheet off the wall and placed it on the floor. More posters beneath. Newspaper clippings too. Another missing person. A man this time. A climber from Bordeaux who'd vanished four years ago. Pinned next to that was a yellowed newspaper clipping, slightly more recent, detailing the grim discovery of the remains of a man in the Alps. Unidentified, due to what they referred to as 'animal activity'. But had the gendarmes decided it was the missing Bordeaux man? Another newspaper clipping outlined the discovery of the body of another climber. An Englishwoman whose remains had been found a little under two years ago.

Henrik knew only too well the dangers of places as unforgiving as the Alps, but–

Noise. Someone was coming. Henrik spun on his heel and rushed for the door. He sneaked a peek, as best he could, along the corridor to the waiting area, but because of the angle could hardly see anything.

He stooped as he stepped out into the corridor, trying to be discreet.

Not discreet enough.

Two eyes peered his way from beyond the door. Henrik didn't even pause to consider who the eyes belonged to. Instead, he spun again and raced for the fire exit. The door banged open behind him.

'*Ne bougez pas!*'

Don't move?

Henrik paid no attention to that. He ran as fast as he could.

Slammed the bar across the fire exit and swung the door open. An alarm blared. Cold air blasted into Henrik's face.

He didn't care. He just ran, and ran, and ran.

24

Ryker left Lyon as soon as he got back to the Jeep. He'd spent no more than a minute checking Hofman's body, keen to scarper from the crime scene, but had found virtually nothing on him. No watch, wallet, laptop, briefcase. Perhaps his death was supposed to look like a robbery. Ryker certainly didn't believe that was what had happened. But why had someone murdered Hofman? Because they knew Ryker was getting close to something?

Who had killed him? A hit organised from prison by Aziz?

So many questions, but Ryker decided to leave the city while he had the chance, rather than to stick around and try and find any more answers there. For one, he had plenty of electronic data to sift through, from the information on the thumb drive, to Hofman's phones, but he'd do that in his own time, somewhere that felt safe. Lyon didn't feel safe, and a doubt in Ryker's mind that perhaps somehow Hofman's murder would be pinned on him wouldn't go away.

He arrived in St Ricard not long before midnight. The first day he and Henrik had arrived, the hotel and lodging options had been limited, particularly given they'd come in peak season, but late at night Ryker expected he had no chance of finding lodging.

So he went to the one other place he could think of.

He wound down his window and pressed the button on the intercom and waited. No answer. So he pressed again. Then a third time. Finally a crackle as his call was answered.

'*Qui est-ce?*'

A sleepy male voice. Bruno, Ryker thought.

'It's James Ryker.'

Silence, then *click*. Silence again. He'd gone. Ryker waited a minute. Nothing. He pressed the intercom again. It was answered almost immediately this time.

'Mr Ryker,' Monique Thibaud said. 'What are you doing here?'

'Looking for a place to stay.'

A short wait, before, 'Come in.'

Bruno and Anna were both up and dressed by the time Ryker arrived at the front door, though their weary eyes suggested they'd had to get out of bed. No night duty then? No sign of Jules still either. Monique had on a silk kimono-style dressing gown, her eyelids were heavy, her cheeks droopy. Tiredness, but also the lack of her neat make-up, the absence of which made her look a lot older too.

'You're a very unusual man, Mr Ryker.'

He shrugged. 'I'm helping you. I thought you'd be kind enough to return the favour.'

'If you're playing games...' Bruno said, cracking his knuckles as he spoke.

Ryker ignored him.

'Bruno, could you make up the room at the back?' Monique

said, before turning to Ryker again as Bruno skulked off. 'There's an en suite there. It's quiet, warm. You'll be comfortable.'

'Sounds perfect.'

Anna set her eyes on Ryker. He couldn't read the look. Somewhere between inquisitive and–

'You had a busy time in Lyon,' Monique said. A statement. How much did she know?

'Definitely busy.'

'You're back here sooner than I expected.'

'I've got a lot of thinking to do.'

'You can tell me all about it in the morning.'

'I might do.'

'I'm going back to bed. Anna, please can you show our guest to his room.'

And with that Monique turned and walked to the stairs.

Ryker and Anna remained standing, her eyes fixed on Ryker.

'I can't decide whether the look you're giving me is because you want to kill me or screw me,' Ryker said.

'You'll find out soon enough.' She turned away. 'Come on.'

They reached the top of the stairs just as Bruno came out of the room at the far side. Six doors off the landing in total. All except for Ryker's were closed, though he noted light seeping out from underneath the door second on the right – Monique's room? What about the hired help – where did they sleep?

Bruno glared at Ryker as they neared.

'Sweet dreams,' Ryker said to him.

Bruno glared but didn't respond.

Anna and Ryker reached the bedroom doorway. Ryker stole a glance inside before he stepped forward, seeking out whether a threat awaited him inside. He saw none. The room was nice. Double bed. Old wooden furniture. Clean.

Ryker turned around. Anna remained in the doorway. A satisfied look on her face. Neither of them said a word. His comment moments ago about them screwing was a joke. Intended to rile her. But did she seriously have that on her mind?

Her smile broadened. A playful smile. She reached forward and Ryker was caught in two minds, both about her intentions and his response...

She grabbed the doorknob and pulled the door toward her a couple of inches. Then lifted her right hand into the air. A key hung from her thumb and forefinger.

'See you in the morning,' she said, before closing and locking the door.

'I'll be here waiting for you,' Ryker said, but he got no response.

He stood and listened as she padded away.

Then got to work.

First up, he powered on Hofman's phone – the one he'd taken from the man himself, rather than the two older phones from Hofman's desk which he'd already figured had been cleared back to factory settings. Disappointingly. Through the day he'd deliberately kept this device off, limiting Hofman's – or anybody else's – ability to track it. He stared aghast at the vast amount of missed calls and messages, including multiple from his wife and son, following Ryker's break-in. He felt sorry for them. Sorry that they'd been drawn into something that wasn't their doing. He wondered at what point they'd find out that Julian was dead.

But he didn't dwell.

He downloaded the phone's data onto a newly purchased second-hand laptop, then did the same with the data from the thumb drive. With the transfer in progress, he pulled the battery and SIM from Hofman's phone and destroyed both.

After that he used a simple analysis software that would

organise and catalogue all of the data he'd collected, and left it to run overnight.

At a little past 1am, Ryker finally lay back under the sheets of the bed and closed his eyes.

———

Not a long sleep, but a much better sleep than he'd had the previous two nights – a combination of the soft, warm mattress and sheets, and genuine tiredness catching up with him. When he woke at 6am, he was soon alert and ready. The house was quiet around him, and he didn't even think about attempting to pick the lock and escape his room, or snap the more fragile window lock to jump out. He wasn't a prisoner. And he had work to do. After showering and dressing, Ryker sat down at the small nightstand-cum-desk and woke up the laptop.

He worked away for nearly three hours, his belly intermittently growling with hunger, before he finally heard signs of life outside his door. He looked away from his screen, awaiting a knock or the sound of the key turning in the lock.

Nothing. But he was sure someone was standing outside there. He rose from his chair, slowly, then softly stepped across the carpet.

'Morning,' Ryker said when he came to a stop at the door.

No response, but he heard the shuffling feet of whoever had been there, moving away.

Ryker waited, but heard nothing more. He stretched, then moved to the window and pulled open the curtains and took in the view now that morning had finally arrived. A gloomy day, but the snowy mountainscape was still pleasant enough.

He glanced over the gardens and spotted Bruno trudging across the snowy lawn to an outbuilding. Not a shed, but a decent-sized brick structure, probably as big as some houses.

Was that where the workers lived? Or something else?

His brain rumbled with what Hofman had told him of the rumours of the tunnels beneath the house. The secrets buried there. Had Hofman meant that literally? Bodies buried there?

Ryker would try and find a way to get a look.

Bruno disappeared inside the building before a knock came on Ryker's door.

'Yeah?' Ryker said.

'If you want food, come downstairs,' Anna answered.

The door unlocked but remained closed. Ryker moved across and opened up. Anna was already halfway across the landing. No one else in sight. He wondered again who'd been outside his room moments before. Anna? Bruno? Monique?

He parked the thought, put away the laptop and other equipment in his bag, stuffing it behind the wardrobe, out of sight, then moved on out, closing the door behind him.

———

Monique's home had a grand dining room with a dark-wood, oval table and twelve chairs, but breakfast was served at the much more everyday pine table in the farmhouse-style kitchen. Only Monique and Ryker ate. Fresh orange juice, coffee, pastries and jams. Simple, but good.

Anna stood watch, looking bored and irritated. Bruno and Jules were nowhere to be seen.

'Did you sleep well?' Monique asked after a few minutes of subdued silence.

'Very well.'

'But not for long. You were up early.'

How did she know that?

Ryker thought back to the room. A camera perhaps? Was she that sneaky? He'd check later. He hadn't bothered last night as really it didn't make much difference as he wasn't doing anything in there that he didn't want others seeing.

'Yeah. I was up early,' Ryker said. 'Habit.'

Perhaps she'd only heard him because of the shower, or the creaking floorboards.

'Are you going to tell me what you've found out?' Monique asked.

Ryker chewed a mouthful of croissant as he thought.

'I heard that Julian Hofman is dead,' she said.

The way she said it... was she pleased?

'And do you know who killed him?' Ryker asked.

She glowered for a moment, as though offended. As though Ryker was accusing her.

'He mentioned some things about you,' Ryker said.

'He did? I didn't even know him.'

'That's what he said too. I'm not sure I believe either of you.'

She didn't respond to that.

'He said he'd heard rumours. Of you secretly buying back a stake in Franck Thibaud champagne.'

'If I had a euro for every silly rumour I've heard about me and my family–'

'You'd be even richer than you already are.'

Monique glowered. 'Have you found out any information on Sophie?' she asked. 'That's why you're in St Ricard, isn't it?'

'Partly. Have you found out any information on Henrik?'

'Actually, yes.'

Ryker swallowed then paused. She had his full attention, and she knew it.

'There was quite a scene last night,' Monique said. 'Apparently a teenager broke into the gendarmerie station. He was found roaming around inside but ran off. His description – his actions too – certainly sound a lot like your boy.'

Ryker didn't know whether to be heartened or horrified.

Before arriving at Monique's house the previous night he'd parked up and walked the short distance into the woods, where they'd left their backpacks previously, but everything had gone. Ryker had hoped that meant Henrik had been back and taken it all, but he'd decided against roaming the vast area in the cold and dark to try and find him. But news that he was in St Ricard… Ryker hadn't felt so positive in a long time.

Breaking into a police station? Ryker wondered what had caused Henrik to do that, and what he'd found.

'I'm assuming they didn't catch him?' he said.

'You've obviously taught him well. Or, not so well, depending on your view of the law.'

Actually, Henrik had learned such skills himself, though Ryker had hardly discouraged him at any point.

'You know yourself, St Ricard isn't a big place,' Monique said. 'If he's here, you'll come across him soon enough. Of course, so might the gendarmes, or some other people who he's wronged.'

'They might do. But don't the gendarmes answer to you?'

She shot him a disgusted look. 'Those men and women uphold the law here. They don't *answer* to me, but they do listen to me.'

Ryker decided not to bother arguing that one any further.

'I asked you about Sophie. Have you found anything to help me?'

'Not exactly,' Ryker said. 'But perhaps you could help me?'

The frown suggested she didn't like the sound of that.

'I think I've helped you quite enough already.'

'Did you know about the other missing persons in St Ricard?' Ryker asked.

'Excuse me?'

'I was searching the internet to learn about you. This town. I found out a lot of interesting things. One thing that stood out? At least three other missing persons here over the last few years.'

'In the Alps?' Monique said. 'It's actually not so unusual. A lot of inexperienced climbers who think they know best realise the hard way that they don't. Some experienced ones too.'

'Or maybe there's more to it than that.'

'What are you saying?'

'I told you. Missing persons. Perhaps accidents in the Alps. Perhaps something else.'

Monique squirmed. 'What are you expecting me to say?'

'I expect you knew about these people, one way or another. Small town like this, you having so much sway over its residents–'

'I don't think–'

'Then your own brother and his family get murdered. Then your own niece goes missing–'

'Are you seriously suggesting that–'

'Why haven't you told the police that Sophie is missing?' Ryker asked.

Monique paused. 'What makes you think I haven't?' She fidgeted a little in her chair.

'Because, unlike those other missing persons, there's been nothing public about her disappearance. No posters on lamp posts, no news reports, no search parties.'

Monique stayed silent.

'So my guess is you don't think she's been kidnapped. You don't think she's dead having fallen off a cliff edge somewhere. You think she ran away.'

Monique still said nothing.

'If I felt it necessary to tell someone else about her no longer being here,' Ryker posed, 'say... the gendarmes–'

'Please don't.'

Interesting.

'Because?'

'Because this is an issue I want to resolve alone.'

'Except you're not doing it alone, are you? You've drawn me in.'

'No, Mr Ryker, you brought yourself here, to my door. Twice. Remember?'

'Yeah. I remember. But I still haven't worked out why you're now so keen for me to help you.'

'You don't trust me?'

'Not at all.'

'You don't think our interests are aligned?'

'I'm not sure I really know your interests. And I'm sure you don't care much about mine.'

'I'm disappointed you think so little of me.'

'Are you?'

Neither said a word for a few moments. Anna shuffled a couple of times. A reminder she was still in the room? Or simply showing her discomfort at being there but having no part in the conversation.

'When did Sophie leave?'

'Disappear,' Monique said. Ryker raised an eyebrow. 'I think I prefer *disappear* to *leave*. The words have very different connotations.'

'Okay. But when?'

'You want the exact date? It was the thirtieth of November.'

'That's quite a while ago.'

'I'm aware of that.'

'Tell me in detail what happened. When did you last see her? Who else was here? What was said? What mood was she in? When did you realise she'd gone? What was the window of time for her... disappearing? Has there been any contact since? Signs of life?'

Monique shook her head, looking a little overwhelmed by the barrage of questions. But they were questions whose answers should have been burned in her memory, if she truly cared for her niece.

'We ate dinner that night,' she said. 'Just the two of us.'

'Tweedledum and Tweedledee weren't around then?' Ryker said, indicating over to Anna who rolled her eyes in response.

'Yes. They were. Bruno was out on errands, but Anna and Jules were in the house. Just not eating with us. We finished around 8pm. Sophie went to her room–'

'Which room is it?' Ryker asked.

A short pause. 'Upstairs, the first on the left.'

'Overlooking the front of the house?'

'Yes.'

'And then?'

'And then I watched TV. I went to my bedroom around eleven.'

'Did you check on Sophie?'

'No.'

'Why?'

'Because…' She sighed. 'She's a teenager, not a baby.'

'No,' Ryker said. 'That's not it.'

'Our relationship is complex. The truth is, we're not all that close, but that doesn't mean I don't care for her a great deal.'

'But a young woman who lost her family in the most horrible way, and you don't even have the decency to say goodnight to her?'

'You're talking to me about decency?'

Ryker shrugged.

'Anna alerted me in the morning that Sophie's room was empty.'

'Anything else missing? Clothes? Jewellery?'

'Nothing obvious.'

'Phone?'

'Her phone was gone, but it hasn't been turned on since.'

The way she said that suggested she'd tried to track the device, though Ryker didn't bother to clarify how.

'What time did you check her?' Ryker asked Anna, who glanced to her boss before answering.

'Around eight.'

'So a nearly twelve-hour window,' Ryker said.

'Yes,' Monique confirmed.

'Anything else that could help to narrow it down? CCTV cameras? Alarm?'

'We only set the alarm when Ms Thibaud is in bed,' Anna said. 'It would have been around eleven thirty that night.'

'And there are cameras?'

'Downstairs, yes,' Anna said. 'And outside too. But they don't cover everything.'

'And they didn't capture her leaving?' Ryker asked Anna. 'Or anyone else arriving?'

'Nothing. The cameras are motion triggered so they only record when they're activated. There's nothing for that night. We still have the records to show that if you feel the need to check.'

Ryker felt he might do.

'Any contact since?' he asked.

'Nothing at all,' Monique answered.

'Did she have a bank account of her own? Credit card?'

'Both. Neither have been used since.'

'You have access?' Ryker said, well aware that he sounded dubious about the fact.

'She's seventeen. I'm her legal guardian, so yes, I have access.'

'Could she have another source of funds?'

'Only cash, as far as I know.'

'How much?'

'I have no idea.'

'Her bedroom window,' Ryker said, thinking about the layout of the house, 'is at the front, to the right of the front door?'

'Yes,' Anna said.

'Isn't the camera covering the entrance directly below there, but pointed away, to the entrance?'

'Yes.'

'So she could have climbed out of the window and dropped down the other side of the camera, and stayed out of its sight.'

'It's possible,' Anna said. 'Except the window still locked.'

Could someone else have locked it after?

'I think you're suggesting then, that Sophie sneaked out before the alarm system was armed,' Ryker said. 'At some point between eight and eleven thirty.'

'*Sneaked out*,' Monique said, turning her nose up. 'I'm sorry, but I don't think I've ever suggested she did that. I–'

'Either Sophie left here on her own, or with someone else, yes?'

'Well, obviously, but–'

'As I've said before, you've never indicated to me a worry that she's been kidnapped, or has come to harm, so is there anything to suggest someone else was here that night?'

'No, but...'

'Then isn't the most obvious answer that she simply walked out?'

Monique didn't answer, and Ryker wondered why it was so hard for her to simply state the obvious. Unless she was still not being straight with him. Had Sophie been kidnapped but Monique wouldn't admit it because it would expose wrongdoing by her somehow?

'So,' Ryker said, 'sticking with your line, that she left here of her own accord, brings me to perhaps the most important question,' Ryker said.

'Which is?' Anna asked when Monique said nothing.

'What was so bad about living here that a girl whose brother and parents had recently been murdered would choose to leave?'

Monique looked livid.

'And then you choose not to tell anyone about her disappearance,' Ryker added.

'I told *you*.'

'I found out,' Ryker said. 'That's different. Which makes me question if you're being truthful with me about what happened that night. And you're happy to have my help to find her, but not official help from the police or other authorities. Why is that?'

A buzz from out in the hallway. The intercom.

'I'll go,' Anna said, rushing off as though desperate to get away. Monique, too, sat poised, ready to get up.

'Saved by the bell?' Ryker said.

'Ms Thibaud!' Anna shouted from out in the hall.

Monique said nothing more as she shot up from her chair and walked out.

25

Ryker left the house feeling agitated. He hadn't spoken to Monique again. She was busy chatting in her office to the man and woman who'd earlier interrupted breakfast. Who they were, Ryker had no clue, but he took the opportunity to leave the house quietly, noting the registration of the Renault parked up outside as he left in case it'd later become important. He thought about sneaking to that outbuilding before he left, but decided against it given Bruno and Anna were skulking around, watching him like hawks. He'd get the chance eventually.

He took all of his belongings with him. Not that he didn't feel he couldn't return there again, but because he trusted Monique and her little gang even less now than he had done the night before.

Why was she so cagey about what had happened to Sophie? There was a chance it was simply down to some sort of embarrassment, not only that the teen had walked out like that, but that she'd *wanted* to walk out.

But all that presumed that Monique was being wholly truthful about the night of the thirtieth of November, and Ryker really didn't believe that.

He drove the Jeep into town, a little surprised that there'd been no question from Monique about his continued use of her vehicle. After parking up he made a return trip into the woods, but once again found the hiding place there empty. Did Henrik have their things, or someone else? In the daylight he noticed a lot of footprints leading to and from the spot, some to the town, some up the mountain, but it was difficult to tell which were the most fresh, and Ryker again decided against going on a long and potentially fruitless ramble to find Henrik.

Instead, he left his belongings there, deciding at least there was less chance of the items getting into the wrong hands – i.e. Monique and her cronies – that way, then made another call to Jen Worthington as he descended back into town.

'Have you got anything for me?' he asked.

'A lot of information. How much of it is relevant, it's hard to say.'

'Can you put it into a Dropbox?'

'Already done. I just need an email for you so I can send you the link.'

He told her the address of the new account he'd set up earlier in the day.

'Can you give me the upshot?'

'I can. None of the email addresses you gave me, nor the company name, seem to have any link to Aziz Doukha, or to Monique or any other Thibaud.'

Which, strangely, Ryker had come to the conclusion of too, given his searches through Hofman's data.

'But I do have a name for each of the people Hofman was communicating with. Some profile information too.'

She read out the names. Antony Petit. Pavel Anarkov. Thomas Kessner. Ryker had figured them all out already from his search of Hofman's data, but Jen likely had more detail on each than he'd been able to discover so far.

'None of these people are on any of our databases as known criminals, but one of them, Anarkov, is a very wealthy man with a lot of close links to the Kremlin, the government in Switzerland too. He's also got a rather large stake in a Russian bank.'

Ryker chewed on that. He'd already figured Anarkov was a very rich man, but the government links, and the bank stake, were news to him. The information did all point to one thing though: corruption. The dam project, one way or another, was mired in corruption and dirty money. Was Monique in cahoots with that group of people, or an opponent? Her reaction to Sophie's disappearance made some more sense if either of those was the case. Perhaps she'd come up against Hofman and the others because she wasn't able to milk the project with them already in place, enriching themselves. The fallout had led to Sophie's disappearance – kidnapping? – and Monique's decision to keep it a secret, for fear of exposing herself. Instead, she'd enlisted Ryker's help and set him off after Hofman.

'Thanks,' Ryker said. 'I'm meeting with one of those guys soon. I'll let you know what I get from him.'

'I heard Julian Hofman is dead,' Jen said.

As well informed as he expected her to be.

'He is.'

'Anything to do with you?'

'Not directly.'

'Watch your back, James,' Jen said, before ending the call.

Her words still on his mind, Ryker kept alert as he walked through the town's streets. No sign of Henrik. No signs of the gendarmerie. As he approached the café, not far from the bar, Fabrique, he spotted a familiar face on the other side of the window. Amelie. Sitting at a table with her chums, hot chocolates and piles of pancakes in front of them.

Ryker inwardly groaned as he stepped inside. Not because

he hadn't wanted to ever see her again, but because the timing was less than convenient – once again. He looked the other way...

'James?'

What else could he do?

He stopped as the door closed behind him and turned to her.

'Amelie, what a surprise,' he said.

'I thought you'd left town after... you know.'

'Still here.'

'I figured. I saw your son yesterday.'

'You did? Where?'

She frowned at his inquisitive tone. 'He was heading up to Grimaldi Lodge. I thought maybe that's where you're staying.'

Ryker said nothing as he thought.

'Is it?' she asked.

'What?'

'Is that where you're staying?'

'No,' Ryker said. 'It's not.'

'Oh, I thought–'

'Sorry, Amelie, it was nice bumping into you, but I've got to go.' The men he'd come to see looked like they were about to leave.

'Oh. Okay. Perhaps I'll see you in the bar, later?'

'You never know,' he said with a smile that he hoped would keep her at ease.

Then he turned and headed for the men, sat opposite each other in a booth. They spotted him walking over. Looked a little wary.

'Gentlemen,' Ryker said as he sat down on the bench facing away from Amelie, blocking any attempted exit for the elder of the two men. 'Glad I caught you.'

'I'm sorry, but... who are you?' the younger and perhaps

more bullish of the two said, who had wavy hair on top, shaved to the bone on the sides. Trendy. At least he obviously thought he was given the confident look in his eyes.

'I don't know you,' Ryker said, glaring at him, before turning to the man next to him. 'But you must be Thomas Kessner.'

TK. One of Hofman's mystery acquaintances. Except not so mystery as to remain a secret to Ryker after his hours of digging and cross referencing.

A decade or two older than his companion, Kessner had a round face and red cheeks. He wore expensive, smart-casual clothes and a very expensive gold watch, but had on heavy work boots, and his coat, folded next to him, was functional rather than fashionable. Ryker understood the muddled look. That of someone of seniority in their business, but whose job commanded the need for both office work, and dirty site work. The younger man was definitely more of an office pen-pusher, even had his shiny black office shoes on. They wouldn't be so shiny later, Ryker thought.

'I... yes, but who–'

'I'm really sorry,' Ryker said with a put-on sigh and a solemn shake of the head, 'but I don't think Julian will be joining you today.'

That shut them both up. They looked at one another then back to Ryker.

'You heard what happened to him, didn't you?' Ryker added.

The two men glanced at each other.

'I didn't do it, before you ask.'

'Who are you?' Kessner asked.

'James Ryker.'

He held out his hand. Kessner didn't move.

'We should go,' the young man said, about to get up.

'Actually you'll sit down before I pick up that fork and stick it through your eyeball.'

He stayed put.

'You're going for a site inspection today?' Ryker asked Kessner. 'At the dam?'

Kessner glared but kept his mouth shut.

'Is that a yes or a no?'

'How do you know–'

Ryker grabbed Kessner's thigh under the table and dug his fingertips in between the muscles, a hotbed of nerves. Kessner squirmed, his face creasing, as though he was trying his best to show no reaction.

'Yes or no?'

'Yes,' Kessner said.

'Great. I'll come with you. You can tell me all about how you know Julian – sorry, knew Julian – and all about your dealings together.'

Nothing from either of them.

'You can also tell me if you know anything about who killed him last night.'

'This is ridiculous,' Kessner said, his cheeks reddening further.

The door opened behind Ryker, drawing the young guy's attention. Ryker glanced over his shoulder.

Seriously?

Renaud and Coupet.

'Don't,' Ryker said to the young man.

'Lucas,' Kessner said, as though imploring his friend not to do anything stupid.

Lucas did relax a little, looked back to Ryker. But the gendarmes were already on their way over.

Ryker took his hand from Kessner's leg. Sat back in his seat. Caught Amelie's eye for a split second as he glanced over his shoulder again. She and her friends stared over with interest.

Would this only encourage her keenness in him or kill it for good?

'Good morning, officers,' Ryker said to the two new arrivals who came to a stop at the booth, eyeballing Ryker and his company.

'I heard you were back,' Renaud said. 'But you've been keeping quiet. Unlike your son.'

Ryker shrugged. 'Teenagers, right?'

'Don't test us,' Renaud said. 'You won't like the end result.'

'You gentlemen okay?' Coupet asked, looking from Kessner to Lucas. Did the gendarmes know these two? Neither were from St Ricard, but they'd likely been in the town plenty.

Lucas squirmed, as if he wanted to shout for help.

'We're fine,' Kessner said. 'Just trying to enjoy some breakfast.'

'You're not eating?' Renaud said to Ryker.

'Actually, I already ate with Ms Thibaud,' Ryker said. 'I stayed with her last night.'

He kept a straight face, but the officers looked seriously put out by his words. A couple of other punters glanced over too, as though the conversation had taken an unexpected turn.

But Ryker had had enough. He made a show of checking his watch.

'I think it's time for us to go, isn't it?' he said to Kessner.

The older guy didn't seem to like that idea at all, but Ryker held his eye until he caved.

'Yes. It is.'

'Excuse us, please,' Ryker said to the officers. They reluctantly stepped back as Ryker and Kessner and Lucas got up from the booth.

'Enjoy your day,' Ryker said to Renaud and Coupet.

'*Au revoir*,' Coupet said. 'Or to you in English, goodbye, until we meet again.'

Ryker smiled at him then headed for the door. Amelie's friends looked away as he approached, as though they hadn't just been glued to the conversation. Amelie remained staring. Ryker winked at her then moved out into the cold, Kessner and Lucas in tow. He stopped on the outside and looked back through the glass. Coupet and Renaud both glared still.

'Come on then,' Ryker said to Kessner. 'Let's go and have a look at this dam.'

26

Henrik hadn't stopped shivering for hours. On a calmer night he would have slept by the fire once more, but the wind had been so cold and fierce, whistling around his tent, dragging with it any semblance of heat from inside. Not to mention the sinister shadows looming on the fabric as the moonlight caught hold of branches all around him. As used to spending time on his own as he was – even in the wilds – he didn't want another night out in the Alps alone. Which didn't leave him many options for tonight...

But first things first. He had a busy day planned.

Hopefully a chance to get warmed through at some point too.

Ella strolled out of Grimaldi Lodge at eleven on the dot. She did a double take when she saw him standing in wait. She looked even more alluring than the previous day somehow.

'You look cold,' she said to him, sounding only a little sympathetic. Was she still angry with him?

'Frozen.'

'Where are you staying?' she asked. She seemed a little

dubious – because of his shivering, or because of him waiting there for her again?

'Tent.'

She shook her head. 'At this time of year? Better you than me.'

'Tell me about it.'

'Your dad really knows how to treat you.'

They fell into an awkward silence. Ella fidgeted, as if she didn't know what else to say.

'You want to talk again?' she suggested.

'Yeah,' Henrik said.

'My mum is home today, so...'

Henrik shrugged. 'Doesn't matter. I thought we could do something else anyway.'

She raised an eyebrow as he reached into his pocket and took out the tickets.

'Day trip?' he suggested with a smile.

Thankfully she said yes, though on realising that the tickets were for the TGV from Lyon to Marseille, he thought he noticed a look of suspicious recognition in her eyes as to why he'd chosen that destination. Still, she said nothing about it until they were on the superfast – and warm and comfy – train in Lyon, and both were finally relaxed. He more so than her perhaps, given the tension that had coursed through him as he re-entered the city.

'We're going to see Michel Lemerre,' Ella said as Henrik shuffled in his seat to take his coat off, deliberately moving a little closer to her as he did so, leaving their shoulders and hips and thighs brushing.

'Yes,' he said, avoiding her gaze as he looked out of the

window to see the last of the city disappearing, and the French countryside rolling into view.

'Why do you need me?' Ella asked.

'I don't,' he said, looking at her now. 'I wanted you to come with me.'

'So you like spending time with me?'

'A lot.'

'If you wanted to see me again, to treat me, you could have taken me to Paris or somewhere else.'

Henrik laughed. 'Maybe next time.'

'You're very sure of yourself, aren't you?'

He shrugged. Was he? He'd never thought so. At school, when he'd actually gone, he'd been a loner. A bit of an outcast really. No real friends, not interested in the work, but perhaps his lowly position in the playground hierarchy had been more down to him than other people – in general, he just didn't like other people much. But he certainly didn't lack self-belief – when he wanted something, he made damn sure he got it.

'I still can't stop thinking that you wanting to talk to me is only an excuse to find out more about Sophie and her life.'

'Or perhaps finding out more about Sophie and her life is my excuse for talking to you?'

'Isn't that the same thing?'

'Not even close.'

'So which is it?'

'A bit of both,' he said with a cheeky smile which earned him a playful hit on his arm. 'I didn't *need* you to come with me today. But I really wanted you to. I don't know how long I'll be in St Ricard, and...'

He trailed off, not really knowing what he'd intended to say.

'What happened to you?' Ella asked.

He tried not to look at her but realised she was staring and slowly turned to face her as he thought about how to answer her question.

'What do you mean?' he asked, sounding as lame as he felt for sidestepping the question. The mood had darkened, and both knew it.

He got what she was asking about. His past.

Even though they hadn't spoken at all about it before, he'd sensed that she'd sensed something. One reason why he was drawn to her, especially as whatever worries she had about his past, it hadn't put her off him. Yet.

'Is he really your dad?' she asked.

He paused before he slowly shook his head.

'Are you in trouble?'

'Because of Ryker? No. He's... he looks after me.'

'But who is he if he's not your dad?'

'He's like me, I guess.' Henrik sighed. 'He has no home. No family. Neither do I.'

'He seems... dangerous.'

'He saved my life. More than once. But... he is dangerous. If you get on his bad side.'

'Has he ever hurt you?'

Henrik scoffed. 'Of course not. He's not like that. I didn't mean he'd hurt me. He hurts bad people. He does good.'

She didn't look so sure. But she'd never even spoken to Ryker. Only seen him kick the crap out of a group of guys in a bar. She didn't know Ryker like Henrik. How many people did?

'You want to know about me?' he asked, sounding more agitated than he'd intended.

'Only if you want to tell me.'

He thought, then sighed, then said, 'I was born in Blodstein. A tiny place in the north of Norway. The nearest city is Trondheim, but it's not a big city really, and I think I probably went there a couple of times my whole life.'

'You're from a small town, like me.'

'But I don't think my life is like yours. You have a nice house, loving parents.'

'My parents are the worst,' she said, her face screwed in annoyance. 'They don't let me do *anything*.'

Henrik laughed, his flippant response not easing her tension, but he assumed she was referring to typical teenage issues rather than the life or death shit he'd had to deal with. Was that unfair?

'I didn't know my dad at all,' Henrik said. 'My mum was a drug addict and I was taken from her when I was two. I lived with my foster parents for years, and I really loved them, even if they struggled with me. I wasn't... easy on them.'

He paused then and the look on her face suggested she sensed his dismay. He hated how he'd treated them.

'They died in a car accident. After that... I was lost. I stopped going to school. I didn't settle with any of the families they put me with. Eventually I ran away.'

'And then James Ryker found you?'

Henrik laughed, though the circumstances of their first meeting were far from funny.

'You could say that. I was kidnapped. By men who'd found out my dad was a Russian gangster. I was his bastard. He didn't even know.'

She looked seriously worried now. Her eyes flitted about, as though she was concerned someone was listening. Would she get up and get off at the next stop and rush off home? No. She relaxed. Put a hand on his leg. Sympathy.

'You're serious?' she asked.

'Yes. Ryker saved me from them.'

'Why?'

'Because that's what he does.'

'That's why you're both in St Ricard?'

'Helping others? I guess so.'

'But who does he work for? He's like... a spy or something?'

'He doesn't work for anyone.'

She seemed really unsure about that.

'Your real dad–'

'He was the worst human I've ever met.' Wasn't he? Although that Aziz guy... 'He's dead now.'

'Ryker killed him?'

Yes. He had. But Henrik didn't confirm it. Instead, he held her eye until she looked away. He looked down to his lap. Realised his hands were shaking. Why?

'I'm glad you told me that,' she said, putting her hand over his to hold them still. 'I'm glad you told me the truth. Even if I don't understand all of it.'

'No,' Henrik said. 'Most of the time, neither do I.'

On the glorious Mediterranean coast, Marseille was noticeably warmer and brighter than St Ricard, even in the depths of winter. Henrik felt overdressed in his cold weather gear, but at least he'd warmed through. The ultra-efficient journey from Lyon had taken a little under two hours – far faster than travelling by car or other means – and by early afternoon they walked around the Marseille Centre campus of AMU, one of five main campuses of France's largest university.

'I didn't think it'd be so big,' Henrik said, in awe at the array of historic, sprawling buildings dotted through the site. University was something he'd never really thought lay ahead for him. Given his life recently, it was surely even more of an impossibility now. As he looked around, that fact made him more sad than he'd expected.

'Me neither,' Ella said.

'He lives in the building over here,' Henrik said, pointing toward an angular seventies' building with an outer concrete shell. Four storeys tall and more than a hundred yards wide. Quite out of place next to the far older and more ornate buildings that surrounded it.

'How do you know?' Ella said.

'I asked.'

'Asked who?'

'His parents.'

'What did you tell them?'

'How do you mean?'

'About who you are?'

'I said I was a friend from St Ricard and I wanted to surprise him for his birthday.'

'How did you know when his birthday is?'

'Social media. Although it's not actually for a couple of weeks yet.'

'Michel's not on social media.'

So she'd checked on him already?

'*He's* not. But his friends are.'

She didn't look convinced. Either because she thought he wasn't telling the truth, or because she didn't like his snooping. He *was* being truthful, although not entirely, as he'd done a lot more searching than a simple social media trawl and call to Michel's parents. His other activities included calls to banks, utility companies, mobile phone companies, pretending to be Michel, trying to get access to his records. With limited success. No need to mention all that now.

'This is it,' Henrik said as they reached the locked outer door.

'So what next?'

'Next you get us inside.'

Henrik smiled at her and reached forward and pressed a

button for Michel. A couple of seconds later a crackly male voice answered. Ella shook her head at Henrik, but he silently urged her on.

'Hi, yes... er... is Michel there?' Ella said. Henrik tried not to smirk, but she looked so uncomfortable. She hit his arm, as though he was breaking her concentration.

'No. He isn't.'

'Oh... it's... this is... Marie. I really, really wanted to see him.' Was she trying to sound seductive? 'If you know what I mean? Can you help?'

A moment of silence, before, 'Come on up.'

A buzz as the door unlocked. Henrik couldn't contain his smile any longer. Ella tried to hold hers too but failed.

'Well done,' he said to her.

'Idiot,' she said, thumping his arm again – not quite as playfully as earlier.

Even at fifteen, Henrik had seen student accommodation before. He'd lived with students for a while, having befriended a group of wayward teens in the months before he'd been kidnapped in Norway. The space occupied by Michel and his room-mate, Theo, was exactly as Henrik expected given his own experiences. A bit of a dump. Piles of clothes – clean or dirty, who knew. Dirty crockery, empty beer cans and spirits bottles.

'Where's Michel?' Henrik asked Theo who had messy long hair and wore linen shorts and a scruffy T-shirt like he'd just got out of bed.

'He's not here,' Theo said, as grumpy as he looked. Perhaps because he'd expected a hot and horny teenage girl to appear at his door, rather than Ella and Henrik intent on giving him a grilling.

'Then where?'

'You're not his friends, are you?'

'We're from St Ricard,' Ella said. 'I've known Michel for years.'

'And you?' Theo said, indicating Henrik.

'He's with me,' Ella answered.

'So where is he?' Henrik asked.

'If you were his friends, you'd know. Michel hasn't been here for weeks.'

Henrik looked across at the mess.

'I've a new room-mate now,' Theo said, as if picking up on Henrik's thought. 'Daniel. He's not in.' Then a broad smile. 'Think he got lucky last night.'

'So where's Michel?'

'You know as much as I do.'

'You don't know where he went?' Ella asked.

'He said he was going home.'

'To St Ricard?' Henrik asked.

'I'm only saying what I heard. He was on the phone to that girl he's obsessed with.'

'Sophie?'

Theo shrugged. 'Said he'd see her back home.'

'His parents left St Ricard a few months ago,' Henrik said. 'They still think he's here, so he hasn't gone back to them.'

Theo shrugged once more. 'We've had a couple of letters for him recently but that's it. They haven't called or anything.'

'And you're not in contact with him?' Ella asked.

'We weren't very good friends. We shared different... interests.'

'Such as?'

'Have you met Michel?'

'I already told you. I'm from St Ricard.'

'Everybody knows everybody in St Ricard?' Theo said, in such a way as to make the idea sound ridiculous. Henrik already didn't like the guy. Something creepy and knowing and snide about him.

'Yeah,' Ella said. 'We do.'

'Do you have any way of contacting him?' Henrik asked.

'I have a number. I haven't tried.'

'Why not?'

'To be honest, it's better that he's gone.'

'Better how?'

'There was talk... he got thrown off campus. Drugs.'

Henrik glanced at Ella, as though enquiring whether that sounded right, or not. She'd suggested to him that Michel was confident and brash, but popular – and successful – with the girls. Young women too. He'd had his fair share of tourists, apparently. But even though their relationship hadn't been long or formal, Sophie had mellowed him. Ella had never mentioned to Henrik anything about Michel having a problem with drugs, but then... perhaps he'd changed after leaving home and going to university.

'Which drugs?' Henrik asked.

'Does it matter?' Theo responded.

'Bit of a difference between cannabis and heroin.'

'Not on campus. Zero tolerance.'

'When did he get thrown off campus?' Ella asked.

Theo shrugged again, appearing a little bored by the conversation now. 'Couple of months maybe.'

'You still have the letters that came for him?' Henrik asked.

'No. You're not the first people to come asking after him.'

'Who else?'

'Two men. Older than you. How old are you, anyway? Thirteen?'

He grinned at Henrik who didn't bother to respond, even if he did feel his cheeks redden a little. Did Ella notice?

'What were their names?' Ella asked.

Theo held her eye as though thinking – or was he just staring at her. He had an ugly glint in his eye that Henrik wanted to get rid of. He balled his fist.

'Don't remember. Some shitty Muslim name.'

'Aziz?' Henrik asked, receiving a curious glance from Ella. He'd not told her anything about him. 'Or Ramiz?'

'Don't think so. But that was the problem with Michel. He had all these characters around him. Like the guy from Lyon who supplied his drugs...' He looked up to the ceiling as though searching for the name there.

'What guy?' Henrik said, his brain already rumbling with possible answers, and the consequences.

'Big black guy. Him and all his nasty friends.'

Henrik whipped out his phone. Googled. Found the image in one of the first results.

'Him?'

Theo squinted as he stared, but then gave his casual shrug once more.

'Could be. They all look the same to me.'

'Only to racists and imbeciles,' Ella said with a sullen glare. Then she turned to Henrik.

'I think we should go,' he said. Not just because he felt either he or Ella were about to smack Theo in the face, but because he desperately needed to make a phone call.

27

Ryker drove. Even if it meant his hands were occupied, he wanted to be in control of where they went. Kessner gave directions, but Ryker knew the route already, from his earlier review of satellite imagery.

Although the site of the dam was less than three miles from St Ricard, they drove on for more than fifteen miles because of the circuitous route needed from the town to make it around the peaks.

'Sometimes, in the summer, it's possible to go that way,' Kessner said, pointing to a road on the right. 'But it's closed at least six months of the year.'

Ryker had figured the same from the maps he'd seen, though he was surprised at Kessner's apparently relaxed tone now. He was in the passenger seat next to Ryker. Lucas was in the back, behind his boss. Ryker glanced at him every now and then in the rear-view mirror. He didn't look happy. Not scared at all, just really angry. Neither Kessner nor Lucas had protested further about why Ryker was with them. Had asked no more questions. Perhaps they thought there was safety for them at the top of the mountain?

They carried on and were soon on a final ascent where roadworks and barriers indicated they were approaching the mammoth worksite. Here the snow had been churned with the earth beneath it by heavy machinery. Stretching off in all directions were deep grooves cut into the land, snaking away, where tracked beasts had roamed. Not for a few days though. The fresh layer of snow covering everything was evidence of that.

'How long since the site was closed?' Ryker asked. He'd read about the closure in the local paper. Bad weather – winds and sub-zero temperatures rather than heavy snow – had hampered progress more than once over the winter. The main work crew – salaried employees – were probably fine with that. They all got paid for staying at home. But the big boys at the construction companies, and the shareholders they answered to, were likely all desperate to get started again so their bonuses and profits weren't further eroded. A meeting was due to take place that morning to determine whether or not conditions had improved enough for work to restart.

At least, that was the official reason for Kessner being in town. But as Ryker had seen from the email trail between him and Hofman and the other, there was also a second motive. Hofman had been set to meet Kessner in St Ricard that morning to discuss their 'problem'.

'It's been five days,' Kessner said. 'Every day costs us tens of thousands of euros.'

'Damn Mother Nature,' Ryker said. 'You try and make a few hundred million building a dam in one of the snowiest, coldest regions of Europe, and look what she does?'

He glanced at Kessner, whose face remained passive. Apparently he didn't appreciate Ryker's sarcasm.

'Take this next left,' Kessner said a few seconds later,

pointing to the closed metal gates. 'Otherwise we'll be at a dead end at the top.'

Ryker didn't respond. He also didn't take the turn, instead carrying straight on, the quality of the track almost immediately disintegrating from flat, hard, compacted ground, to horrendously bumpy churned mud and snow.

'I said–'

'I heard what you said. But I want to get the scenic view.'

He looked across at Kessner again. Now he didn't look so confident.

'This is–'

'Shut up, Lucas,' Ryker said, without bothering to look at the younger man.

The tension in the car remained noticeably higher – for the two passengers at least – as Ryker drove the Jeep upward, jostling to keep the vehicle under control on the near impossible terrain. The top of the mountain came into view. Ryker had intended to go right up there, but as the Jeep went over a divot the back wheels sank into the ground. The tyres spun. Even the four-wheel drive, even the super-grippy tread, could do nothing to help.

A shame, as the Jeep had been useful for him the last few days. At least he'd already stashed his belongings elsewhere.

'Looks like we're walking,' Ryker said.

Neither of his 'guests' looked very pleased about that.

Ryker stepped out first. Kessner and Lucas a few seconds after. Ryker walked through the mess of mud and snow to where they were face to face, whispering.

Ryker was a couple of yards away when Lucas spun around, penknife in his hand which he swooshed toward Ryker as he lunged forward.

'Go!' Lucas shouted. To Kessner, presumably. Except Kessner didn't move.

Ryker dodged left to avoid the knife and sent a punishing gut shot to Lucas, who doubled over, coughing and spluttering as the knife came free. Ryker shoved forward, clasping his hand over Lucas's head and slamming it into the side of the Jeep.

Lucas collapsed to the floor.

A fist coming for Ryker's head. He ducked and grabbed the hand and squeezed. Hard. Then threw a punch to Kessner's kidney. A brutal shot that caused Kessner to screw up his face in agony.

'Don't blame me if you're pissing blood.'

He let go of Kessner's fist and the man stumbled back. Ryker grabbed Lucas from the ground and hauled him back into the Jeep.

'Stop whimpering,' he said as he took Lucas' wrists and slung the rope around them, then wound the rope around the headrest in front before tying the knot as tight as he could. 'You'll be much warmer in here. And those nice shoes won't be ruined.'

Ryker slammed the door shut. Looked to the keys in his hand. Then to Kessner, who now looked petrified as he clutched at his side.

'More than one way off this mountain,' Ryker said. He clicked the button to lock the Jeep then pulled his arm behind his head and flung the key fob as far as he could. It fell out of sight beyond a snowy ridge.

'What are you doing!' Kessner protested, looking like he might chase after the key.

He didn't.

'You can either follow me, or I can drag you the rest of the way,' Ryker said.

Kessner said nothing.

'So?'

'But... where?'

'I thought you knew this site?' Ryker asked. He got nothing in response. 'This way.'

He set off. Took two steps before he turned to Kessner who still hadn't moved.

'Okay,' he finally said.

'Good choice.'

They got moving.

'I... I... still don't understand. What do you want from me?'

'I'm here... *we're* here because of the Thibauds. You're going to tell me everything you know about them.'

'I... but...'

'Save it,' Ryker said, cutting him off with a wave of his hand. 'Just use this time to think about what you'll tell me. The truth will work out much better for you. It might even save your life.'

Ryker looked over. Some of the colour had drained from Kessner's cheeks, though perhaps that was down to them being out in the cold as much as anything else.

They didn't have to walk much further. As they approached the ridge, the land opened out in front and below them. The view... spectacular. About as mesmerising as Ryker had ever seen. The Alps rose all around them, the sweeping view stretching miles in every direction. Behind them, St Ricard was nothing but a pinprick. In front of them, sturdy metal barriers stood at a rocky edge. Just below the edge, the walls of the dam curved around to the other side of the valley. A hundred yards, perhaps a little more, a little less, but probably twice as high as it was wide. A mammoth construction.

Ryker came to a stop. Kessner did too. Below them orange and yellow hulks were dotted here and there, though there was no buzz or whir from the frozen machinery.

'It's something, isn't it?' Kessner said with genuine pride in his voice, as if forgetting his predicament.

'It certainly is.'

'Four years of my life. So far.'

'Let's take a closer look,' Ryker said, slipping through a gap between two fences.

'But...'

He turned back to Kessner, who kept looking over his shoulder.

'Don't run,' Ryker said. 'You won't get away from me.'

Kessner said nothing.

'I get it,' Ryker said. 'You're scared. And you know there are men on the other side, the way you wanted me to go. The site is closed but there's always a skeleton crew. Security. Engineers. Surveyors. Whatever. But they can't help you now. You'll never get to them before I get to you.'

But Kessner wasn't convinced. He turned and tried to bolt. Ryker raced after him and only a few steps later reached out and grabbed him and yanked, and Kessner slipped to the snow.

Ryker dragged him past the fences as he scrabbled in the snow, then yanked again to toss him forward. Kessner's body slid on the icy verge and he screamed as he slipped out of view.

Ryker rolled his eyes then set off in pursuit. A couple of steps before he decided to fall to his backside and slide down after him – quicker that way.

They didn't descend for long. The land in front of them flattened out and they both came to a natural stop. As Kessner scrambled to his feet, Ryker grabbed him again and pulled him further along, closer to the cliff edge, all of twenty yards adjacent to where the dam wall started.

'How high is it?' Ryker asked.

'W-what?'

'The dam. It looks *damn* big. How high?'

'Th-The tallest part is two hundred and twenty-one metres.'

Ryker whistled, genuinely impressed. 'Any idea what happens to a body falling that height onto rocks?'

'No, I–'

'You're about to find out.'

Ryker took hold of Kessner's hand and yanked him forward, swinging the man like a pendulum. He cried out as he lost his footing. Ryker grabbed hold of a fallen tree trunk to hold him steady as Kessner's body dropped over the edge of the rocks.

Ryker strained as Kessner dangled. He renewed his grip on the trunk, causing Kessner to drop a couple of inches further, eliciting a horrified shriek.

'I've got you,' Ryker said.

'What are you doing!' Kessner screamed.

'Currently? Holding your life in my hands...' Ryker said, wincing from effort. 'But I'm not as strong as I used to be. My hand... the scar you see. Some bastard drilled a hole right through it. It's never been the same. All sorts of nerve damage. Sometimes I get pins and needles. Sometimes I lose all feeling. The cold seems to make it worse.'

'You're insane!'

'Maybe I am. Now would be a good time to talk.'

'I don't know what you want!'

'Yes you do. Hofman. You and him were involved in a scheme. Tell me about it.'

'What scheme?'

'This is your... only chance.' And Ryker meant it. His grip weakened by the second. 'There's a kickback,' he prompted. 'To you–'

'Okay! Yes. There's a kickback. From our investors in the Middle East and Russia. Ten million euros. Each.'

'Hofman, you, and...?'

'Antony Petit! Pavel Anarkov!'

The same names Ryker had heard before.

'So what's the deal?'

'We finish the project, we get paid! It's that simple.'

'Except it's not simple, is it? Hofman is dead.'

'I... I...'

'Who ordered it? You?'

'Me? No! It was... it was Anarkov!'

'Why?'

'Because we couldn't trust Hofman! He was about to talk. It was... it was you?'

Ryker pushed that idea away. Had he caused Hofman's death?

'What about Corinne Thibaud? Anarkov have her and her family killed too?'

'W-What are you talking ab–'

'Seriously?'

Ryker jolted, and Kessner squealed again.

'Okay! Yes, Corinne Thibaud was a problem. She was opposed to the project for years. Even after we broke ground she and her climate activists tried to scupper us at every turn!'

'So you and your friends had her and her family killed?'

'What? No!'

'You're sure about that?'

'Of course I'm sure!'

'Then why is Corinne dead?!'

'I don't know, but... I'm not a killer. I'm a businessman.'

'I've seen the emails. *You* made the problem go away.'

'I paid her! I paid her off. Two million euros.'

Did Ryker believe him? Hell of a time to lie.

'The Thibauds can't help but stick their noses into everything around here! Even now Monique is causing chaos for us because she wants more control!'

Which Ryker had been about to come to. The new problem.

The one Hofman had been due to speak to Kessner about. Monique Thibaud.

Kessner's face twitched. As though he'd said something he shouldn't have.

'You kidnapped Sophie Thibaud to get back at Monique?'

'Kidnapped? What are you talking about!'

'Do you know where Sophie is?' Ryker bellowed.

'No!'

'Then what has Monique got to do with you? This project?'

Kessner shook his head. Ryker released his grip ever so slightly and Kessner screamed and squirmed.

'A few seconds,' Ryker said. 'That's all you have.'

'Not just this project. She controls everything around here!'

'And?'

'And what? She's mad! You must have heard the rumours! The bodies under the house. The cellars. All she's ever wanted is money and power and she'll do anything to get it!'

Ryker's brain whirred. Kessner's face creased with panic.

'Monique has a lead voice on the environment council for the Alps national park. Nothing gets built here without her approval. Corinne was a problem not just for us, but for Monique. How was she supposed to milk us with her sister-in-law in the way!'

'You're saying she had Corinne and her brother killed?'

'Who gains the most from their deaths?'

'Why?'

'Because she's a greedy bitch!'

Kessner slipped further down and squealed like a pig. Ryker really didn't have time to dwell.

He dug his heels into the ground and released his hand from the trunk and swung it downward.

'Grab it,' he said.

Kessner strained to reach up. As soon as he had the double

grip, Ryker twisted his body over, taking Kessner with him, who managed to scramble up and to safety.

He lay on the snow, looking to the sky, panting.

Ryker got to his feet, his hands and arms and shoulders on fire.

'You fucking pyscho–'

'Save it,' Ryker said. 'There's an outcrop fifteen feet below. A broken ankle or two perhaps, but you'd have had nothing more.'

Kessner shook his head in disgust.

'Monique Thibaud. You need to tell me everything.'

Kessner stared at him, huffing.

'Obviously Monique didn't do it herself.'

'So what? You're saying she hired those two gangbangers from Lyon?'

Kessner laughed. 'She's a bit more sneaky than that.'

Ryker waited for more. None came.

'I'll put you back over the edge again,' Ryker said, jerking forward and causing Kessner to flinch and cower.

'Okay, okay!' he said. 'The boyfriend. Sophie Thibaud's boyfriend. Michel Lemerre. Rumour is, Monique paid *him* to organise the hit. He's a lowlife and *he* brought in those others. But it went wrong. Lemerre, or the others, fucked up. Sophie got away. The two goons got killed as Monique covered her tracks. Lemerre's family disappeared from St Ricard not long after. Lemerre himself? Sophie? Well, have you seen either of them recently?'

Ryker hadn't, but he didn't bother to confirm. Apparently Kessner didn't need an answer.

'They're probably buried in the tunnels under her damn house.'

Ryker opened his mouth to say something to that, except the next moment he spotted movement out of the corner of his eye. The sudden confidence on Kessner's face suggested he'd seen too. Ryker looked back the way they'd come. Several shapes appeared there, by the fences. Men on skis. Men on snowmobiles. Men with dogs too. One of the men pointed in Ryker's direction. A chorus of shouts and barking erupted.

'Shit,' Ryker said as the rescue party descended.

28

Kessner, still lying in the snow, laughed. A hearty, patronising laugh. Ryker grabbed him by the scruff of his neck and pulled him to his feet. The three snowmobiles, engines whining, raced toward them; the skiers, the men on foot with the dogs, moved behind.

Ryker looked further down the slope. A treacherous and icy descent that way, but was it his only option? Well, other than jumping over the edge where he'd had Kessner dangling moments before.

The snowmobiles reached him, circled around. With helmets and big visors on, Ryker couldn't see the faces, though one of the drivers was huge, and wore a gendarme uniform. Coupet. No doubt Renaud was among the men further behind. The rest of them? Who knew.

'You're in trouble now,' Kessner crowed. 'Bet you wished you'd killed me when you had the chance.'

Ryker ignored him, thinking. He hadn't expected the assault, but more than being worried, he wondered how they'd got to be there at all – had the gendarmes followed from the café? Who were the others in this group? He held on to Kessner, as though a shield, in case anyone decided to come at him. Coupet and Renaud would have sidearms. The others?

The snowmobiles came to a stop. Coupet jumped off his and pulled his visor up. Yes, Renaud was there too, holding on to one of the dogs, Ryker realised. The men crowded around.

'We were waiting for you to mess up,' Coupet said. 'Didn't take long.'

'Glad I didn't disappoint you.'

One of the other men twitched, as though about to come for Ryker. He twisted toward him, pulling Kessner's wrist in between his shoulder blades – a hammerlock.

'Any closer and I'll snap his arm.'

Enough of a threat to keep the guy at bay. For now. But what about when they all rushed forward?

'So what now?' Ryker said. 'You know Ms Thibaud won't be happy if–'

'Fuck the Thibauds,' Kessner said, his confidence surprising Ryker. 'Fuck them all.'

A sneer spread across Coupet's face. 'I think the reign of the Thibauds in St Ricard is about to come to an end.'

A mutiny? Kessner had said himself Monique Thibaud thought she ran the town. But times change, and the new money flowing into the area – from Petit, Anarkov, others? – was talking. Perhaps Monique hadn't paid enough people enough money.

Did Monique know of the impending rebellion? Most likely yes, given she'd tipped Ryker off about Hofman in the first place.

'I'll be sure to explain that to her when I next see her,' Ryker said.

Coupet opened his mouth to retort, but before he did, Ryker swung around and tossed Kessner away and the guy stumbled and scrambled and slipped onto a patch of ice and slid out of view. Two men raced off after him – would he fall over a cliff edge before the men reached him?

'Oops,' Ryker said, as Coupet lunged for him.

He had just enough time to ready himself for the juggernaut hit, and both of them thudded down into the snow, sending a plume of powder into the air. Even though he'd taken the hit, Ryker reacted more quickly, hauling his knee up into Coupet's groin then hammering his fist into his ribcage. Coupet winced, then roared in anger and Ryker was sure if he'd stayed there the big man would have pummelled him, but Ryker managed to worm free. He bounced to his feet, smashed his heel down onto Coupet's head to keep him on the ground – for a while at least.

A dog leaped at Ryker. Its teeth sank into his forearm. Ryker grimaced in pain, tried to pull the beast off but its jaws were clamped. The dog was only doing what it'd been trained to, did he really want to hurt it? No need. Its master called it off. But as Ryker cradled his bleeding arm, he looked around; he saw he had nowhere to go. The men crowded around him. Well, all those who hadn't gone to help retrieve Kessner.

Coupet groaned and propped himself up on his arm. Ryker scanned the angry mob. As well as Renaud, a third gendarme was among them, a couple of the guys from the bar too – Hugo, was it?

And Lucas. Though he remained a little further back, not one for confrontation, apparently.

'What now?' Ryker asked Renaud. 'You're going to arrest me?'

Renaud snorted. 'No.'

'He's okay!' came a shout from out of sight. Ryker had guessed as much, yet the confirmation did nothing to ease the anger of the men around him, it seemed.

'Just get it done so we can get out of here,' Lucas shouted, a horribly snide look on his face, as though he enjoyed the idea of Ryker's suffering. Ryker would take the look away soon enough.

Sensing the big man regaining his focus, Ryker ducked to

the ground, sending his knee into Coupet's face at the same time as he lifted the gendarme's sidearm. Renaud went for his gun too but not quickly enough. Ryker pulled the trigger. A bullet zinged into the snow by Renaud, but it wasn't enough to hold him back so Ryker fired again. A hit. On Renaud's hand. No choice but to drop the gun now.

But even with the weapon in hand, Ryker was seriously outnumbered. The dogs were released again, men rushed forward. Ryker fired more warning shots as he ran and weaved and jumped onto Coupet's snowmobile.

He fired off the rest of the magazine, then tossed the gun at the on-rushers as a makeshift weapon. Someone grabbed the back of his coat but Ryker shrugged him off, an elbow to the face kept him away. He twisted the throttle and the engine revved and Ryker turned the handlebars sharply, kicking up snow and ice as the snowmobile spun in a circle. Then he shot off, not heading down, not yet. Lucas. Like a rabbit caught in the headlights.

Ryker held out his bleeding forearm. Lucas tried to duck but Ryker's bone smashed into his nose, poleaxing him. A few broken teeth. Broken nose perhaps. He'd hoped for much worse for Lucas.

He turned the handlebars again, spun again. Then headed down. Swerved to avoid an onrushing snowmobile. The men and dogs and skiers gave chase. Ryker thought he'd get away easily but the rough terrain hampered the hefty vehicle. A dog yapped at his side. A skier was right behind him. Ryker weaved between trees, braking hard all the time to keep control and not crash, struggling to pick up speed. A snowmobile blasted past, jumping over a small ridge. Were they trying to get in front to box him in?

Soon the dogs fell back, running out of steam, but the skiers kept up. The final snowmobile was catching him too, the rider perhaps more experienced than Ryker, or just taking more risks.

A skier right by Ryker's side. The snowmobile in front of him swerved, the rider braked, perhaps hoping to bring Ryker to a stop. Except Ryker decided not to brake at all, but took a hard left, right into the skier who tumbled and clattered away.

The third snowmobile had caught up. Two riders on there now. The one on the back...

Ryker sensed he was about to jump before he even did it. Ryker pulled the brake and his craft skidded to a stop, sliding left and right as the snowmobile next to him raced forward. The jumper had already set himself for launch and could do nothing as he leaped into the air and splatted into the snow a couple of yards in front of Ryker. He released the brake and twisted the throttle again and the snowmobile thudded over the fallen man.

Then Ryker pulled a right, momentarily catching out the other two snowmobile riders. The skiers? No sign of them. Had they finally drifted?

Ryker tried to pick up speed. He raced through a narrow gap between two hefty pine trunks. At least one of the chasers would have to slow to let their friend past first. Except, Ryker saw over his shoulder, neither of them slowed at all, and rather than wait to follow the other, one of the riders jerked right. Searching for a gap there? But there wasn't one. He obviously realised his mistake as he headed for a clump of trees, and tried to correct himself, but had no time. As he twisted the handlebars, too much too soon at speed, the snowmobile skidded then flipped, sending the driver with it.

Ryker didn't see how he ended up as he headed into woods, but that rider wouldn't be chasing again any time soon.

One more left. Ryker ducked and swerved, weaving through trees again, his speed hampered, but then he came out into a clearing and twisted the throttle as hard as he could. Cold air blasted in his face as he raced along. A rocky edge ahead. What lay beyond? Ryker had no clear view. Worth the risk to try the jump? He sped toward it. His hand twitched on the brake. He released the throttle a little bit.

No. Into view came the drop beyond the ridge. Surely a fatal fall.

Ryker squeezed the brake as tightly as he could. Turned left. A similar move to the fallen rider moments before. He struggled to keep control. The snowmobile skidded, virtually no traction. He was sideways on to the drop, sliding closer and closer to the edge. The back half of the snowmobile teetered, Ryker hauled his body to the left, hoping the shift in his weight would do the trick and save his life...

The front found grip and he shot off again, racing along the cliff edge. He glanced over his shoulder. The rider behind him had been more cautious, and having killed his speed sooner, was now picking up pace more quickly to catch up. For a few seconds they raced alongside each other. The guy was almost close enough for Ryker to reach out and grab...

Trees up ahead. Only one obvious way through. Not enough space for both snowmobiles. Ryker was about to pull the brake but then the other rider swerved into him – aiming to knock him over the edge?

Ryker let go of the handlebars. Leaped from his snowmobile. He caught the other rider around the neck. Ryker's snowmobile crashed over a rock and disappeared from view over the cliff. He tried to stay on the other vehicle, but the rider had lost control, the snowmobile careening left and right, and Ryker was thrown off, into the snow. He rolled and banged and bumped to a stop.

The snowmobile raced off, but the rider couldn't regain control and it ploughed head-on into a tree.

The boom echoed. Snow burst from the tree's canopy. The

rider was flung sideways, his shoulder and side cracking off the trunk before he fell into an awkward heap, unmoving.

Ryker groaned and planted his head back into the snow for a moment as he regained his composure. He looked back the way they'd come. No sign of the chasing pack now.

Body aching, he got to his feet. Took a couple of steps toward the edge of the ridge. A big drop. His snowmobile lay in a smoking heap at the bottom.

He walked – hobbled, really – over to the fallen rider. He hadn't moved at all but the rise and fall of his chest showed he was breathing, though it was obvious his shoulder had dislocated because of the protruding joint, and his leg hung at a horrible angle too.

Ryker crouched down next to him. Pulled off his visor. He shook his head. The guy from the bar. Not Hugo, but his angry friend. Not so angry now.

Ryker checked his pockets. Phone. Wallet. He made a note of the name then tossed both over the edge.

'Good luck,' Ryker said to him before he stood up once more. Still no sign of anyone else around him. He pulled out his phone. The screen had cracked a little but was still working. Blood dripped off his forearm and as he tapped, a red smear spread across the broken glass.

Map. Less than two miles from St Ricard. He had no clue who or what would greet him when he returned, but that was exactly what he intended to do.

Except he took two steps forward then collapsed into the snow. Onto his knees to start with. The world spun around him. He lifted his hand to his head. Hadn't realised he had a cut at the back, blood dripping down his neck.

No wonder he felt so woozy.

He fell back into the snow. Looked up at the misty sky, as

white as the powder he lay on. An optical illusion almost. As if he was actually staring at the ground.

Disorientated, he drifted. Until the phone, still in his hand, buzzed.

He didn't look at the screen as he brought the phone to his ear.

'Hello.'

He thought perhaps the voice on the other end would bring some much-needed clarity and focus, but the sky swirled above him.

'Henrik?' Ryker said. He was sure he'd heard his young friend's voice.

No response. He looked to the screen. Had the call failed?

The phone buzzed again. Ryker answered. Or tried to at least.

'Ryker, it's Jen Worthington.'

He blinked, hoping the swirling above him would stop.

'Ryker, can you hear me?'

'Yes.' But her voice was faint, his own one word answer distant and detached.

'It's about Aziz Doukha. He's out.'

And seconds later, so too was Ryker.

29

'Do you think Ryker's in trouble?' Ella asked, the concern on her face clear.

Henrik brought the phone away from his ear, then sighed as he stared out of the window of the TGV carriage, the tall buildings of Lyon's financial district now in view in the near distance as the train slowed.

'Henrik?'

'Maybe,' he said.

A whole host of thoughts – worries – went through his mind. Perhaps Ryker was dead. Perhaps he was in trouble, as Ella had suggested, tied up somewhere and being tortured. Perhaps he'd simply lost or stopped using his last burner phone – too much heat on him?

The idea that stung the most was that Ryker had simply dumped his phone and walked away and had no further interest in Henrik.

He called one more time, even though he knew the response would be exactly the same as it had been every time he'd tried on the journey back from Marseille.

As before, the call didn't even ring through.

ROB SINCLAIR

He put the phone back in his pocket. Ella nestled a little closer into his side. The feel of her, right next to him... some people described it as butterflies in their stomach, and he understood now what that meant.

'It doesn't matter,' Henrik said.

'What doesn't?'

'It doesn't matter that I can't speak to Ryker.'

She looked like she didn't believe his words. He didn't either, but he had to at least try and sound positive.

'I think I know where Michel is. Theo said he was going back home. To see Sophie.'

'He didn't exactly say that.'

'No. But I've a feeling I know where he is.'

'And you really think he was involved?'

He did, though he hadn't fully explained his thought process to her. Why? Partly because she was so close to what had happened to the Thibauds. She was Sophie's friend, she knew Michel too. But yes, Henrik now believed Michel Lemerre was involved in the attacks in St Ricard. It made sense. Michel was a young man who'd got mixed up in drugs, and with it, perhaps the darker side of life. He knew – was supplied drugs by – Didier Lenglet, the dead man who police claimed to have been one of the two attackers.

'I'm sure he was involved,' Henrik said. 'I just don't know exactly how or why.'

'Blackmail?' Ella suggested.

Possibly. Perhaps Michel wasn't in cahoots with the drug pedlars, but in debt to them. He hadn't been there that night in St Ricard, but he'd known about it. He'd given the killers information, about the Thibaud home, where to find their valuables. Since then he'd disappeared. In hiding, because of what he'd done, or because he felt his life was in danger.

'Come on,' he said to Ella, the train nearly at a stop. He got

268

up from the seat and held his hand out to her. 'Let's get you home.'

She smiled, though it couldn't fully hide the worry in her eyes. She took his hand and they walked to the doors and stepped down onto the busy platform. Rush hour, and the station heaved with crowds of people waiting to get on and off trains going near and far.

Still holding onto Ella's warm, gloved hand, Henrik squeezed through the mass of people, ushering her along. They finally made it through the masses but then Henrik stopped dead as Ella came to his side.

'What is it?'

He didn't answer. Just pulled her across the platform and behind a thick pillar.

'Henrik?'

She glanced over to where he was peeking.

'The policeman?'

No. Not the policeman, but the woman he was speaking to. The woman from Aziz's gang. Layla. As Henrik scanned the people all around him, he spotted the other one too – Vaz. Trying to be discreet.

'Henrik?'

'It's not the policeman,' Henrik said. 'But the police here are probably working with them.'

That was the only explanation. Not only for the fact Layla was speaking so casually to the uniformed officer, but for the fact that both of Aziz's guards were out of prison at all. Did that mean the boss was too?

Henrik gulped at the thought. Them being in the station was no coincidence. Somehow Aziz's crew knew Henrik was there. They'd tracked him. Were waiting for him.

'We need to go,' Henrik said, pulling Ella back the other way.

But they only made it all of two steps before she whipped her hand out of his grip and stopped.

He turned to her, imploring, but her face was creased with anger.

'What's happening?' she said.

'We have to get away from them.'

She didn't say anything else but he saw the doubt in her eyes. The questions over what she was doing there with him. The danger he'd put her in.

'If they see us, they'll try and take us. If they don't kill us, they'll hurt us. Badly.'

But then, if he left her and ran, would they even go after her at all? Would they even know her?

He couldn't take the risk. Aziz had power and reach, and as Henrik had already seen, he had a horribly wicked side. If he wanted to truly punish Henrik, he'd do it in the most grievous way. That meant not only hurting him, but anyone with him, anyone close to him.

'Please? I'll protect you.'

He held his hand out to her. But before she took it Henrik glanced over her shoulder. Layla had spotted him. She locked eyes with Henrik and her mouth turned up in a callous smile.

'Quick!' Henrik shouted, grabbing Ella's hand and tugging her.

She didn't resist, and they were moving quickly even before the shouts from behind them cut through the bustling station noise.

'Where are we going!' Ella shouted.

Henrik didn't really know. Away. That was his only thought. And into the crowd. The busier the area, the more chance they had.

'Police! Move!'

Not shouting at Henrik and Ella, but at the other passengers, who began shouting in turn, some screaming as people pushed and shoved and cleared a path for Layla and the policeman, who now had his gun out.

Vaz was there too. Off to Henrik's right. Struggling to break free from the crowd around him. He shoved an old man to the ground. Henrik ran face first into a woman, nearly sent her tumbling.

'So sorry!' he said, spinning to move around her, which ended with him bulldozing into a much bigger and burlier man.

Henrik practically bounced off him but somehow managed to stay on his feet. For a flash he thought maybe the man was with Vaz and Layla, but as he looked up into his eyes...

'Please, help us,' Henrik said, sounding almost as worried as he really was. 'Don't let them take us.'

With that he tugged on Ella's hand and pulled her away. He turned to look over his shoulder a few steps later. Vaz rushed forward after them. Then the big man stepped in his way. Held his hands out as if to grab Vaz...

Henrik winced. He'd spotted the glinting blade, hanging from Vaz's fist, a split second before it disappeared from view, into the big man's side. He was sure he heard the sickening squelch too. Vaz didn't break stride as he pulled out the blood-dripping knife and the man silently crumpled to his knees, clasping his hands over the wound.

A woman screamed, realising what had happened. Would bystanders assume Henrik, fleeing from the police, had dealt the blow?

'Shit,' Henrik said, trying to move faster still.

Layla and the policeman were closing too. Another policeman up front. Henrik pulled Ella to the right but then felt resistance. He thought at first maybe someone had grabbed her.

'This way,' she said. She let go of his hand and moved away.

'But–'

'Trust me,' she shouted back.

But all he could see that way was a run of three platforms before the end of the main terminal building.

Still, he only hesitated for a breath before setting off after her, taking long, quick strides. She didn't slow at all as the first platform approached.

She wanted them to jump?

Yes. She ran to the edge, then lifted her hands above her head as she leaped into the air – like a long jumper on an athletics track. Except she had no sandpit to land in.

Henrik was in mid-air before she'd landed on the other side. She made it by several inches, stumbled, but then righted herself and Henrik's feet planted down again shortly after, much to his surprise and relief.

'But where–'

'Just come on!'

She didn't let up, pulled away from him. Henrik thought he was fit enough but Ella was like a leaping gazelle. She bounced over the next jump, taking it in her stride. This time she landed just as Henrik took off. She was nearly at the third platform by the time he landed, his back foot slipping right on the edge of the concrete, though his forward momentum saved him.

He glanced around him. Layla was giving chase, but the policemen? Vaz? Up on the bridge off to Henrik's left, aiming to come around at them that way. But Ella and Henrik would still be ahead given the longer route.

Ella made the last jump. Henrik was still two steps from take-off...

His distraction, looking around him, hampered his approach. He was too far from the edge, nearly a foot of platform remaining as he went airborne. The extra distance came back to bite him on the other side. His front foot found contact with concrete, but it wasn't quite enough to keep him moving forward and his body sank down. He reached out, trying to plant his hands so he could roll into the fall.

A booming horn blasted from his right. A hulking train. Coming his way. Not fast, but fast enough, and only a couple of seconds from swallowing him up. His foot slipped and he pushed his forearms down onto the concrete as his shoe hit the track below. He strained and grimaced trying to pull himself up. The train horn blared once more.

'Give me your hand!' Ella screamed.

He looked up to see her on her knees on the platform. He reached out for her, but doing so, releasing his arm from the concrete edge, caused him to slip back again.

Gasps from others around them who'd spotted the upcoming tragedy...

His feet hit the track below and Henrik pushed up as Ella pulled. She rolled over, away from him. Henrik slid up onto the platform as she did so and a rush of air blasted into him as the train rolled past.

'Come on!' Ella shouted.

Both were up on their feet a moment after. No sign of Layla now – she'd have to run right around now the train was there. Vaz? He was ten yards off to their left.

'Over here,' Ella said, making a break to the right. A café up front. Heaving inside.

'We can't go–'

'Trust me.'

He did. They slowed a little as they approached the closed glass door. Ella opened it, then both stepped in. A few heads turned their way but the people inside seemed oblivious to the outside commotion.

'There,' Ella said, indicating the door in the opposite corner.

She rushed that way. Nearly sent a suited man with a tray of coffees flying.

'Sorry!' Henrik said again.

Ella pushed open the door and they were out on the cold, dark streets of Lyon.

'If we'd gone the other way we'd have come out the main entrance,' Ella explained, out of breath. 'Right by where the police always park.'

'But now what?' Henrik asked, his eyes darting left and right. Then. 'No.'

Layla. She ran out of another door further down the street, pretty much skidding to a stop. She looked up.

'Run!' Henrik shouted.

They turned and bolted. But then Vaz blasted out of a door in front. He reached out to grab Henrik but he managed to spin out of the hold and hotfooted it away. He and Ella sprinted, heading around the edge of the station building, and doing a better job of snaking around the people there than the two larger adults who were momentarily out of sight as they rounded a corner.

'Here,' Henrik said.

He darted left and grabbed a metal pole used to hold up the rope barrier for the adjacent bar, then ducked into an archway. A dark, empty space. Henrik grasped the pole in both hands. He heard the footsteps. Slowing.

A shadow crept in front of them...

Henrik leaped out, swung the pole which thumped into Vaz's midriff. Enough force in the shot to cause him to fold over.

Layla...

Henrik wound up again and smacked the pole across the side of her head. A horrible clunk. A bystander gasped in horror. Layla collapsed to the ground. The gun in her hand clattered away. She was out for the count.

But Vaz wasn't. Knife in hand, growling in anger, he went to rise to his feet.

Slam. Thump.

Ella hit him twice with another of the poles. The first blow to his back, the second to his head.

'We need to go,' Henrik said, dropping the pole, then picking up Layla's handgun before reaching out for Ella.

She met his gaze. What was she thinking?

She kind of smiled before she tossed the pole which bounced and banged across the tarmac. Then, hand in hand, they ran away as fast as they could.

30

'Who were they?' Ella asked, sounding angry more than anything else, now that the adrenaline of the chase had worn off. No sign of that smile now. Had it been a real smile at all or just nervous relief?

'Bad people,' he replied as he rested his head on the seat of the ageing bus which chugged along the dark street, out of Lyon.

Ella tutted and turned away.

'You've brought me into this mess,' she said. 'I didn't ask for that. The least you can do is be honest with me now.'

A fair point. But how to explain?

He just went for it.

'They work for a man named Aziz Doukha.' He looked over at her. He didn't think the name meant anything to her. 'He's a really bad man.'

'Why would they want to hurt you. And me?'

'Me and Ryker came to Lyon to ask questions about Lenglet and Touba. You know, the two men the police say killed the Thibauds. Both of them, directly or indirectly, worked for Aziz.'

'So he was really the one who had the Thibauds killed?'

'We thought maybe, but he said not.'

'You've spoken to him?' She looked really confused.

'Kind of. He was going to kill us. But the police arrived.' He sighed again. 'It's complicated.'

'The police? But the police were helping those two in the station.'

'I know. I don't really understand either. But Aziz was arrested that night along with all of his gang. I don't know how they got out of prison. But it looks like they're coming for me now, for revenge. Ryker too, probably.'

'And me.'

He closed his eyes. 'Possibly.'

'If we get back to St Ricard, the gendarmerie can help us.'

She sounded quite sure about that. As though they were people she knew and trusted. But he'd turned her world upside down and he feared she was about to see just how ugly and unsafe it really was.

'No,' he said. 'I'm not sure they can help us.'

'Why?'

He didn't answer. The look of worry on her face ramped up further.

'So is there anyone who can help us now?' Ella asked.

Just one person, Henrik thought, but didn't say. James Ryker. Except Henrik had no clue where he even was.

———

The return journey to St Ricard was long and tiring and tense for both Henrik and Ella. They took three buses, by far the least direct route, but hopefully less predictable and harder to track that way. Cheaper, actually, than on the way out to Lyon.

'Do you think they'll be waiting for us when we arrive?' Ella asked, the worry in her voice clear.

He hadn't realised she was awake. For the last half hour

she'd had her eyes closed, her head rested on him, half on his shoulder, half on his chest, her body turned toward him, her legs curled up onto the seat. He'd loved it. The comfort and closeness. Calmness too. Such a contrast to the danger they'd run from in Lyon, and that he knew still lay outside the bus somewhere.

'I don't know,' was all he could say in answer.

But there was a chance Ryker was back in the small town, wasn't there? If he was still alive at all. Did he even know that Aziz and his gang were free?

The thought of Aziz made Henrik shiver. Maybe he and Ella should have kept on running.

'Do you think...?' Ella paused and lifted her head from him to sit up straight. Another chill went through Henrik as the warmth from her body receded. 'Did the same people hurt Michel? Is that why he's missing?'

The truth was, the thoughts of all the people Henrik had met in Lyon and St Ricard made his head hurt. Monique Thibaud and her guards. The gendarmes. Aziz and his gang. Michel. Sophie. He believed all of them probably had dark secrets, one way or another, and he really didn't know how all their lives and their activities intersected.

He was so confused and frustrated trying to figure it all out. And look where his efforts were leading him. Into trouble, over and over. What frustrated him even more was that he and Ryker being in St Ricard in the first place was all down to him. All of the trouble was down to him. He'd so wanted to be like Ryker. The noble warrior. Riding into an unknown town to help the victims of a horrible crime. He'd never expected events to spiral so spectacularly out of control. He could have avoided bringing all of this mess onto himself.

With them both remaining on edge, the rest of the journey passed by in near silence. Eventually the bus pulled to the stop in St Ricard that consisted of nothing but a small shelter. Henrik saw no one lying in wait, whether Aziz's crew or the gendarmes or whoever. No one else got off the bus with them and they both remained standing on the frozen pavement as the chugging diesel engine faded into the distance.

'I can take you home,' Henrik suggested. Most likely the safest place for her – unless they could find Ryker.

'No,' she said, circling her arm around his. 'I'm not leaving you now.'

He smiled at her. She didn't return it, but the look of determination in her eyes still warmed him.

'Before we got off the train in Lyon,' she said, 'we talked about Michel. You know where he is, don't you?'

'I think I might do.'

'And do you think Sophie is with him?'

He couldn't answer that. He didn't even know if Sophie was still alive.

'She could be, couldn't she?' Ella added, hopefully.

'She could be.'

'I think if we can find them. If we can really find the truth, we'll be safe. The police... someone in the police or the gendarmerie has to be good still.'

'I think so.'

'Then let's finish this. Let's go find Michel.'

'Let's do it,' Henrik said, his determined stare matching hers, as his fingers snaked around the grip of the gun in his pocket.

The night was as cold as any since Henrik had arrived in France, and despite their big winter coats, hats and gloves, both were shivering as they made the final approach to the dark and boarded-up Thibaud residence.

ROB SINCLAIR

'Why would he come here?' Ella asked as they moved through the gates, sounding doubtful.

'Because it's familiar. Familiar is safe. And he's hiding. Theo said Michel was going home. St Ricard. But his parents aren't here anymore, so where else?'

She shook her head, as though she didn't understand.

'It's a natural instinct,' he said. 'When I first met Ryker, when he first saved me from the men who'd kidnapped me, we didn't run away. We headed right back to my home town Blodstein. I took Ryker to an abandoned warehouse I used to hang out in. I knew it was safe. I knew the men wouldn't look for us there.'

'You stayed there long?'

'No. Not at all. But not because we couldn't, but because we had to find answers. Ryker...' Henrik paused and laughed. 'He doesn't give up easily. And he doesn't like to sit around doing nothing. We took the fight back to them.'

'And here we are,' Ella said. 'Back in St Ricard. We could have gone anywhere to hide, but instead we came here. To keep on fighting.'

Henrik didn't respond. Largely because he couldn't be sure of her tone. Was she impressed by him, or mocking him?

'I think you're probably a lot like him actually,' she added.

Whether or not she'd meant it as one, he took that as a compliment.

'But Michel,' Henrik said. 'He didn't come here to fight back. He came here to hide. And I think he's still here now.'

He said those last words in almost a whisper, the house all of twenty yards in front of them.

They kept to the edge of the treeline as they moved further forward. Certainly no obvious signs of life here. No smoke trailing up from the chimneys, no lights visible around the window edges, though the glass was so thoroughly boarded he wasn't sure that

280

meant much. As they reached the back of the house they cut across the lawn to the brickwork and pulled to a stop and listened. No sounds except for a distant creature in the woods – an owl perhaps? – and the gentle rustle of piney branches.

Ella was shaking now, though Henrik didn't know how much of that was through cold, and how much was fear.

Henrik stepped along the wall. Ella followed closely behind. He reached the patio doors. The board had been pushed back in place. Henrik crouched down and pulled it away, as carefully and quietly as he could. The glass panel beneath it remained broken.

'Come on,' he whispered, looking back up to Ella. She really didn't look keen, but he turned to the hole again and crawled through then paused a moment on the inside.

No sounds. No smells. No lights. Just like last time.

'Come on,' he said, even more quietly now as he held a hand out to her.

The next moment her head poked through and she wriggled across the floor to squeeze through the small gap. They both straightened up then looked over the dark space in front of them. Nearly, but not quite pitch black, because there was just the faintest outline of light around the closed door in front of them.

'He's here,' Ella whispered.

'*Someone's* here,' Henrik responded as he edged forward.

He reached the door and slowly turned the knob, trying not to make any noise at all. The slightest of creaks from the inner mechanism. Henrik froze as his heart pounded in his ribs. Ella was trying to control her breathing but it was getting faster and deeper by the second.

'Grab something,' he said to her.

He couldn't see the reaction on her face but felt her move

away. A couple of seconds later she came back to his side, a lamp in her hand. Better than nothing.

He pulled the door open. The light – an electric lamp or torch, he thought, because there was no flicker like there would be from a fire or a candle – came from the adjacent room at the back of the house. The smell, too, of food now. Soup, perhaps?

No sounds at all though. The house remained eerily quiet all around them.

Henrik moved toward the light, every step taking an age as his brain rattled with thoughts, not just as to who he'd find here, but what he'd do.

He pulled the gun from his pocket. Reached the door which was ajar. Used his free hand to push it further open. One inch. Another.

Movement behind him. Shuffling feet. A scream.

Ella.

Henrik spun. Held the gun out. Ella moaned and struggled.

'Stop or you're dead,' the man said. To Ella.

Henrik tried to process the voice; he could still see nothing of the man standing there except the faintest outline of shadow. He reached out behind with his foot and kicked the door further open. Not much light spilled out, but it was enough to make out the two figures in front of him. Ella, her pleading eyes boring into him. A knife rested against the skin on her neck.

Behind her a man. Tall, broad, and young.

Michel Lemerre.

31

Darkness had arrived when Ryker finally came to. He had no clue what the time was – his phone wouldn't power on. He groaned and pushed himself up in the snow. His body was rigid, frozen. He shivered violently as he got to his feet. The moon was high up in the sky, the light radiating off it mostly smothered by cloud, but enough to provide the smallest illumination to the area around Ryker. The smashed-up snowmobile remained, but the fallen rider had gone. Had he come to and hobbled to safety, or been rescued?

If someone had rescued him, why had they left Ryker? They could have killed him. Captured him.

He looked around. Nothing he could see up the mountain where he'd come from. In the opposite direction a haze of orange hung in the night sky – light seeping from St Ricard. Did that light mean it was still relatively early in the evening?

Ryker set off in that direction.

Dried blood caked the back of his head. That was a good sign, really. At least he didn't have a gaping wound there, though his head throbbed and there was a lump the size of a golf ball around the area.

He used nothing but his natural instincts and the thin moonlight to help guide him to the light of the town. More than once he had a near miss where he was a step away from a deathly drop before he realised his mistake. More than once he lost his footing and slipped and slid, though luckily, each of those times, he slid across ice and snow rather than over a cliff edge.

His brain rumbled with thoughts with each step he took. Monique Thibaud. He had to find her. Kessner claimed she was responsible for the murders of her own family members. That she'd used her niece's low-life boyfriend to set up the crime. That she was responsible for the deaths of Lenglet and Touba too. A clean-up? It did make some sense.

Money and power were the drivers. Corinne – Monique's sister-in-law – had tried her best to scupper the dam development. Had taken a backhander herself in the process from Kessner and his shady accomplices. But Monique craved a clear path to full control, to milking the developers for everything she could, like she had been doing for years within the community. So she'd set up the murders. Except Sophie had survived the attack. A thorn in Monique's side.

It made sense, didn't it?

Except, Ryker wasn't sure it did, fully. Was Monique really that dark?

And, more to the point, if Corinne had already been paid off, as Kessner suggested, why would Monique still need her out of the way? It was Kessner et al. who were Monique's blockers, not her family members.

Ryker was still missing part of the puzzle.

He'd find it.

He didn't know exactly how long the trek took, though he guessed it was at least an hour until the buildings of St Ricard became visible, and nearly the same again until he made the final approach.

He didn't go into the town itself. There was nothing there for him. Except perhaps the stragglers who'd made it home alive from the fight in the mountains. But he didn't intend on confronting them again tonight. He had more important business.

He approached the house from the back, stomping through the thick snow to get there. His clothes were wet and cold, snow having reached between every seam and gap. When this was all over, he really wanted to get away from the Alps. Find a warm corner of the world for a while. He pushed those optimistic thoughts away. Reached the perimeter wall of the house. Looked around him. Listened for sounds from beyond. Nothing.

He scaled the wall and crouched down on the other side. Right by the large outbuilding. The one he'd seen Bruno head to before. Curiosity got the better of him. He'd heard rumours from multiple sources now. Tunnels, buried secrets. Was any of it true?

Champagne was in the Thibaud family name. Officially they held no stake in the business anymore, but Hofman had claimed Monique was secretly buying a stake back. Why?

Kessner, on the other hand, had said Monique had her own family killed. That she'd perhaps even dispatched her niece and her boyfriend underneath the house. Or could they just have been held hostage down there for some reason? Outlandish, perhaps, but that didn't mean it wasn't true.

Keeping his eyes busy, looking back toward the house, Ryker moved across and pushed on the door handle of the outbuilding. Unlocked. He slowly, carefully, opened the door and stepped inside.

Darkness. He felt around the wall and found a light switch. Not a very good light, but good enough.

He looked around. He'd had all manner of thoughts as to what he'd find in here. An extravagant tool shed. A dormitory for Bruno, Jules, Anna et al. A prison for Sophie and Michel. Tunnels below? Perhaps it was a combination of all of those. In front of him was a near empty room, except for a couple of bunk beds and a few odd tools, and an arched doorway, steps leading down the other side. Could Sophie be down there?

Ryker crept forward but could see nothing down the dark stone stairs, and could hear nothing either. He was about to start the descent for a closer look when something caught his eye. On the floor by one of the bunks. The light bounced off it, causing it to glisten. Liquid. Two small patches, on the wooden planks. Ryker crouched down and touched with his finger, though he already knew what it was.

Blood. Ryker looked to the bottom bunk. The sheets were all a mess, a bulky form beneath. Ryker reached forward. He took hold of the top sheet with two fingers and held his breath as he peeled the fabric back.

Two glassy eyes stared at him. Jules. Dead. Definitely dead.

A noise outside. The wind in the trees? Ryker left the dead man and moved to the door. Opened it. No one there. The noise had come from further away, by the house. He couldn't see anyone, but he did have a clear line of sight to Monique's house, and he could tell someone was home by the light spilling out from several windows.

Whatever lay below, it was the people in the house that Ryker needed to focus on for now. He made a beeline for the nearest corner, where he knew the two cameras at the back of the house left a blind spot.

He pulled up against the wall. Looked and listened once more. On the other side of the house, at the front, he spotted several vehicles parked up on the drive. Interesting. The car he'd seen earlier in the day when he'd left Monique with her visitors was no longer there. So who were her new visitors?

A shadowy recollection of him lying in the snow burned in his mind. The phone call. Jen Worthington.

It's about Aziz Doukha. He's out.

And coming for his revenge? It would explain why Jules was dead in his bunk. Were the others already dead too?

Henrik?

Ryker pushed that thought away. He heard voices beyond the walls and glass of the house but it was too difficult to make out words, or even who'd spoken. He moved along to the nearest window, grabbed a rock from the flower bed there, and smashed it into the glass before he darted around to the back corner once more.

Heightened talking inside. The front door opened, voices that way. The back door opened too. All of ten yards from Ryker. He went that way. Two dark figures emerged. Both were armed. Except for the rock in his hand, Ryker wasn't. One of the figures held a curved machete, the other a handgun. Ryker, light-footed, raced toward them. They moved toward him, but in the darkness they didn't see him until it was too late.

The one with the gun lifted the weapon. Ryker lifted the rock. He crashed the heavy stone down onto the gunner's arm. A cry of pain. A woman? Ryker smacked her around the head with the rock, then spun her around and grabbed her neck as the machete swooshed down toward him. The blade cut deep into her shoulder, only missing her neck by inches. A horrible sound. A horrible wound. But not as bad as it could have been.

The other attacker, a man, wrestled to pull the blade free, it was wedged so deep. Ryker let go of the woman and pushed her aside and the man, still holding the machete, went with her. He finally dislodged the blade. His friend collapsed. Ryker flung the rock. Headshot. Enough of an impact to cause the man to lose his balance. Ryker raced forward. A straight forearm to the throat sent the man sprawling to the ground, gasping for breath. Possibly his last.

Ryker kneeled, to grab either the loose gun or machete...

Neither. Voices behind him. He darted for the open door and into the house – the empty kitchen – just as a series of spotlights in the garden flicked on.

Ryker pulled up on the inside of the doorway and glanced back outside. The two people he'd tackled lay crumpled, blood circling out around the woman. Two more black-clad men reached them. Checked them. Radioed.

Movement to Ryker's left, from out in the hall. Then a man appeared in the doorway there. In the dim light Ryker had to double take to be sure who it was.

Vaz – Aziz's guy from the tower block.

The goon – in his nice suit – smiled. Ryker wanted to wipe it off. But instead he dashed back outside. Jumped. Spun. A roundhouse kick to the head of one of the men out there. The other lifted his weapon. Ryker grabbed the machete from the floor. Flung it like an axe. The blade spun and splatted into the man's side and he let rip with his assault rifle as he fell to his knee. Not for long. Ryker smashed him in the face with a front kick and he keeled over.

Ryker wrestled the gun free as Vaz ran outside. No time, or space, to properly aim and fire, instead Ryker swiped the gun and caught Vaz on the side of his head. But Ryker could do nothing about the knife which nicked his side.

Ryker dropped the gun to free his hands and grabbed Vaz around the neck and they fell to the ground in a tangle. Ryker on top at first. He smacked Vaz in the face with a fist, but then the knife swooshed toward him again. As he held the blade at bay, Vaz used the distraction and soon they tumbled and he was on top, the knife clasped in both hands.

The blade pointed down toward Ryker, no more than two inches from piercing his chest. He fought with everything he had to stop the fatal blow. A horrible smile spread across Vaz's face. He knew he was winning this battle.

Ryker summoned all his inner strength, then in swift motion he shifted his upper body across, knowing he'd be unable to hold the knife at bay that way, but at least the blow wouldn't be as deadly. He reached up as the knife plunged down. Into his shoulder. He ignored the pain and opened his jaws. He sank his teeth into Vaz's neck. Clamped shut. Then he yanked his mouth away taking a chunk of flesh with it. Vaz roared in pain.

Ryker spat the flesh out and threw Vaz off him. The knife remained protruding from his shoulder. He pulled it out, reached for Vaz and hauled him up, an arm around his neck to hold him. With his other hand...

Squelch.

Vaz groaned and jostled, but not for long. Not with the knife inside him.

'Don't fight it,' Ryker said, quietly into his enemy's ear. 'Your renal artery is severed. I pull this knife out... you're dead. Unless one of your friends here is a damn good surgeon.'

Vaz said nothing, but his protests calmed down. He got the point.

'Now move.'

Ryker shepherded his hostage along. Into the kitchen. He'd made it three steps when two more men appeared in the hall. Not faces he recognised, but their calmness, their clothing, showed who they belonged to.

'It's okay,' Vaz shouted. 'Let us through.'

'You won't leave this house alive,' one of the two men said to Ryker

'You think?' he responded.

The two men stayed in position. One held a hunting knife. The other, yet another machete. What was it with these guys?

Only when Ryker was a yard away did the men finish their standoff and move aside.

Ryker headed past them into the hall.

'Which way?' he asked, though he thought he already knew because of the light coming from the formal dining room.

One of the men nodded that way. Ryker sidestepped over, his gaze not leaving the two men for more than a second. He moved into the dining room. Five people in there. Three were tied to chairs; Monique, Bruno and Anna. Layla was standing by her boss who was seated for the spectacle, and looking horribly pleased with himself.

'James Ryker,' Aziz said. 'So glad you decided to join us.'

———

32

'If you hurt her–'

'Who are you?' Michel said, a sneer on his face.

Ella squirmed. Henrik's finger twitched on the gun that hung by his side. Had Michel even spotted the weapon yet in the darkness?

'I asked you a question,' Michel prompted, tugging on Ella's hair to pull her head back and expose more of her neck, as if a further threat of what he'd do.

'I'm no one,' Henrik said. 'But you know her. You know Ella.'

'You shouldn't have come here.'

'Let her go.'

No reaction at all from Michel, his face remained in a snarl, the dim light shining on it making his features look haggard and sinister.

'I said, let her go.'

Henrik raised the gun, slowly, so as to not cause a sudden reaction from Michel, whose eyes found the weapon, and Henrik noticed the confidence slipping from his face.

'Shoot him!' Ella screamed.

Henrik pulled the trigger.

Not entirely a conscious reaction. An impulsive response. A pre-emptive response, really.

The big problem was that Henrik had no skill with a firearm. The kickback sent the barrel jolting upward and the bullet flew up into the ceiling at the far end of the hall. Plaster dust burst into the air on impact. Still, the booming shot caused both Michel and Ella to reel.

She kicked out. Stamped on Michel's foot. The knife came away from her neck. Henrik pulled the trigger again. Had set his pose more rigidly this time, but Michel was moving quickly and stooped down as the bullet sailed over his head. He dashed across the hall, to a doorway for a darkened room at the front.

Henrik rushed forward and grabbed Ella. Her eyes were teary. A dribble of blood snaked down the delicate skin on her neck.

'You're okay,' Henrik said.

She nodded in response.

'Michel!' Henrik shouted out. He looked at Ella once again. 'Get behind me.'

She did so, crouching down, as though she expected Michel to race out into the open at any second. He still had the knife. Was there another weapon in that room too?

Henrik glanced over his shoulder, into the lit room behind him. A big torch, sitting on a side table.

'Grab the light,' Henrik said to Ella.

She looked unsure. She shook with fear.

'It's okay,' he said. 'I won't let him hurt you.'

'We should go. Henrik, please.'

'No.'

They stared – glared? – at each other for a few moments before Ella took one, then two steps backward. Then she spun and darted for the torch, grabbed it, raced back and pretty much skidded to a stop by Henrik's side.

'Slowly,' he whispered to her, before taking a step forward, the gun held out, both hands around the grip.

A bang from the room in front of them. Both of them flinched. Another bang. A scrape. A scratch.

'He's trying to get out,' Ella said.

Henrik agreed. Michel was trying to force the window, and the boards on the other side.

Henrik moved forward with a bit more confidence and purpose. He reached the doorway and pulled up on the adjacent wall. He sneaked a peek but could see nothing in the dark room, the beam from the torch not reaching inside.

'On three, shine the light for me,' he said to her. Ella nodded. 'One, two... three.'

She stepped into the doorway, torch beam arcing outward. Henrik dashed into the room. His eyes darted left and right. Found Michel. The far left of the room. Scrabbling at the window frame. Like a rat trying to claw its way out of a cage. He paused, perhaps realising his attempt at freedom was fruitless. He turned. His face caught in the torchlight. Not as sinister as before. No knife in his hands. The blade lay on the floor, a couple of feet in front of him.

Michel's eyes flicked down to the knife then back up to Henrik.

'You'll never reach it in time,' Henrik said.

'No? Probably not before you fire. But you're not exactly a good shot, are you?'

'Take the risk if you want.'

Silence for a few moments.

'You'd really shoot me?' Michel questioned, almost mocking. 'You'd really risk killing me? You're a kid. What are you? Fourteen?'

Henrik didn't respond to the taunt.

'He's someone you shouldn't underestimate,' Ella said, and

despite the tension in the room, Henrik beamed inside at her words.

'You have no clue, do you?' Michel said to her.

'Actually we do,' Henrik said. 'We know about you and Didier Lenglet.'

Michel shook his head but kept his mouth shut.

'He sold you drugs,' Henrik said.

Michel's face twitched but still not a word.

'So what was it?' Henrik asked. 'Did you only do it for the money?'

'Do what?' Michel barked back, his tone angry and confrontational now.

'Were you there that night?' Ella asked. 'Did you help Didier Lenglet kill Sophie's family?'

Absolutely no reaction on Michel's face. Until he burst out laughing. An irritatingly sarcastic laugh.

'You two. Seriously? You've been watching too much *Scooby-Doo*. Look...' He pulled at his cheeks. 'No mask. It's just me. Simple, boring, Michel.'

'You did it,' Henrik said. 'I know you did. You did it for the money. How much did you get?'

Michel shook his head.

'Did you pull the trigger? Or were you too scared? Yeah, that was it. You had Didier do all the dirty work? Coward.'

'You stupid boy. You have no clue.'

But Henrik didn't believe a word.

'And where's Sophie now?' he asked. 'Your girlfriend. She was supposed to die that night. Did you let her escape because you got scared, or was it just a stupid mistake?'

Michel breathed in heavily as he glared daggers at Henrik.

'You probably hoped she'd die out there. Did you have to pretend when she came back? Pretend to her you were happy? Or did she already know what you'd done?'

Still no response from Michel.

Henrik shook his head. 'That's it. She knew. That's why her aunt protected her. Kept her away from the press and the police. Away from you. Except you couldn't let her talk. You had to make sure. And that's when she disappeared. Is she dead now too?'

'No. I'm not.'

The soft female voice came from out in the hall. Henrik spun around, gun pointed that way. Ella did the same with the torch.

Sophie Thibaud stood right there, calm as anything, at the bottom of the stairs.

'Do I look dead to you?'

No response.

'Do I look at all distressed to be here with Michel?'

She didn't, and Henrik's brain whirred. What had he got wrong?

Sophie took a step forward. Ella took a step back, toward Henrik, who swung the gun from Sophie and back to Michel, confusion consuming him.

'Sophie?' Ella said.

'What's going on?' Henrik blurted, not very impressed that he couldn't think of anything stronger to say.

Sophie came inside, met Michel in the middle of the room

'As I was trying to explain to you, I didn't kill Sophie's family,' Michel said, still sounding angry. 'I love her.'

'But... Didier–'

'Yeah, I knew Didier. That doesn't mean I wanted him to kill Sophie and her family, you imbecile.'

'Then why–'

'Sophie, you've got a lot of explaining to do,' Ella butted in.

'I know. I will.'

'Then do it now,' Henrik said, still pointing the gun at the two in front of him, still not sure what to think.

'Please,' Sophie said. 'You don't need that here.'

'But...' Michel paused and looked to Sophie, then back to Henrik. 'You came here because of Sophie, didn't you?'

No response from Henrik or Ella.

'You came here to help me,' Sophie said, a look of admiration on her face.

'Yes,' Ella said, when Henrik didn't respond.

'You know why we're here,' Sophie said.

'Hiding,' Ella suggested.

'We had to get Sophie away,' Michel said. 'Before she got hurt too.'

'Hurt by who?' Ella asked.

'But now... the four of us together. Perhaps we can make a difference.'

'Hurt by who?' Ella asked again. 'Who are you afraid of, Sophie?'

'Her aunt,' Michel said, in such a way as to suggest Henrik and Ella really should have got that by now.

'Monique?' Henrik clarified.

'She did this,' Sophie said. 'She had my family killed. She wants me dead too.'

'Why?' Ella said.

'She killed Sophie's family. She's been clearing up ever since,' Michel said. 'Lenglet and Touba first of all. Her two assassins. But Sophie was the one she really needed to get rid of.'

'Why?' Henrik asked again.

'Isn't it obvious?' Michel said. 'With Sophie gone, she becomes the last Thibaud. She owns *everything*.'

'But the four of us together,' Sophie said, her face brightening, 'I think we can stop her.'

33

'Let them go,' Ryker said.

'Excuse me?' Aziz responded, his face turning sour in a flash. Then his eyes rested on Ryker's hand. The knife stuck into Vaz's side.

'Renal artery?' Layla asked, no emotion in her voice.

'I see you're a man of action, James Ryker,' Aziz said. 'But are you willing to execute my friend to make your point?'

Ryker didn't answer.

'That would make you no better than me.'

'I never said I was a good person.'

Aziz laughed. 'What a tough guy. I have to admit though, I am still confused why you're here at all.' He turned to the bound Monique, next to the similarly tied-up Bruno and Anna. 'What you're doing working with this woman.'

One of the two men by the doorway twitched and Ryker twisted that way a little. Vaz groaned as the knife dug a little deeper. The move was enough to halt whatever attack the man had thought about. For now. Apparently he cared more for Vaz than the boss did.

'You see the reason for me being here is simple,' Aziz said.

Ryker waited for the explanation he expected to come but Aziz went silent.

'Layla, please untie that one,' Aziz said, pointing to Anna.

Layla moved over and worked on the ropes behind Anna, who moaned as she stared at Ryker. Or perhaps she tried to say something, but couldn't with the gag in her mouth.

Layla pulled Anna to her feet.

'Give her something useful.'

Layla nodded and moved to the pristine, gleaming, dark-wood dining table. Shimmery metallic objects lay on the wood, but not the expensive silverware usually expected on the plush furniture. Layla picked up a meat cleaver and walked back to Anna who stood resolutely. Would she try to fight back? Surely there was an opportunity here. Anna was no slouch. But something about the supreme confidence of Aziz...

'Take it,' Aziz said to her.

'Don't do this again,' Ryker said.

'Do what?' Aziz replied, still looking at Anna and Layla. Then he turned to Ryker. 'This is what I have to do.'

'Revenge,' Ryker said, trying to buy time. For what? Aziz raised an eyebrow. 'The simple reason you're here is revenge.'

Aziz didn't respond.

'I understand now. Monique had your people killed. Didier Lenglet. Ramiz Touba.'

'She also organised that raid at my offices which not only saw people I employ killed, but me put behind bars.' Aziz spoke with genuine bitterness. 'And you left me there, in that car park. Which is why I'm coming for you and your boy too. So thank you for helping me in that regard. But Ms Thibaud should have realised... she might have had the power to get me arrested, but she doesn't run Lyon. I do. This will be her one and only lesson.'

'What's your name?' Aziz asked Anna. Layla took the gag out of her mouth.

'Anna.'

'And your friend there?'

'Bruno.'

Aziz laughed, though didn't explain to anyone why.

'Take that cleaver. Hit Bruno. Again. And again. Keep going. Until I tell you to stop.'

Bruno squirmed and moaned. Monique shook on her chair, squeezed her eyes shut.

Anna didn't move. Layla took out a handgun and pushed the barrel to Anna's temple.

Ryker, in the same position, would attack from there. Why didn't Anna?

She took the cleaver in her shaking hand.

'Don't,' Ryker said.

Anna caught his eye. Then she shook her head.

'Wait!' Ryker shouted. Vaz writhed at the interruption and Ryker twisted the knife a little. The two men by the doorway both flinched, ready to pounce... but stayed put. He had everyone's attention. But what next? 'I didn't tell you why I'm here.'

Aziz groaned and looked back to Ryker, exasperated. Ryker didn't have much time.

'I'm here because I was looking for Sophie Thibaud. I wanted to find her and I wanted to find out who murdered her family.' He looked to Monique. '*She* did. Monique Thibaud organised the killings of her own family members. Lenglet and Touba pulled the triggers that night, but she pulled the strings. That's why I'm here. To find out why. To find her niece. And to have *her* punished.' Aziz nodded, as if in agreement. 'But the right way. You want Monique Thibaud to suffer? Let's see her in jail the rest of her life. Her family name forever tarnished. Her wealth gone to waste.'

Monique moaned, her imploring eyes staring at Ryker. Aziz's

face screwed, like he had a mouthful of razor blades. He turned away from Ryker.

'Anna, do what I told you to. Now.'

Anna found Ryker's gaze once more. She looked at him pleadingly...

What could he do?

Boom.

The gunshot echoed. Time slowed for Ryker. He watched Anna's body crumple as the spatter of blood and brain and skull erupted out of the side of her head. Wispy smoke rose up from the barrel of Layla's gun.

Nothing else for it. Ryker yanked the knife out of Vaz's side then sank it straight back into him. Once. Twice. A quick end. He turned as one of the men by the door opened fire. The bullets hit Vaz in the chest. Ryker ducked down and propelled the dead man away from him, right into the other two, then leaped forward as Layla opened fire.

The bullets raked the wall by him. He reached out and grabbed the head of the first man he got to and smashed his skull against the stone wall. The impact was horrific, and as he let go a smear of blood and hair streaked down the paintwork.

Ryker spun and lunged, took out the next man below the knees and as his gun came free his body somersaulted and he landed on his head with a crack. Broken spine? If not, he was certainly out of action for this fight.

Ryker, crouched low still, reached for the gun in front of him.

'Uh-uh,' Layla said.

She stood two yards away. Her gun pointed at Ryker's head. He slowly brought his hand away from the weapon on the floor.

'You are really fucking annoying, do you know that?' Aziz spat, still seated in his chair as though the death and chaos around him was nothing but an irritating inconvenience.

Layla circled Ryker. She kicked the gun from his reach.

'On your feet,' Aziz said.

Ryker slowly rose up.

'Now move to the table.'

Ryker did so. Well, why wouldn't he? That's where the array of weapons lay.

'Take the cleaver.'

The cleaver which lay on the floor just beyond Anna's lifeless hand.

Ryker bent down and took the weapon though winced as he did so. The pain in his injured shoulder was worsening, not to mention his head wound. He'd tried to ignore it, tried to not let the weakness show, but as he straightened up again he saw the look in both Layla and Aziz's eyes.

Layla moved behind Ryker. He glanced over his shoulder to see her lift a carving knife from the table.

'Do it,' Aziz said to Ryker. 'Do to Bruno what Anna couldn't.'

'No,' Ryker said. He didn't even have to think about it.

'There won't be a bullet to your head, my friend.'

'You think you scare me?'

'Have you any idea what I can do to a man?'

'Not much, I think. You get your minions to do your dirty work for you.'

Aziz jumped up from his seat, his face reddening, as though about ready to launch himself forward.

Did he have it in him?

Movement behind Ryker. He spun. Too late. Layla drove the knife into Ryker's already injured shoulder. He shouted in pain, creased over. Dropped the cleaver. Layla darted back out of range, her movements lightning quick and light-footed, like an Olympic fencer.

'I could show you,' Aziz said. 'If I really wanted to. But you know what? I prefer to watch. Now do what I asked.'

'No,' Ryker said.

Layla came at him again. Ryker tried his best to defend but she was too quick. The blade glanced across Ryker's bicep. Not a bad blow, but yet another that took a little bit of his strength and resolve and focus.

'She'll do this to you all night long,' Aziz said.

'She'll have to.'

Layla moved again. Ryker was ready this time... but then... the attack never came. She feinted and ducked away, back out of reach as she stared at her master.

Aziz turned to the doorway. Ryker hadn't heard anything out there. But they both had. Earpieces?

Sure enough, moments later, footsteps. Ryker tensed. He looked over at the tools on the table. Could he get one?

A woman strode into the room, assault rifle held in both hands. Where the hell had she come from? Ryker tried to show no reaction to the next people he saw.

Henrik, his shoulders sunken, his eye swollen nearly shut, and he limped badly. With him, the girl from the bar. Ella, he thought Henrik had said she was called. Sophie Thibaud came next, and a young man Ryker didn't recognise – Michel Lemerre? The two young women cuddled and cowered. The young man kept his head bowed. Blood streamed down his head and neck from a wound somewhere in his hairline.

Behind them, another of Aziz's crew came into view. A shotgun in his hands. He remained standing in the doorway.

Aziz burst out laughing.

'This night just gets better and better. Who do you people think you are?'

Aziz moved toward the four, looking over them in turn. Henrik caught Ryker's eye. He looked... defeated. What had happened?

'I know you,' Aziz said, standing in front of Henrik. 'So, as with your dad, this saves me the trouble of hunting you down later.' He moved on, past the other three. 'But I don't know any of you.'

'They're all kids,' Ryker said.

Monique's moaning returned and Aziz looked to her, and then back to Sophie.

'Ah, yes. I see the resemblance. She's a Thibaud. But these two?' He looked to Ella and Michel. 'Just kill them so we can keep this moving.'

The man with the shotgun stepped up behind Ella.

Ryker spun and stooped and grabbed the cleaver from the floor and flung it at Layla. The blade rotated at speed as it headed for her. Ryker didn't wait to see where it hit. Instead, he darted the other way.

He grabbed the woman with the assault rifle. Henrik turned and lunged for the man with the shotgun. He fired. No hit. Ryker twisted the woman's arm and threw her to the floor and kept on twisting until her arm snapped and she screamed and released her grip on the weapon.

Ryker took hold of the rifle but then he cried in pain when Layla dove at him and sank the knife into his side. Aiming for the renal artery, like he had with Vaz? She missed the sweet spot, but she did enough to cause Ryker to drop the rifle.

Layla darted off to apparent safety, but the shotgun went off again. Whether a deliberate aim or not, a series of holes opened up along Layla's back and she collapsed to the floor. An unexpected end to an accomplished fighter.

Bruno moaned at the same time – had he been hit by a wayward shot from the blast?

Ryker looked back to Henrik who wrestled with the shotgun man still. So too, did Sophie and Ella, clawing at his back. Michel was on the ground. Not dead, but certainly groggy from something.

Aziz...

Going straight for Ryker.

Ryker sank down, balled his fist and sprung up like a jack-in-the-box. He caught Aziz under the chin with a sweet uppercut. Aziz flew back and landed in a heap.

Ryker looked to his left. Sophie had a gun in her hands.

Bang.

Chest shot. The man with the shotgun collapsed to the ground.

A strange silence took over in the room.

Subdued. Relieved. Horrified.

Henrik hugged Ella. Sophie kept hold of the handgun as she reached out and helped Michel to his feet.

Across the other side of the room, Aziz stood up, propping himself by the fireplace. All alone now. Unarmed too.

Layla lay unmoving, but Ryker moved over to check her. He'd take no chances with someone like her. He moved her onto her back. Alive. But only just. A punctured lung, perhaps two. Ryker could tell by the horrible wheeze with each pained breath.

Monique Thibaud stared on, her wide eyes like snooker balls. Bruno's head was bowed but he was breathing still.

Ryker heaved a sigh then moved over to the chairs.

'Make sure he goes nowhere,' he said to the youngsters, indicating over to the groggy Aziz.

Ryker kneeled down and untied Bruno first. He remained in his seat. He was badly injured, but he'd survive if they got him to a doctor quickly enough. Did he deserve that?

Monique Thibaud, somehow, remained unscathed.

Ryker moved to her, was about to loosen her ties, when Henrik spoke.

'Leave her.'

Ryker looked up.

'She killed my family,' Sophie said, looking on the verge of tears.

Ryker looked from Henrik to Sophie to Michel, to Ella.

Aziz laughed. Ryker straightened up.

'Interesting,' he said.

'What is?' Michel said as he stepped closer to the table. Henrik and Ella huddled together. 'She's a killer.'

'Really? Only, I heard *you* were responsible,' Ryker said to Michel.

The young man scoffed.

'After all, it was you who knew Didier Lenglet, wasn't it?'

Monique moaned on the chair. Ryker got on with loosening her ties.

'Don't,' Michel said.

Ryker ignored him.

'You can't let her go!' Sophie shouted. 'Please!'

Monique's hands were loose, but Ryker left the gag in her mouth and put his hand on her shoulder to keep her seated.

'Well this is exciting,' Aziz said. Ryker wished he'd kept his mouth shut. 'I thought you already said Monique Thibaud was a killer? That she wanted her niece dead. That *you* wanted her to pay.'

'I said what I had to say to delay you,' Ryker said.

'Will somebody please explain what's going on!' Henrik shouted, drawing everyone's attention.

'Despite what more than one person has told me, your aunt didn't have your family killed,' Ryker said to Sophie. 'But, I'm pretty sure you know that already.'

'Yes she did!' Sophie shrieked, looking rattled. 'All she's ever wanted was my family's money! She would have killed me too! It's why I had to run.'

'You're partly right. All she's ever wanted is power, money, an unblemished reputation, and she'll go to lengths for all of those. But she didn't have your family killed. She didn't need to.'

'She hated my mum,' Sophie said. 'She had to kill her–'

'Because of the dam project? No. You see, your mum's protest was already dealt with. Maybe you didn't realise that. That there were other shady characters involved there. They were the real threats to Monique not getting what she wanted.'

'Ryker,' Henrik said, 'what are you–'

'You two did it,' Ryker said, looking from Sophie to Michel.

No confirmation, no denial, because the next second Aziz made a move. Desperation or had he spotted an opportunity?

Bang.

He shouldn't have bothered. Aziz's body slipped down the marble and to the floor, a hole above his left eye oozing blood.

Sophie whipped the gun from him to Ryker, but Ryker was already moving. Michel grabbed a filleting knife from the table, a snarl on his face as he went for Ryker, but he hadn't betted on Bruno who stuck a leg out and Michel went stumbling.

Sophie opened fire. Missed Ryker. Henrik and Ella didn't move – frozen in confusion or fear?

Michel, determination on his face, drove the thin blade into the back of Bruno's neck. With little effort several inches of metal disappeared and Bruno's body quivered. He pulled the knife out.

Ryker was almost on him.

'Don't move.'

Sophie. She held the gun to her aunt's head.

Michel laughed. A horribly callous laugh as he wiped the bloody blade clean on Bruno's shoulder.

'I don't understand,' Ella said, sounding on the verge of tears.

'That's because you're a fool, Ella,' Sophie crowed, glancing to her friend.

'I understand,' Henrik said. 'Michel *was* the second killer. With Didier Lenglet. I knew it. But...'

'But you didn't exactly take a lot of persuading otherwise,' Michel said with a laugh.

'For the money?' Ella asked. 'Is that all it was, Sophie? Your parents' money?'

'No,' Ryker said. 'I don't think so. I think it's because they wanted to.'

'Actually, I'd say it's because of love,' Sophie said, gazing at Michel.

'Did you have to pretend?' Henrik asked Sophie, sounding disgusted. 'The night your family was killed, did you pretend you were scared?'

'I *was* scared,' Sophie said.

'But we did what we had to do,' Michel said.

Enough. Ryker didn't really care for the explanation anymore. He launched himself for Sophie. Would she really blast a hole in her aunt's head? Maybe. But there was enough doubt with Ryker descending. She tried to aim at Ryker but he slammed into her and took her from her feet and crashed her back into the table. Her lower back folded painfully and the gun clattered free and she slid to the floor – out of the fight for sure.

Ryker turned as Michel lunged with the knife.

'Henrik, no!' Ryker shouted. But Henrik didn't listen. He dove in and swung a fist to the side of Michel's head. Michel slashed at him and a gash opened up in the belly of Henrik's coat and he stumbled back. Michel wound up for a killer blow...

Ryker grabbed Michel's knife hand. His other hand took the young man around the neck. He hauled Michel from his feet. Let go of the knife hand. Took hold of Michel under his armpit and threw him into the wall. His back cracked off the stone and he collapsed to the floor. Ryker crouched down. Twisted

Michel's arm. Not much effort needed before the knife came free. Then he elbowed Michel in the face and his head lolled.

Ryker got back to his feet and looked across the room. Absolute carnage. About the biggest mess he could recall seeing in a single room.

'You okay?' Ryker said to Henrik, who was panting, on the floor, being comforted by Ella.

'I've had worse.'

An unfortunate statement for a fifteen-year-old.

'Any more surprises?' Henrik asked.

'I fucking hope not,' Ella said.

Ryker forgave her the profanity. He fished a phone from Michel's pocket, used the fallen man's thumb to unlock it, then called the police.

34

Ryker's eyes sprang open when he heard the door. He shuffled up in his hospital bed a little, as though he was in any fit state to launch an effective counter-attack if there was a threat...

No. No threat. Well, not an immediate physical threat anyway. The man who walked in was smartly, but dully dressed in a grey suit. His thick moustache was at odds with the shiny bald head, the only hair on top was that around his ears. Ryker had met him once already, and even before the man had introduced himself that time, he'd guessed what he was at least.

'*Bonjour*,' Inspector Lafayette of the Police Nationale said with a friendly smile.

'I've had worse,' Ryker said, in French too, though Lafayette gave him a curious look as though he didn't understand. Was Ryker's French that bad?

Lafayette moved over to the chair by Ryker's bed but he didn't sit down.

'The nurse tells me you're asking to be discharged.'

'I don't want to stay here longer than necessary,' Ryker said. 'And if I'm well enough, I'm free to go, aren't I?'

On Lafayette's visit yesterday, the answer as to whether Ryker would face any charges hadn't been fully clarified, though Lafayette was clearly suspicious of Ryker and his actions. He did still have a twenty-four-hour police guard outside his hospital room, as did Henrik a few doors down, but Ryker felt the guards were there more for his and Henrik's protection, rather than to keep them contained, and Ryker had been allowed to roam the building a couple of times, and had been to see Henrik plenty.

'Sorry, you can't go yet,' Lafayette said, which was a stronger response than Ryker had expected.

Had something changed?

'Yesterday I asked you a lot of questions about who you are,' Lafayette continued. 'And why you came to St Ricard. Your relationship with the Thibauds. And what happened in that house two days ago.'

'You did.'

'And I'm not sure I liked your answers much.'

Ryker didn't say anything. Which was Lafayette's point really. Ryker had given the policeman little detail in answer to his questions. Insisting only that he and Henrik weren't the bad guys. That they'd acted in self-defence. That Aziz Doukha was a psychopath who would have killed everyone in that room who didn't work for him. And that Michel Lemerre and Sophie Thibaud were responsible for the murders of the Thibaud family. He'd also told him what he knew about Hofman, Kessner, Petit, Anarkov. Ryker had never met those last two, but he firmly believed they were responsible for Hofman's murder. What other crimes had the corrupt group committed over the years?

Okay. So he'd said quite a lot really. But he hadn't explained it much. He was still trying to make sense of it all himself.

'Tell me again, why did you go to St Ricard at all?'

Ryker sighed and looked the other way, to the window where

the blinds remained closed, even though it was the middle of the day. There wasn't much of a view anyway. Just another wing of the hospital.

'Mr Ryker, if you help me, I will try to help you.'

'What do you want from me?' Ryker said, turning back to the policeman.

'We'll need witnesses for when we prosecute Michel Lemerre and Sophie Thibaud. And possibly Kessner, Petit and Anarkov too.'

'You've arrested them all?' Ryker asked.

'Kessner yes. The other two? We haven't even found them yet.'

'I'm not sticking around to stand in a courtroom months down the line.'

Lafayette sighed. 'I thought you'd say that.' He shuffled in his satchel and pulled out an A4 pad, then took out his phone too. 'So I came prepared.'

'You want a statement?'

'Yes.'

'And if I do that I can leave?'

'As long as I'm happy with what you tell me.'

Ryker thought about it.

'There is one other thing too,' Lafayette said.

'What?'

'Ms Thibaud has asked to see you.'

'Monique?' Ryker asked, although he could see no reason why it'd be Sophie.

'Yes.'

'Why?'

'You'll have to ask her. But I need a statement from you first. I don't want you two comparing stories.'

'Where is she?'

'In jail.'

Ryker took a moment to think. He still had so many questions about what had happened in St Ricard, both in his time there, and before. Aziz Doukha was dead, but not all of his crew were. Layla had somehow survived though was in a drug-induced coma. Three others belonging to Aziz's outfit had been taken alive from Monique's home too. Ryker had no interest in speaking to or even coming across any of those people ever again.

As for Michel and Sophie? Both had been arrested on suspicion of murder, related to the attack on Sophie's family. Ryker had met a lot of bad people in his time. Cold-blooded murderers. Sadists. He couldn't recall seeing two people with those traits who were so young and so... normal?

But as much as they intrigued him, he had no intention of ever seeing or speaking to them again.

Monique Thibaud? Ryker still wasn't sure he really understood her. He also didn't know if she was truly bad or not. She'd lost a lot the last few months, but he also believed she'd organised the deaths of Didier Lenglet and Ramiz Touba – revenge. Although she'd made a mistake with Touba. An innocent man, at least for the Thibaud murders. Though Ryker felt little sympathy for the death of an assassin who worked for someone as grotesque as Aziz Doukha.

Did Monique Thibaud deserve punishment?

'Okay. I'll talk to you. And then, if the nurses will let me leave here, I'll go and visit Monique.'

Two hours later Lafayette left, satisfied. He said he'd need a few more hours to speak to Monique before Ryker could see her in the jail. Likely cross-referencing what Ryker had told him with her own version of events. Would she have told the

police the truth? Would she have told the police anything
at all?

Ryker grimaced with each step he took as he shuffled along
the hospital corridor to Henrik's room. The knife wound to his
side was far from the worst injury he'd ever had but with the
blade having pierced his abdominal muscles it made walking,
moving at all, painfully difficult. His shoulder... the sling helped
to keep things steady but he didn't know how long it'd be before
he had full use of his hand and arm again. Weeks, possibly
months, though at his age, and with the knocks he'd taken for
years, perhaps he'd never regain his full strength there again.

As for Henrik...

Ryker opened the door and thanked the policeman there
then moved inside.

He stopped and stared. Fifteen years old. Not the first time
Henrik had been hospitalised with nasty wounds. Because of
Ryker?

'How you doing?' Ryker asked.

'I hate it here,' Henrik groaned as he shifted up under the
covers.

Ryker similarly groaned as he sat down in the chair next to
the bed. Then he laughed.

'Look at us,' he said.

Henrik smiled. 'You look a lot worse than I do.'

'Thanks.'

'Lafayette came to see me earlier,' Henrik said.

'Yeah. Me too.'

'Did you tell him much?'

'I told him everything.'

Henrik raised an eyebrow.

'I want to get out of here. I wanted him off my back.'

'So you're free to go now?'

'Yeah.'

Henrik sighed, looked dejected.

'What?'

'I can't believe I made such a stupid mistake.'

He'd said this multiple times now.

'You didn't,' Ryker said.

'Yes I did. I found Michel. I'd already discovered that he knew Lenglet. I thought he was the bad guy, that they both did it for the money. I could have shot him before we ever got to Monique Thibaud's house. But seeing Sophie threw me. They manipulated me. So easily.'

Ryker thought again about the wickedness of the two youngsters. Sophie might not have pulled the trigger to kill her family members, but she'd bought into it. For love, she'd claimed. Was that really it? Or did the need for money and power – control – come into it for her too?

'I got it wrong as well,' Ryker said. 'Not in the house, at the end, but before that. I was looking too big, I guess. I saw the dam project, saw the conspiracy there, the corruption and criminality that big money so often breeds... but this time, the answer, to the Thibaud murders at least, was so much more simple.'

'Sophie's family weren't the first people he killed,' Henrik said.

'I know. I saw the news. The missing persons. Maybe others we don't yet know about.'

Ryker had even found the news articles about those himself, but had never properly linked them to what had happened to the Thibauds.

'Best not to think about it,' Ryker said.

'But I can't stop thinking about it. I saw the faces of the other people he killed, when I was in the police station. I don't think the gendarmes even knew they were looking for a murderer. They thought they just had a series of missing hikers. I should have figured it all out sooner.'

'None of that is your fault.'

Henrik sank a little. 'No. Maybe not. But I was there in that house with them. I should have known. I should have stopped them there and then.'

'That was never your responsibility.'

'I should never have left you.'

Henrik held Ryker's eye and neither said a word for what felt like an age.

'I thought... I thought. I *wanted* to be like you. I thought I could be.'

'You're more capable and resilient than you realise. But you don't need to be me. Look how it works out.'

Henrik smiled, then grimaced in pain.

'Ella... she came to see me.'

'She's okay?'

'Better than we are. But I... I let her down as well.'

'You haven't let anyone down.'

'I did. I lied to her. She knows I'm only fifteen now. She didn't take it well. I'm not sure she'll forgive me. I really liked her. I've messed everything up.'

Ryker smiled again and Henrik screwed his face in irritation.

'What?'

'Nothing,' Ryker said. 'Just... if I were you, concentrate on being a teenager. It suits you. You'll enjoy it more than... than what we've been through.'

Henrik held Ryker's eye once more. 'I think you might be right.'

Ryker looked at the clock on the wall. Five minutes until his ride arrived.

'I need to go,' he said. He grasped Henrik's hand for a moment and squeezed it gently.

'Go where?'

'Monique Thibaud wants to speak to me.'

Henrik looked confused.

'Yeah. That's what I thought too. I'll tell you all about it when I come back.'

Henrik nodded. Ryker got to his feet. He was at the door when Henrik spoke again.

'Ryker.'

He turned.

'Thank you.'

'For what?'

'For protecting me. I never asked for it. And I didn't make it easy for you. Lying to you. Leaving you to try and do things on my own. You never... you stuck by me. No matter what. No one's ever done that for me.'

'More fool them,' Ryker said.

'You've taught me so much. You never asked for anything in return. I owe you my life. Thank you.'

Ryker smiled and headed out.

35

The room in the prison was bland and dark. No natural light. But it was clean and Ryker had certainly seen far worse. Two guards brought Monique into the room. Her hands were cuffed together as she arrived but the men unlocked the chain before they sat her in a chair then exited the room. Monique wasn't a high-risk prisoner, and perhaps she still held some sway over the authorities given the light-touch treatment.

'I wasn't sure you'd come.'

'I was too intrigued not to,' Ryker said.

He looked over her. She'd aged several years in the last two days. Her hair was straggly and thinning, her face heavily wrinkled with big, dark bags under her eyes. Confinement, and whatever else weighed heavy on her mind, wasn't going well for her.

'How are your injuries?' she asked, indicating his shoulder.

'Bad, but I'll get over it. Probably.'

'Is Henrik okay?'

'He'll be fine. For him I think it's the mental rather than physical toll that I'm more concerned about.'

'He's resilient. Perhaps more so than you realise.'

ROB SINCLAIR

Ryker said nothing.

'I still don't fully understand your relationship together, but I see how much you care for him. He's very lucky to have someone like you to look after him.'

'Why am I here?' Ryker asked. He had nothing to say to this woman about his relationship with Henrik.

'Because I sensed you wouldn't be staying in France for long. And I wanted one opportunity to explain.'

'Explain what?'

'Me.'

Why did she even care?

'I'm not a bad person,' she said.

'It's not me you'll need to convince.'

'When Sophie came out of those woods... I've never felt such relief. I thought I'd lost my whole family.'

She paused, as though she expected Ryker to say something.

'You said to Aziz Doukha you thought I did it. You thought I had my family killed. You're not the only person to have said that.'

'I also told Aziz *why* I said that.'

'But did you ever suspect me?'

'Perhaps at one point.'

'That upsets me. But I'm also interested to know why.'

'Because it fitted. To a certain extent. The dam project. Corinne's attempts to scupper it. The dirty deal she did with Hofman and Kessner and the others.'

'But that was Corinne, not me.'

'But there was more to it. You've got so much control in and around St Ricard. You stood to gain the most from the deaths of your brother and his family. You'd inherit their fortune. You'd get free rein to control anything and everything in your town.'

'You really think I care that much about money and power?'

'I do. Yes.'

'Then you still don't know me at all. I told you the first time I met you about my family history.'

'And I understood your pride.'

'Exactly. My pride, and my honour, for my family name.'

'So much so that you've been buying back a stake in Franck Thibaud on the sly? Offshore shell companies to hide your interest.'

She didn't respond.

'And the tunnels and cellars under your home? How long have you been bottling counterfeit champagne?'

She sneered at him, but he'd been doing his homework since they last met. He'd had plenty of time on his hands in the hospital.

'Why?' he asked.

'I told you before. Every bottle of Franck Thibaud bears my name. Every bottle has to be the best.'

'So you flood the market with fake bottles of your competitors. Bad wine, to sully their names. You make money from an illegal operation, and you help to preserve the integrity of a brand that you secretly now own part of again. It's quite an interesting take on pride, I have to say. A rich person's take, that's for sure.'

'It's for my family.'

'Like having Didier Lenglet and Ramiz Touba killed was?'

'Yes. Exactly.'

So she was admitting to that? Would she admit it to the police too?

'And you set me off after Hofman because you thought he and his buddies were responsible. You thought they'd taken Sophie too, further leverage over you and whatever scheme you were trying to swing with them on the dam project. Which was why you didn't go to the police when she disappeared. You wanted her found, but you wanted them properly punished, and you also wanted to keep your prospects alive with that project, and your name clean.'

She didn't respond to that.

'Did you hope I'd kill them all for you?'

'I heard the police haven't located Petit or Anarkov yet.'

'Apparently not.'

'Petit is just a very rich businessman,' Monique said. 'But Pavel Anarkov? I met him once. It'll be interesting to see how he responds to this.'

'You're saying he'll come after me?' Ryker asked.

Monique didn't answer.

'If he does, so be it,' Ryker said. 'You'll need to watch your back too.'

'I always do.'

They both fell silent for a few moments.

'Did you never suspect Sophie?' Ryker asked. 'She was your niece. You must have–'

'Looking back? Perhaps the signs were there. I tried so hard to look after her. To protect her from the police, the media. But she hated me for it. She said I wanted her to be a prisoner in my home. That wasn't true, but the more we fought, the more I realised something wasn't right. I wouldn't let any of her friends see her. But Michel... he came to the house. More than once. Then he snuck in one time. Bruno found him in her room. I went crazy at them both and...'

She trailed off, looked away, as though reliving the moment, likely more painful now that she knew the truth.

'I should have realised sooner.'

They fell silent again, and Ryker didn't know if he had anything else to say. Once more he wondered why Monique had even bothered to ask him there. Perhaps as some sort of catharsis. She felt better for talking, and she wanted to change Ryker's opinion of her? Perhaps it was simply because she wanted to exert her power still. Over the police, the prison guards, Ryker.

'I'm sorry,' Monique said.

Ryker didn't bother to ask exactly what she was sorry for. Not long after and he was at the door. The guards opened up.

'Goodbye, Monique,' Ryker said.

She said nothing in return.

Night-time had arrived when Ryker made it back to the hospital. Having been discharged, he needed to find somewhere to stay for the night, though he wouldn't go far, given Henrik remained there. Perhaps he'd simply stay by Henrik's side until morning and think about his plans again tomorrow.

Ryker turned the corner and looked along the corridor. He stopped. No police guard outside Henrik's room. He moved forward at pace, ignoring the pain in his side and his shoulder. He reached the door. Pushed it open.

He closed his eyes as his brain stabbed with remorse and regret and something else he couldn't even describe.

The room was empty.

'Mr Ryker?'

He turned to the nurse.

'He's gone?'

'He left earlier. A taxi came for him. I thought... he said he was leaving with you.'

'No.'

'Oh, but...'

'It doesn't matter.'

She looked confused but after a moment a doctor called for her and she scuttled away to do whatever she needed to.

Ryker's brain swam. The last conversation with Henrik rattled in his mind. Henrik's parting comments.

Thank you... For protecting me. I never asked for it... you stuck by me. No matter what. No one's ever done that for me... I owe you my life.

Ryker hadn't realised it at the time, but it wasn't just a thank you. It was a final goodbye.

For the best?

He really didn't know.

With a well of emptiness opening inside him, Ryker turned and walked away.

THE END

ABOUT THE AUTHOR

Rob specialised in forensic fraud investigations at a global accounting firm for thirteen years. He began writing in 2009 following a promise to his wife, an avid reader, that he could pen an 'unputdownable' thriller. Since then, Rob has sold over a million copies of his critically acclaimed and bestselling thrillers in the Enemy, James Ryker and Sleeper series. His work has received widespread critical acclaim, with many reviewers and readers likening Rob's work to authors at the very top of the genre, including Lee Child and Vince Flynn.

Originally from the North East of England, Rob has lived and worked in a number of fast-paced cities, including New York, and is now settled in the West Midlands with his wife and young sons.

Rob's website is www.robsinclairauthor.com and he can be followed on twitter at @rsinclairauthor and facebook at www.facebook.com/robsinclairauthor

A NOTE FROM THE PUBLISHER

Thank you for reading this book. If you enjoyed it please do consider leaving a review on Amazon to help others find it too.

We hate typos. All of our books have been rigorously edited and proofread, but sometimes mistakes do slip through. If you have spotted a typo, please do let us know and we can get it amended within hours.

info@bloodhoundbooks.com

Printed in Great Britain
by Amazon